Michael Heath

The Separating Sea

Cover design by Hamish Braid

This book is a work of fiction. Names, characters, places, and incidents either are products of the author's imagination or are used fictitiously. Any resemblance to actual persons, living or dead, events, or locales is entirely coincidental.

The author can be contacted at michael@mhconsult.com

First Printing: February 2016

ISBN-13: 978-1523630677

ISBN-10: 1523630671

For KLG

"Life is not a series of gig lamps symmetrically arranged; life is a luminous halo, a semitransparent envelope surrounding us from the beginning of consciousness to the end."

Virginia Woolf
Modern Fiction (1919)

Before…

Bubbles and blood. It was the absence of both that struck her. The blow had been heavy; his surprise genuine. He must have registered her murderous intent in a micro-second, much too short for that recognition to give way to fear, his eyes opening wide by a degree almost impossible to notice.

After the blow his young body reeled comically and slid – to her pleasure and surprise – silently into the enveloping water. She lifted her arm again, the stone still gripped to deliver a second blow; but a second blow wasn't needed.

As the pale, thin, white body arched upwards she gripped his hair with her right hand and pushed into the small of his back with her left. Easing him down into the water again, feeling his chilled torso slide smoothly against her thigh.

She then calmly looked up but all were occupied with their own dramas: lovers splashing each other in a watery courtship; children noisily flopping around from the inside of supporting inflatable rings. She turned back to see if there was any movement. But there was none.

She was certain he was dead.

1

Keys. Purse. Mobile. Hope Dunne placed her hand on each for reassurance. Noticing that all three were not quite equidistant on the kitchen counter, she smoothed the phone a little to the right. Perfect.

She'd lately discovered the ruse of placing her empty cereal bowl in the sink before opening the Weetabix sleeve and dropping two brittle biscuits into it. Now there were no annoying crumbs to wipe up. Withdrawing the bowl, a simple splash of water and any escaping flakes were effortlessly washed away.

Hope permitted herself a little smile of satisfaction with this latest manifestation of her ingenuity. Measuring out the cold milk, she stopped abruptly: the correct balance had to be achieved.

The first mouthful was always synchronised with a reassuring glance at the kitchen clock. Mum and Dad had had their early morning tea. Once her cereal and coffee had been dealt with, there was just time enough left for cleaning teeth, contact lenses and making her – now aired – single bed.

A tortured squeaking suddenly distracted her: it was the cat pawing outside at the kitchen's UPVC back door. She rolled her eyes – her mouth still full of muddy Weetabix – realising that she had forgotten to feed Pardew.

It was the cat's normal habit to follow Hope as she trudged wearily downstairs after her shower but, this morning, Pardew had already liberated herself through the one-way cat flap just as a reluctant, watery sun had shyly lifted over Ruislip.

Hope undid the locks and opened the door; a clean morning breeze ushered Pardew into the kitchen. A small, matted area of fur, speckled with blood, indicated that she'd been in a fight and Hope bent down to inspect it.

"I told you, Pardew, trust nothing and nobody. When will you ever learn?"

Hope decided that the wound would soon heal and set about organising Pardew's meal. She tore off the lid of the cat food and, immediately, its awful fragrance insinuated itself into the very roof of her nasal cavities. She hated the smell. Strange, she thought, whatever the cat food's 'flavour', the same shocking stench disgusted her senses.

Pardew leaned disinterestedly over the bowl and, realising that it was the very same brand and flavour she'd eaten only one week before, decided it was neither worthy of attention or ingestion. With a feline *froideur* she walked away, taking one sneering glance back at Hope before padding haughtily towards the stairs.

Hope sucked in her cheeks (she had resolved only the previous week to stop swearing to herself every time she became annoyed), released them and turned to the last of her Weetabix, now stodgy and unappealing in her bowl. Rushing her coffee, she decided to get back on schedule and clean her teeth. She looked at her watch, fully aware what the time was, but still comforted by the gesture.

And then her mobile rang. She recognised the number.

2

"Oh, I forgot to make my bed!"

Caught in a queue that stuttered towards the traffic lights, there was no one to acknowledge her sudden outburst. She felt very uncomfortable. What would Mum and Dad think? Will they see the unmade bed and, annoyed at her untidiness, make it for her? The idea angered her; she liked looking after herself. It was a small gesture of control in a house she had no control over.

The realisation that she, as a woman approaching 56 - intelligent, impeccably dressed and meticulously groomed - should be preoccupied with what her parents might think of her unmade bed, struck her as perfectly incongruous. But the situation was what it was.

She'd already decided that, once her now elderly parents were no more, she'd sell the family home and move away to somewhere nice. She couldn't decide between a London flat (although each successive year that option seemed to recede as London house prices relentlessly climbed) and a cottage in the Cotswolds.

Her thoughts were immediately driven away by the impudent blaring of a car horn telling her that the queue was now moving. Hope looked in the rear-view mirror, put the car into a crunched first – and stalled.

Restarting the engine, she crept insolently forward – as slow as she could to upset the horn man – and thought of this morning's mobile call. Hope had heard nothing when she answered but knew he was there. Why hadn't he said something? She'd repeated 'Hello' several times.

From her bag – crouched crablike on her passenger seat – she heard the mobile ring again. Keeping her eyes forward her left hand probed and pushed in the fake leather folds. Hope became increasingly irritated: first that she couldn't locate the phone, second that it emerged in her hand upside down.

"Hullo?"

"Hope, it's Gavin. I needed to apologise."

Hope sucked in her cheeks for the second time that morning. "You disappeared."

"I was… I had to go. Thuong called. Wanted to know where I was."

"I'd only gone to the toilet. Why did you run off like that?"

"I didn't run off. I've just said…"

Hope pulled the phone away from her ear, trying to distance herself from the irksome conversation.

"Come on, you know how it is, Hopey".

The intimate corruption of her name was Gavin's attempt to defuse the argument. She knew that.

"Well, let's talk when you come round tonight."

"Well, Thuong's not going out now, so I can't…"

"Forget it. Bye"

Hope felt better for killing the call so quickly. The coldness she'd cleverly invested in the word 'Bye' brought a keen satisfaction. Gavin didn't need to be like that. He'd obviously got what he wanted last night – and then he wanted away.

Peevishly, she picked up the phone again and turned it off. He might call back. And she might not have the strength to ignore it.

3

"Morning, Martina. Morning, Jay."

Hope walked briskly, flanked by desks on one side and small, gaping offices on the other. Her bag was quickly placed down before she opened the third drawer down of the filing cabinet and pulled out her washed mug. She leaned over and opened the window, it's metal rims brown and flecked with rust, to let the morning air into the stuffy, small sales office of Jupiter Rent A Car.

"Coffee anyone?"

Martina smiled: "Please, Hope." Her attention immediately returned to the hypnotic lure of her PC screen, simultaneously pushing her unwashed cup towards the edge of the desk.

"Never say no," beamed Jamilla, her large eyes widened to accentuate the all-too-familiar innuendo. Hope's face conveyed complete indifference. She didn't like those sorts of jokes and knew that, if she displayed any enjoyment or reaction, it would only encourage Jamilla's smutty humour.

A cesspool is the best place for smut.

Minutes later, Hope stood, arms folded, by the expectorating coffee machine. All three mugs were placed neatly – and separately – in front of her. Her own mug was a greater distance from those of Martina and Jamilla, as if fearing some airborne contamination. The line of all three had been positioned perfectly parallel to the edge of the laminated work surface; handles exactly following a secret ley line only her eyes could discern.

The most dreadful thought revealed itself to her. Why was she, in her own country, always making coffee for a Paki and a Polack? Both were younger than she was. Was that right? Surely that wasn't fair? Making coffee for two immigrants when they ought…

"One of those for me?"

"Oh, morning Gavin." She could feel the heat rise in her face as she blushed.

He swung energetically out of the kitchen area back into the corridor. The slightly large dark blue suit jacket buttoned over the first budding of a middle-aged paunch.

"Good weekend?" He called back.

"Very good, thank you."

How did he do it? How did he fall back into the role of her manager so casually, so naturally? She could hardly believe it was the same man who – passionately and entirely – had given himself to her in her lounge the night before.

She felt an old familiar storm rising inside her, a commingling of conscience, passion and love. It surprised her how well she managed to control the maelstrom that swirled inside her yet never revealing it to those she worked with. How long could that last, though? She'd often said herself that people who have affairs in offices think nobody suspects, when the truth is that everybody not only suspects, but knows for certain.

She pulled down an extra mug and placed it close to her own, although still making sure that its handle fell into the correct alignment with the other cups. Hope carefully took a teabag, kissed it and dropped it into his mug. Gavin preferred tea. There was something very nice about that. Something rather English and sophisticated.

4

"Ready!"

Hope walked sullenly into Gavin Laing's confined, tidy office with lips pursed and eyes averted. She closed the door behind her; it was always more private. She knew that Martina and Jamilla would be 'all ears'. She'd even noticed that Martina often knew about some events even though they'd yet to be formally announced. She concluded that it was obviously something Martina had genetically acquired from her parents, who'd lived for most of their lives under the yoke of communism and had probably survived by developing just such an instinct for divining the, as yet, unrevealed.

"With you in a moment, Hopey. Bloody predictive text..."

Hope's pursed lips were now beginning to ache. She released them momentarily as Gavin's unblinking gaze concentrated on the screen of his iPhone.

"Off she goes." He placed the phone carefully to one side of his keyboard. "To business: who's in and who's out?"

Hope despised that line. The same line he'd used ever since he'd joined the sales team as Sales Manager two years previously. Was it two years, she wondered? Almost two years. How wonderful to be so close to the man you loved.

Gavin leant back in his chair but kept his pen tapping on the desk in a manner that showed rhythm was not his strong point. He had the round, freshly scrubbed face of a child that had only recently emerged from his Sunday bath; an appearance even more accentuated by the boyish way his hair was smoothed back from his forehead. Hope thought that he'd probably been over-mothered, and that his preening self-confidence and fierce competitiveness, had probably stemmed from that.

"Keith has you in for ten. He needs two hours, so I've bumped Rhona to one and that leaves you with the sales team conference at two-thirty. Thuong..."

He had the arrogance of a man that knew he'd always possess looks that women – and men – would notice. Hope knew that she was not the only one who found this attractiveness hard to resist, but she had to block those troublesome thoughts from her mind.

"Bumped Rhona?" asked Gavin, who was now looking in a side drawer, "Why'd you bump Rhona?"

"Because she's a scheming bitch who everyone knows you're screwing."

"Because she's a scheming bitch who everyone knows you're screwing."

"Keith has? Must be important."

"No: we're supposed to be important. Otherwise what was last night about?"

"Fine." Gavin slammed the drawer closed. "Have you let Rhona know?"

"No, she can turn up on time and I'll take great delight in giving her the bad news."

"That's good. Have you seen my file for the ICES project?"

"Yes, I've shredded it."

"Well it was here last night."

"So was I, Gavin."

"You're right; must still be at home. OK, make sure you email Rhona. Anything else?"

"Only my existence."

"That's good. Thanks, Hope."

Hope smiled weakly. She'd seen TV actors smile weakly – often when they'd unexpectedly been let down – and had been practising the look in the bathroom mirror after cleaning her teeth. Gavin hadn't noticed. Maybe her smiles were *too* weak. Perhaps a stronger weak smile might create more… what was that word..?

It was *frisson.* It had been her February word. Every month she had tried to teach herself a new word, one that would help her to develop a more sophisticated vocabulary. Once the word was chosen she had to find at least two opportunities a week to use it. French words always best won her approval; they sounded so superior and demanded that you season the sound with a moderate French accent as it looped from your mouth. All of the French words had been winners: *frisson*, *penchant*, *éclat*, *metier.* She was convinced that they were all Southern French in origin. Warm and scented with mountain thyme. Were there mountains in the south of France? Did they have thyme growing on them? She liked to think they did.

Yes, she mused as she left Gavin's office, she needed to find a way to create more *frisson*. A tension that was…

"That's the elephant in the room, Simon."

Martina Grabowski was using her low, throaty telephone voice; a combination of beautifully articulated English infused with the salacious twang of a Polish Marlene Dietrich. Its flirty potentiometer was already turned to 9, one notch more and the business was hers. She always laughingly dismissed it as her 'man-catcher' voice.

"Martina's such a whore" thought Hope. "And that Rhona's an evil, evil cow. I bet she's already got her fat Scottish claws into Gavin. They're all such fuckers."

Martina suddenly looked up and returned Hope's kind, radiant smile.

5

"Hope. Stand here, please."

"Why, Miss?"

"Don't ask 'why'. Get up and get here!"

As Hope's pushed back chair scraped across the parquet flooring, she could sense Neil Dowling's sniggering. She calmly walked to the appointed space – next to the classroom nature table at the front of the class – whilst keeping her unblinking eyes on Miss Fisher the entire time.

Neil Dowling kept his arms folded - too neatly and too high – across his chest. The over-eager folding of arms that only a sinner of real experience could demonstrate. His head was held up and slightly back; his eyes open wide and lips crushed shut.

The lesson continued. A dome of dark, bloated clouds had hung all morning over West London and was now releasing the first spots of rain which streaked down the wide classroom windows. Hope slowly realised that, from this standpoint, the classroom looked very different. She was viewing a daily routine from a distinctly individual angle. From side on, Miss Fisher resembled their priest: earnest, expressive yet remarkably dull.

She quietly released her right hand from behind her back and eased the too-tight elastic of her knicker leg. A pine cone escaped from the nature table and bounced on the floor. Hope immediately retrieved it and put it neatly back, hoping that the gesture would appease the anger of Miss Fisher. Miss Fisher glanced, irritated, towards Hope but soon fell back to discussing the subtraction sum on the blackboard.

"And so what would that leave?"

Neil's hand rocketed up in a fascist lunge.

"Neil?"

"Seven, Miss Fisher."

"Right; Neil, sit down."

Hope stood astonished. Minutes earlier 'Sticky' Dowling had been whispering to her about Miss Fisher's severely-tight hair bun. This ceaseless volley of jokes had soon overcome her resistance until she'd snorted out in laughter. And now here she was, shuffling from foot to foot in the class 'sin bin' whilst Neil nurtured his 'chosen one' image with the teacher.

Gradually, as the lesson progressed and the other children began to copy out Miss Fisher's next sum, Hope became increasingly anonymous; even Neil seemed to be working completely unaware of her existence or the empty chair – still in the position Hope had left it – next to him.

Hope resolved – very slowly – that she had a real hatred for Neil. She crossed her fingers behind her back and began to think of scenarios where she could hurt him. She imagined different situations that all culminated in an appallingly violent outcome. She then began to sift through them, pleasurably, for the best opportunity that offered the most sustained agony.

Drowning, she concluded. She wasn't sure how; she was just certain that it was going to happen.

6

4 April 1968

My dearest Neil
Kneel here and put your head
On this breast
I have a stone
Against your neck…

Over the succeeding months, she'd kept returning to the five lines she'd already written but, try as she might, couldn't think what to write next. Resignedly she folded the small sheet back up and carefully lodged it between the wooden cross-strut of her bed and the mattress.

She knew it was easy to kill someone. What would they think of her then? Quiet Hope that no one ever really noticed. She'd tried so hard to stand out at school but, come the moment, her nerve always seemed to fail her. The other children in the class were always so assured, so accomplished. Their parents were also blandly normal. At school, when her class were congregating in the playground, they seemed to make up really funny things to say all of the time, things she genuinely laughed at; but her own comments drew no laughter, no approbation. They just slid away unnoticed.

She pulled her poem out again. She needed a final line. It will come, she thought. Nobody thinks I amount to very much, but I do.

She recalled that Neil hated swimming.

Her mind drifted towards perfect futures. How fortunate that she will have been nearby, browning herself on that sticky afternoon. Splashes, volleys of laughter, screams and then… one awful, haunting, shattering scream.

'Sticky Dowling's sticky end' Hope inwardly called it. A too-hot day in July chilled by a collective awakening to death. The busying of hands. The silent, uncomprehending weeping; the sheltering of young children ushered by towels to a distance. And through it all, through the manifold gulps and breathy staccato of grief, Hope would hear the lap, lap, lapping of the lido. Utterly indifferent.

She'd keep her promise.

Sitting on the floor with her back to the bed, she felt the enveloping warmth of the late afternoon sun break over her. God was the sun and the sun was God. She knew that, and felt this bright brilliant shaft to be His approval.

7

With her modest lunch completed, Hope continued reading her book, hunched over with her arms neatly folded beneath for balance. As her eyes followed the line of the sentence she realised that none of it was going in. She wasn't even sure where she was in the plot.

Accepting that her mind was too agitated, she set the book to one side and resolved to write a poem. After all, Jamilla and Martina were out at lunch, Gavin upstairs in a meeting room with Rhona, so she had no one to interrupt her.

Pulling out a piece of clean A4 paper, she waited for a line to percolate up. It would have to be about Gavin. Weren't they all really about Gavin?

You seemed so cool to me today…

Yes, that had a nice lilt. She rhythmically counted the syllables out on her fingers.

Eight beats. She'd recently noticed that all her poetry seemed to be composed now using eight iambic beats: da dah, da dah, da dah, da dah.

This morning when our glances met…

This was going nicely and she was already anticipating 'forget' as the rhyming crown of the final line in the stanza.

When once we'd had so much to say…

'When once'? She put a line through and rewrote beneath:

Last night we'd had so much to say…

Yes, much better. The next line burst up and surprised her:

And danced our little dance away…

A five-line stanza! Was it too much like a limerick? Would they publish a romantic limerick? No, she decided, it wasn't a limerick, and once more basked in the pleasure of this unexpected inspiration.

The last line. It has to end in 'forget'.

But quickly you've so soon…

No, that was the wrong tense for 'forget'. She chewed the end of the pen and thought how she might approach it from a different direction.

Oh Gavin, how could you forget?

Gavin? When it was published might this be too personal? Perhaps replace 'Gavin' with 'my love'? It worked, but seemed a bit old fashioned. What about 'lover'?

It was always the final line she struggled with. It was supposed to be the *coup de grace* to the stanza after all.

Oh, lover how could you forget?

At first she wasn't sure whether this was the right line, but the more she whispered it to herself, the more she became convinced that it would work.

She wrote the poem neatly out again, pleased with what she now had.

You seemed so cool to me today
This morning when our glances met
Last night we'd had so much to say
And danced our little dance away
Oh, lover how could you forget?

Hope felt a deep pleasure at what she'd written. She rechecked each line for the eight beats, twitching each finger in turn as a physical reassurance.

Hope liked to tell people that the only lessons she really enjoyed were the poetry lessons. But that wasn't true. Try as she might, she could never actually recall any poetry lessons. Of course she would have had some, but they would have just been a small part of the English Literature syllabus at school.

She'd told herself that, one day, she was going to round them all up into a book. Maybe go to Waterstones and see who the publishers of poetry were and then put together a letter and enclose some typed-up copies of her favourite pieces. She relished telling people. She thought how she might reply to the letters she received from admirers telling her just how helpful her work was in mending their broken hearts. Perhaps she might call the collection '*Therapy*'. What about '*Love Therapy*'? Even better, '*The Therapy of Love*'.

How glad she was that she had already decided so much. But when she looked down once again at the poem, her spirits sank.

The dreaded second stanza. She had begun so many poems, but so few had more than one verse.

8

"What sort of party?"

"A nice party, Dad. If it wasn't then I wouldn't go."

Hope's Father looked up from his dinner. "You can't tell who's at a party. How'd you know? How'd you know who's going to be there?"

Hope calmly smoothed out her skirt, removing cat hairs with long strips of sellotape. She didn't answer immediately; she knew it was best to appear calm and unconcerned.

"Mrs Curran is letting Bernie and Mary go. She wouldn't let them go if it wasn't right.

Denis Dunne grimaced and put down his knife and fork.

"For the love of God, Hope, I need to know you're safe. I don't want you drinking and everything. You're not old enough."

"You know I don't drink and it's a school thing anyway. They don't allow you to drink."

"But it's not at the school. It's at the Church Hall. So what'll they be serving at the bar all night? Tap water?"

Hope decided that she'd probably removed as much cat hair as she was going to, and put the sellotape roll back on the table. She held parts of the skirt up to the light and picked off the remaining hairs with her fingers.

"Dad, if I don't go then they'll make my life miserable. Stuck-up Hope. Thinks she's too good to socialise with us. Do you want them to make my life miserable? 'Cos that's what they'll do."

Denis looked strained and stared down at his food. Hope noticed how thin his hair now was; and for the first time realised that creases had begun to deeply etch into his face.

"I'm not sure. What would your Mother have said?"

"She'd have been all right with it. Anyway, she's not here so it's what you say that counts. She met you at a party, didn't she? You told me she did."

"A dance. Not a party."

"Same thing, Dad." She passed behind him and looped her arms around his shoulders, kissing the top of his head.

Eventually, he gave up on his meal - the fish fingers were too cold now anyway – and hauled himself up and took his plate into the kitchen, smiling at Hope as he did so. An unconvincing smile, but a smile nonetheless.

"Have you eaten?"

Hope nodded, passing behind him to open the kitchen door wider.

"You're going to have to decorate this kitchen, Dad."

Denis looked around but said nothing. Hope took this as a positive sign that he was at least weighing up the possibilities of her going. When he said 'no', he could be unshakeable.

Hope walked out into the garden and saw that he'd cleared away the weeds from the rose beds. In recent years, Denis had mown the lawn but seldom could find the spirit or energy to do anything else. As a result, a few beleaguered pots were choked with weeds and the paving stones down the side of the fence were mottled with algae and bird droppings.

She crouched down and watched a Small Tortoiseshell butterfly settle on a buddleia's lower branch, flicking its mosaic wings closed and open again to catch the warm evening sunlight.

A distinct ripping noise caught her attention. Denis was pulling a long sheet of old wallpaper from the kitchen wall.

9

Hope gave out the coffee silently. She had contemplated a sarcastic remark that would have implied how wrong it was that she should have made the drinks yet again. But as she entered the office, she saw that Jay was away from her desk (so that's a waste of a drink) and Martina had wedged the phone to her ear with her bony shoulder whilst typing carefully into a spreadsheet.

She noticed a post-it note on her screen placed dead-centre where Gavin always left his post-it notes. She became flustered: what if he had written something indiscreet? What if he *could* make it this evening? What if Thuong had changed her mind? Her mind reeled with the possibilities that were both mortifying and thrilling.

She leant quickly across and peeled it away.

You forgot my coffee. G.

She picked up her pad of post-its and wrote neatly: *You forgot you're breaking my heart. H.*

She went into Gavin's neat office where the cedary trace of his after shave still hung in the air. She thought that the hum of his PC sounded like the distant roar of a city heard from some overlooking mountain. Would Gavin be with her? Sitting behind, gently nuzzling his face into the nape of her neck, with his arms enveloping her as she took in the hazy view below? Would they soon make love? Had they already made love?

With a deep tenderness, she pressed the note on to his PC screen with her forefinger.

It read: *Sorry, I was busy. H.*

10

She was thinking of Neil. That morning, as she'd walked into school, she'd been humming *'I Can See Clearly Now'*. She wasn't completely sure of the words but knew what it meant. Her life was going to be a bright, bright, sunshine-y day. Up to now, the dark clouds had her blind. The devil was off her back. God and goodliness were pouring into her.

Yes, she could see clearly now. she told herself this again and again.

And during double Geography, it was into this calm, clear mind that the final line to her poem presented itself: *'And you will gasp for air'.*

She hastily scribbled it down.

"What are you up to Miss Dunne?"

"Everything, Mr Templeton, and a sad old alcoholic geography teacher like you would probably be appalled. Or maybe you'd like to watch?"

"Then do try and finish it. You've just under half an hour."

Now she was ready. The poem was complete. For three years she'd hoarded it in different places in her bedroom. She would write it out again, she decided. Take a fresh sheet and copy it out in its entirety, neatly. Perhaps, if her parents were out, she might find one of the candles they kept for the power cuts and build a small altar where she could incant the words.

Then she'd have to find Neil. Get close to him.

An idea percolated up into her mind that made her give a small shriek of surprise. She remembered that, with her parents, she'd been walking by the side of the large lido reservoir at Ruislip and seen Jehovah's Witnesses being baptised. She distinctly recalled their white, scrawny male bodies, wearing only swimming trunks, being lowered into the water by overweight men wearing white T-shirts. It was all very exciting and a large crowd had gathered in a human fringe around the water's edge. She was sure they'd even baptised an Olympic wrestler.

It was a moment of raw inspiration. Divine inspiration. That was it: He had spoken to her and she was His vessel. Now she knew what she would have to do.

That evening, whilst her Dad watched *Coronation Street*, she went quietly upstairs and reached behind her old David Cassidy poster for the folded note sellotaped there. For over three years she had kept her unfinished poem and now – at last - it was time to replace it with something complete. Her small hands trembled with excitement as she gently unfolded the paper and smoothed it out on her desk.

After dating a fresh slip of paper, she wrote the poem out again, adding the final grisly denouement:

13 November 1972

My dearest Neil
Kneel here and put your head
On this breast
I have a stone
Against your neck
And you will gasp for air.

Hope took the scrap of paper that bore the original verse together with some matches she'd stolen earlier from the kitchen matchbox. She pulled the bedroom door quietly behind her, descended the stairs and, heart pulsing with the excitement of the event, slipped out through the back door.

Earlier, the November evening had closed in quickly with low clouds and spluttering showers. Hope groped in the dark reaching out for the side wall to help navigate along the long garden path up towards her father's shed. When at a safe distance, she methodically ripped the paper her poem was on into small strips. She then tried to bundle the small ribbons of paper together but, so fine had she torn them, they were soon caught by small gusts of wind that lifted them randomly around the garden border.

She gave up, concluding that it was too wet anyway to keep any flame burning for too long; soon, perhaps at the weekend, she would carry out the real deed: the incantation of the previous poem over the burning candle. Maybe she should write the new, complete one out again and burn that instead? Yes, she thought, that would be much better.

The mournful music from the house told her that the adverts were about to start. She giggled and fumbled her way again back to the house.

It may have been dark, but she could see clearly now.

11

Hope mumbled her prayers, hidden in amongst all of the other classes in her House Assembly, under the watchful gaze of Mr Terrance, the Housemaster. She couldn't understand why, if everyone was supposed to concentrate on what the words meant, he could so distractedly repeat the prayer every morning whilst his unblinking stare intently scanned the serried rows of children for misbehaviour.

Mr Terrance had several favourite words, but of all of them it was the word 'behove' he seemed to cherish most. Almost every morning there was an occasion when he would refer to some action that would require 'behove' to substantiate the seriousness of his intent. It often was the essential pivot of phrases such as, "And it would ill-behove any boy or girl who took it upon themselves to..."

Hope wasn't sure what the word meant but knew that 'behoving' was something to be avoided.

At the end of the last prayer, Mr Terrance pulled himself up to his full height with the pomposity of a man who felt himself about to deliver an important address.

"Good morning. As you can see, our assembly this morning is a little different. As we go towards Christmas we should be thinking, not of ourselves and our own selfish wants and needs, but of those around the world who are less fortunate, maybe less loved, certainly less secure. I am not saying that I have a wish that you do not enjoy yourselves, Christmas is a time of rejoicing and familial happiness after all. But as you do enjoy yourself, take a moment to think of those who do not share your gifts and your blessings.

And it is with that in mind that I think we should remind ourselves of those who have laid down their lives just so that you and I can live in a better world. One of those great men was Martin Luther King. The record I am about to play, *Abraham, Martin and John*, refers to King and the tragedy of his assassination on the fourth of April 1968…"

Hope heard no more. This great man, Martin Luther whatsit, had been assassinated on the very day that she had first written her poem. Her breast almost burst with the significance of it all. Yes, it had been the very same day!

As the music filled the classroom where Wiseman House was assembled, she couldn't stem the tears of emotion streaking her cheeks.

She deliberately stayed back after the assembly was over and, when the teachers were busy talking about the day's events, walked up to the Dansette record player where she could see the empty record sleeve leaning against it. She picked it up and turned it over. It was a picture of Martin Luther King. And he was black.

12

Jamilla pushed back lazily into her chair.

"It means 'beautiful. It's Arabic."

"But I thought you were Pakistani."

"Martina! Pakistani? I'm not Pakistani. I don't even look like a Pakistani."

Hope hid her surprise and carried on with her inadequate lunch, trying to gather various shreds of soggy lettuce leaves into a portion big enough to be worth eating. She gave up and pretentiously wiped her mouth on the piece of kitchen roll she'd packed into her lunch bag.

"I never thought you were from Pakistan, Jay. It must irritate you when people get it so wrong."

"Oh Hope, you just don't know. Most people in Britain are so ignorant about my Country. I still get called a Paki even now. Even today! People still think that it's part of the British Empire. That they own it. That they can just be rude and racist. Still, things are better than they used to be. It was far worse for my parents. Oh, the stories they tell. My own father bullied and beaten. And he was so educated. But they didn't want to know. To them he was less than an animal."

Jamilla was getting agitated. Hope could see that Martina had lost interest and was now texting someone – probably her Polack boyfriend she thought.

"It's ignorance, I'm afraid," Hope continued; "people don't understand it so they become afraid of it."

Jamilla stabbed a finger towards Hope. "There you have it! Exactly right. Racism is ignorance. That's what 'prejudice' means: to pre-judge. Make your mind up before you've even found anything out about the facts."

Hope took a sip of water to try and wash the remnants of her lunch down.

"Live and let live. That's what my Father always says."

"Too right. India's a wonderful country. So different. It's got so many beautiful places and many different cultures and languages."

'So why don't all you Pakis go and live there?' thought Hope.

12a

Elizabeth Clancy had just caught up with Hope but found herself struggling to walk at the same pace.

"Why are you walking fast? Slow down!"

Hope stopped immediately.

"Why do you think?"

"'Cos you're mad."

"Mad at who?"

"Not mad at who. Just mad. Like a spazzer."

Hope said nothing and moved on, at a slower pace. She didn't like Elizabeth Clancy and often pretended to not notice her when walking home. She was too much of an all-rounder for Hope's liking. Good at lessons and good at sports. She'd even represented the borough at 200 metres. Or was it the 100 metres? Perfect Elizabeth Clancy. Whatever you could do, she could do better or faster. That was why, if she suspected she might be somewhere behind her, she quickened her pace.

"Guess what I heard? Go on, ask me."

"What have you heard?" sighed Hope.

"No, you've got to guess."

"You're preggers."

"What? No, be serious! I'll give you a clue."

"You've been asked out by Sully."

Elizabeth was speechless. How did she know? Hope was the first one that she'd wanted to tell and she seemed to have known all along. Hope pretended to read the long PG Tips advert down the side of a nearby double-decker bus that was straining into third gear, stuffed with unruly schoolchildren.

She decided that her answer had obviously found its target. Everyone round school knew that Sully fancied Elizabeth and that it was just a matter of time before he asked her out. Pretending to have known for certain all along should shake her. Hope stopped again and pulled off her light blue school cardigan. The heat had built steadily during the day to an insufferable closeness and the areas by the path that were muddy and waterlogged all winter were now as cracked and bleached as an exposed river bed.

Elizabeth decided to change tack and start teasing Hope.

"Are you jealous? I heard you fancied him yourself. I heard that you were hoping he'd ask…"

"Piss off, Clancy."

"So it's true! I knew it was true!" Elizabeth pretended to guffaw, swinging her leather satchel in dizzying circles about her.

"You're welcome to him. Make sure you get him to wipe his nose before kissing him. Not unless you want green lipstick all over your stupid mouth."

For some reason, Hope noticed that this remark had also hit its target. Elizabeth suddenly slowed her pace and flailed for a riposte.

"How do you know, unless you've tried to kiss him yourself?" She knew she was losing the exchange.

"Snotty Sullivan isn't my cup of green tea. Snotty snoggers never were."

"He's not snotty."

Hope turned around and began to walk backwards. "Used to be. Everyone in St Osburg's called him that. Snotty Sullivan this, Snotty Sullivan that…"

Hope then opened her mouth and lurched forward, pretending to vomit.

Elizabeth caught up again, but this time seemed rather deflated. "Well, he's not snotty now."

Hope, triumphant with her mastery of their exchange, walked towards home once more. Ahead, she could see, to her deep pleasure, Neil Dowling nonchalantly leaning against a wall, waiting for them both to catch up.

"Hiya. Going somewhere girls?"

"None of your business."

"Oh, sorry. Bad time of the month? Makes you a bit touchy?"

"Piss off, Dowling" Hope smiled.

Elizabeth brightened up: "Going to the Curran's party Neil?"

"Nah, can't have a proper party in a church."

"Church Hall. Not the Church."

"Yeah, and what sort of party will it be with a Priest there."

"Probably a better one if you're not there," Hope sneered, although she was deeply wishing that he would be.

Neil, throwing his khaki haversack over his shoulder, fell in walking with the two girls.

"Anyway," continued Hope, "What were you thinking of doing that a priest shouldn't know about?"

Neil affected an inscrutable look. "That's for me to know and you to find out, Sunshine Girl."

"You're not that interesting," Hope derisively replied.

She was enjoying this, Hope decided. She felt she had the upper hand with both and, whatever they threw at her, she could confidently bat aside. The three walked on in silence for a while, although Hope still felt a small smouldering knot of indignation in her stomach about Patrick Sullivan asking Elizabeth out over her, even though she couldn't stand him.

They turned to cut through the Council Estate, passing the litter that huddled and twitched around the exposed roots of limp snowberry bushes. Conversation had strangely fallen away and the three stared through the windows of houses they passed, opened wide to try and air the small rooms in the high heat of the late afternoon.

Hope knew that she and Neil would soon be walking on once they had reached Elizabeth's house. Was there one last opportunity to assert her superiority?

Elizabeth started to rummage in her schoolbag for her house key.

"See you then."

"Why's your house Number 12a?"queried Hope. "Is it a flat?"

Elizabeth looked nonplussed at the question; Hope had been in her house, so must know it wasn't a flat.

"I told you. Dad thinks the number thirteen's unlucky."

"Oh yeah. My Mum says that's a real Council-Housey thing to do. She says you wouldn't get that in our street. Would you have that in your street Neil? Probably not."

The second cruel lance had found its home and Hope affected a knowing smile, cocking her head dramatically to one side.

"Come on, Neil. Might catch something."

But Neil looked surprised by the whole exchange and shrugged his shoulders at Elizabeth as if to signify that he wanted no part in it. He waved weakly and turned to catch Hope up.

14

Denis Dunne had, at one time, cut a small, slim figure in Athlone. But early middle age had mutated that slight frame into a thick-set, paunched man. He sat, bowed, in the front pew of St. Osburg's Church.

Seated next to him, pressed against his side, was Hope. No one else sat on the pew with them. They looked utterly alone.

Arranged behind, in no particular order, was a gathering of friends and family. In that red brick, unfeeling building, a dull, silent sorrow sat amongst them. They could all hear the faint whisperings of the passing cars outside, the sounds of which broke like irregular, exhausted waves on a shingle shore.

In 1955, Denis Dunne had reluctantly agreed to go with Frankie Brennan to that evening's dance. Frankie had told Denis that 'He'd had his eye' on Mary Tuohy and that he needed someone to keep her pal occupied. Denis hated the idea of making up a foursome. He knew that Frankie had a rather underdeveloped taste in women, and that the company that they were likely to keep would be similarly underwhelming.

Try as he might, as the pair walked up the Grace Road, Denis couldn't get his tie to sit right. He began to think about leaving Frankie to it; after all, it wasn't for his own benefit he was going.

And sure, wasn't he already walking out with Mary Mullen? If she found out about this evening, how would he explain that away?

Annoyed, he gave up on the tie. His mind started to turn towards the dull prospect of shuffling couples, no drink and a Priest notorious in all Westmeath for walking in and sending them home early. What was worse, his original plan had been to take Mary to the Adelphi to see *To Hell and Back*. He loved Audie Murphy.

Denis could see her even now, standing outside Sean's Bar: as nervous as a sparrow and pulling her bag close to her hip. Her hair unruly, tousled and coal-black. But the eyes. The dark, dark eyes that lifted towards him and held him mute.

"Oh, and this is Carol. Carol, I give to you Mr Denis Dunne."

But Frankie hadn't given Denis to Carol; Denis had already given himself to her. Carol smiled then looked away to avoid the awkward intensity of Denis's stare. Frankie, sensing that Denis might not be competent enough to handle these first moments took matters into his own hands.

"Let's get a quick drink before we trip the light fantastic. Denis, you come with me and give me a hand."

That night, Denis prayed that the Priest would interrupt the dancing so that he could be alone with Carol but, for once, he was irritatingly absent. Denis tried to talk a little with Carol between dances but they were always quickly joined by Frankie and Mary, with Frankie dominating all the exchanges in an attempt to impress Mary at every opportunity. Denis knew he could never compete with the self-assuredness (others would have said 'cockiness') Frankie displayed and used every opportunity to steal secret glances at the petite woman he had met only an hour or so before.

They walked back that night together, trailing Frankie and Mary by a slowly increasing distance. Denis was hoping later to be able to ask Carol if she'd like him to walk her home. Where Frankie and Mary might fit into such a proposal he wasn't sure and dare not hope that fortune would smile on him and magic the other couple away.

"So why Carol? It's a lovely name."

"My mother. She just loved Carole Lombard."

"Right, so it's Carole with an 'e'"

"No, without. Maybe the Priest couldn't spell. Or didn't like the 'e' or something."

"I'm Denis with one 'n'. Me Dad says why waste two letters when one will do."

The thin membrane of clouds was pulling apart, revealing dim stars that shyly emerged from their concealment. The grunts of badly meshing gears of a passing flatbed lorry broke the quietude of the long road.

A stiff silence had insinuated itself between them. Denis thought hard about how to break it and resume their conversation. Before he could speak, Carol breezily interjected: "I'm leaving Athlone soon."

Denis was stunned and shocked by disappointment; he'd only just met this small, precious girl and now he could feel fate wresting her away from him. He tried to not let his disappointment show.

"Leaving? Where to?"

"England. I have to be with my sister Patsy. She's not well and Dad wants me to be with her for a few weeks."

"But you're coming back then? Afterwards, I mean."

"I expect so. See what happens when I'm there. I don't want to be dishing out pills and tablets all my life.

"What'll you do there? I mean, for a job and everything?"

"I'm going to be an actress. Oh, you look surprised? I can dance and sing as well. I've done a few things already hereabouts. I'm bound to get some work in the West End. Everybody says so."

"An actress? I didn't know you were an actress? I thought you worked in Flemmings."

"Well, I do *now*. But not forever. A girl has dreams as well. Bigger dreams than working in a chemist all your life."

"Well, I hope you call me when you're famous. You might need someone to look after you."

Carol abruptly stopped. "You're a bit of a fast worker, Mr Dunne."

Denis would happily have caught the breath he could see rising from her full mouth and swallowed it completely into his own lungs. He'd never kissed someone on a first night out; he wondered if this night might be different. He dearly hoped to God it would. What wouldn't a man give to kiss such an angel?

But Carol gave a small laugh and walked on, almost as if she could sense his ambition.

He walked behind her for a short while. The coat hugged her small frame; it was the first time he'd noticed the slow, languid walk that she would always have, even when - years later - her petite form could never recover its original slimness after the birth of their children.

"Actress, eh? Name up in lights and all that? Miss Carole Lombard." Denis pretended to frame her name in the air with his hands. Carol wasn't sure if he was taking her seriously or not, and the colour rose in her cheeks

"And why not? Stranger things have happened. Although I hope it reads Miss Carol Maguire, not Carole Lombard."

Denis had wanted to say, "Or Mrs Carol Dunne', but knew it was surely asking too much of life. He vowed he would kneel and say a prayer of thankfulness every day if only he could spend the rest of his life with Carol Maguire. Perhaps he might be better praying to St Jude, for wasn't he the patron saint of lost and desperate causes? Oh, he was lost, marooned now in these soft-sharp pangs and emotions; and desperate that Carol might find some small piece of her heart where she could learn to love him.

Denis suddenly felt a push into his side. It was Hope quietly urging him with her left hand to stand up. He did so and struggled with his too-tight black tie.

Such a small coffin, he thought, as he walked behind in small mechanical steps as it was carried by four unevenly arranged bearers out of the Church.

15

"Still drinking?"

Hope raised and gently waved her empty glass in reply.

Gavin hauled himself confidently on to the high bar stool and immediately caught the attention of the barman with an authoritatively raised finger.

"What'll you have, Hopey?"

"Same again, Mr Laing, please."

"And the same again is?"

"Oh, come on Gavin! There's no one here who knows us. We can drop the pretence."

"So that's your 'same' is it? OK… Oh, another dry white wine here, please. On my room."

Hope pushed the empty glass away ready for the replacement. "I'll buy you one back."

"Not at all. Look upon it as a 'thank you'."

"For what? For the months of deceit?"

Jupiter Rent a Car's annual company conference, always held in the first week of July, swept around each year like a rather tarnished carousel horse. To some it was something they always looked forward to, a chance to misbehave away from husbands, wives, partners and families. Others dreaded it as it meant sharing a soulless twin hotel room with someone whom they would have to intimately acquaint themselves: getting an inside knowledge of how they must always arrange their bedside table at home, clothes hanging peccadilloes and the late night secret squeaks and farts they made when they were in the bathroom.

Gavin felt that the first afternoon – the 'kick off' and conference theme - had gone well. His twenty-minute presentation had followed Keith's, his Sales Director, and the well-rehearsed spontaneous jokes had all found their mark.

From just outside the yawning double doors of the lounge, a voice announced itself. "Ah, here's obviously the place to be. Drink anyone?"

Passing into the room came Barry Bufton, the company's training manager, holding his almost-drained beer glass against his chest. Hope's heart sank like a bloodied stone. Bastard Barry Bufton.

"Mr Bufton!" Gavin's tired features were now freshly lit – a shameless skill all salespeople acquire until it becomes second nature to them - and a smile spread wide across his face. "We'd always thought of you trainers as nine-to-five types."

"El Gavino! Good conference? Feel you're getting your message across?"

As Barry remained standing, Gavin noiselessly slid from his stool and edged towards him.

"I'd like to think so. It's an important message. These are stretching goals we're setting these guys."

"But a goal is so important, Gav. It channels energy into real action. That's got to be good for the team." He brought his glass to his lips and sipped, then breathed slowly out before adding, "Affirming too."

Hope's blood-stained rock was now accelerating towards the floor of the lido.

"I need them with me, Barry. Challenging times; big changes. This financial year has got 'Last Chance Saloon' written in big letters all over it for some people. Keith, me, all of us."

Barry cocked his head to one side. "One message. One team. One reward." Each point in Barry's triumvirate was signalled by a newly raised finger.

"Trouble is, if we don't make the numbers this year, it'll be the wrong reward."

"With that approach we'll definitely fail. It's a question of psychology, Gavin. If you engineer your senses towards victory, then that's – without any shadow of a doubt – what your team will walk away with. As a leader, you've got to be a darkroom. Think of the light as doubt that might creep in. Be a darkroom, Gavin. Shut out the light of doubt. Expose your team to victory only and hand them that photograph. Perhaps you might even use my darkroom image at your next meeting? I could do you a couple of slides."

"Seems all the wrong way round to me. They'll just walk away thinking our job is to keep them in the dark."

Hope drifted. She resented Barry's sudden appearance; always bringing his irritatingly persistent 'positivity' that inevitably wore her – and everyone else - down. And then there was his small collection of ill-fitting suits, each of which seemed to slackly gather his limbs up so that he resembled a poorly trussed chicken.

She smiled inwardly when she recalled his flatulence. Occasionally, to his obvious discomfort, an anal rumble had insinuated itself often whilst he was in company. She'd never noticed it when he'd first joined the company, but since the short 'sabbatical' he'd taken some time ago, there seemed to be more and more occasions when he'd discharge a slew of rolling farts.

His consistent response to this was to act as if nothing had happened, but Hope knew it had and attributed his weak sphincter to too much time spent trying to impress his 'University chums' in whichever provincial technical college he'd ended up at.

Le Petomane. Yes, Bufton was Le Petomane in sorry, sulphurous decline.

Despite having once been told that the average bowl of bar peanuts was tainted with 9 different urines, she reached for one all the same. She enjoyed the saltiness of the first peanut and started to mechanically feed one after another into her mouth, her elbow becoming the fulcrum of a lever that effortlessly supplied nut after nut after nut.

When was that fucking retard Bufton going to go? He'd probably been nice looking once. If he'd dressed right. But now he was a shabby non-man, occupying that hinterland that lies between early middle age and death. Greying. Stooping. Embarrassing.

Barry's voice crashed into her thoughts: "Sorry, Hope, we're being rude. Can I recharge your glass? Another tumbler of the unblushed Hippocrene?"

To her astonishment – and vague shame – Hope was holding a completely drained wine glass. Falteringly, she lifted it once more.

"Same again?"

16

"Will you do it?"

Hope leaned forward and opened her eyes deliberately wider, bringing her hands forward to rest on her lap. She leant into Neil, aware that her low cotton top would gape invitingly.

"I told you I'll do it, Neil. But you've got to be honest."

Now she bit her bottom lip. She knew this always imparted a dramatic quality. Seconds slipped by, with nothing but distant, indistinct birdsong witnessing their passing.

"Will you keep your word?" Hope added.

"Yeah. But you're not just…"

Hope laughed. "Leading you on?" She cupped the inside of his right knee with her left hand and, in a small circular motion, splayed her hand outward and inched it slowly up his leg.

"Fuck."

Hope lurched back in her seat, swiftly withdrawing her hand from Neil's thigh as she did so.

"Not now. Dad might be back."

Her attention fixed airily to the front room window, as if she quite expected her Father to climb through it at any moment.

"I'll be quick."

Hope's eyes swivelled back, half lidded and mocking.

"Nah, it'll be all round school. Besides…"

"Besides what?"

"Besides. Just besides."

"But you're going to do it. To me. Underwater."

A smile ghosted across her face. Her eyes hardened as she took in poor Neil. Doomed Neil. Sometimes she could almost love him. Then she would notice how the light would slant across his pustular face and a surge of nausea would erupt into her lungs. Although she remembered that Richard Burton complained of the same condition, the sight made her want to vomit her greasy lunch into his thin-lipped mouth.

Sex. It's all adolescent boys think about. It's certainly all this adolescent boy thinks about. She sat up straight again.

"Piss off, Neil."

"Hmm?"

"Dad's back in a minute. You're going to have to go. And take your little hard-on with you."

17

Carol Dunne couldn't look Hope in the eye. She pretended to tap the ash from her cigarette even though there was none yet ready to fall.

"Are you brave, Hope?"

"Very brave, Mummy." Hope moved into the brief curve of her Mother's body; she could feel the prickly weft of her scented dress against her cheek.

"And do you believe in God?"

"Course."

"And where's the nicest place to be. Here in Ruislip or with our Lord, his Holy Father and the Holy Ghost?"

Hope was confused. This was what Father Thirle, the Parish Priest had once talked to the class about. The Holy Trinity. She'd struggled to comprehend what he was talking about when he had sat with them in the classroom; now, she felt even more unsure in his absence.

"Are you going to see them? Are you going to see Jesus?"

"I think I might be. I think he's asked me to go to them because he knows you're a brave, brave girl." She pulled quickly on her cigarette to mask the emotional surge that was climbing in her chest.

"Can I go? Can I see them with you?"

"No. God needs you here. He needs you to look after Daddy."

Hope could feel - even in these tender years - that the conversation was a charade. Like Father Christmas, she knew to play along with the whole pretence of it all. Only last year, she'd looked in her father's shed for an old racquet and there they were: hers and Stephen's Christmas presents waiting to be wrapped. Even the doll's house furniture that her Mother had repeatedly promised Mummy and Daddy would never be able to afford. She'd never let on that she knew.

"I'll look after Daddy. But I don't want you to go to Heaven."

"You're a good girl, Hope."

Carol Dunne pulled Hope's head to her and pressed her lips and nose deep into her hair.

"I want to be a good girl."

She thought she heard her Mum hiccup.

The room door was gently opened and Denis, ashen-faced and red-eyed, took one step into the room.

"They're here, love."

18

"So what have been our takeaways?"

Barry Bufton opened his arms like a beaming, welcoming landlord, inviting the delegates on his workshop into his better world.

A dowdy, grey-haired woman spotted her chance.

"Well, for me Barry, because of what you've shown us today, I take back new tools and a new way of thinking."

She looked to the other delegates not for approval, but for attention. The late sun had thrown a warming beam around the place where Barry stood, with tiny dust specks picked out as they floated about him.

"Thanks, Sheila." Barry had his head, once again, dipped to one side to stress the degree of sincerity that he wanted to project; his face showed a caring and understanding mask.

"If I've been able to move your approach…."

He now looked pleadingly at the delegates, his intense – curiously menacing - stare fixing them to their seats.

"…to a more right-brained way of thinking, of creating a different you, then to me this time that we have shared together has been a success."

This smugness was too much for Hope. She felt the room inflating with a sense of Barry's ego and had to reach for a pin.

"I thought that all that right-brained, left-brained stuff wasn't true, Barry. That it was just a myth."

Barry remained serene and unperturbed, completely untroubled by Hope's deliberately provocative question.

"No, Hope. You often read this or that about neuroscience and its research. But I can categorically reassure you that we really do have left and right brain dominance. In fact, do you know I welcome your left-brain analysis of all we've covered today? Some might see it as an attempt to derail the progress we all have made in this room together, but I view it differently. Can I tell you how I view it? It's rigour, that's what it is. It's rigour. You've taken the decision to kick the tyres of this concept, just to see if it can stand on its own two feet. Well, kick away, Hope. And when the dust has finally settled, you'll discover that concepts such as right and left-brain thinking will be ready to roar away to their next destination. That's a fact."

As Barry spoke, he failed to register the increasing embarrassment of most of those in front of him. But, as always, he was strangely impervious to it. His stare slowly scanned the group for intellectual submission; Hope noticed how – like the well-oiled dome of a Dalek – his gaze smoothly swivelled from one side of the room to another.

"Now, anybody else? Ah, Eric, your takeaways please."

19

Carol Dunne had finally found an empty bench and, with her sister Patsy's shoes pinching her feet so cruelly, had decided to take a rest.

Eyeing the weed-strewn bombsites, pocked with small forests of spent, feathery willow herb, the insinuating chill of the London wind pried and prodded like a lecherous Uncle into the folds of her thin coat. She had one cigarette left. Smoke it now or save it for the bus? She reached into her pocket for the packet and felt it resting against a box of England's Glory matches. She hesitantly withdrew her hand before plunging it back into her pocket again to retrieve both boxes.

The pigeons had the resigned bearing that conveyed that today was not a good feeding day. Sideways, they eyeballed the likelihood of being fed by the dreary temporary park residents – some standing, some sitting – and accepted that better meals were probably found elsewhere.

The Serpentine seemed to be chilling the air with its icy surface; a flat, glassy sheet that sucked the heat to its muddy depths and exchanged it for a lean, arctic vapour.

If it hadn't been so cold, then Carol knew that she would have wept bitter tears of disappointment and frustration. But the chilling atmosphere, somehow, implied that emotion wasn't seemly. She carefully pulled memory from memory, teasing each apart as one peels one strip of Parma ham from its neighbour. In her mind she held each piece of memory up to the light and viewed, in crushing exactitude, the humiliation that had taken place that morning.

"Stop, stop, stop!"

The accompaniment had frozen mid-bar and Carol looked up in astonishment, staring toward the fourth row of the damp theatre where two self-satisfied men were now intensely debating something that seemed completely unconnected with the prepared routine she had just started.

She stepped back and glanced sideways at the audition pianist. Worryingly, he had taken her music and slapped it dismissively on to the lid of his worn piano. He'd obviously decided he wouldn't need it any more.

She could feel the sweat on her forehead, now chilling her brow in the damp cold of the theatre. It wasn't perspiration borne of effort, she had only got to the end of the first verse and the dance steps she had moved through were light enough and physically undemanding, it was the perspiration of nervous fear. She had made one bitter sacrifice to earn this moment in front of these men and she couldn't allow herself to think that it might have been a worthless exercise.

Still the men were talking. Maybe it was not as bad as she'd imagined? It might be an understudy role? Or perhaps a very minor part? She straightened up and patted down her pleats. Her left tap shoe was chafing her ankle and it was only now that she was conscious of the discomfort. She rechecked the upper part of her leotard for vomit. For some reason, a quarter of an hour before she was required on stage, she had suddenly been sick in the dressing room. She'd been very nervous in her small-scale performances back in Athlone, but never so much that it had made her sick.

Then one man broke from the intense conversation and looked towards Carol, her small figure utterly diminished on such a vast, empty stage. The pianist relit his cigarette and pushed his stool back from the piano so that he could cross his legs…

"Oh, you still here?"

His eyelids lowered like an emotionless cobra considering its prey. He would eat her, digest her, defecate her.

"No, thank you, Miss... run along. Harry, give me a couple of minutes for a pee before the next, will you?"

The pianist hadn't even bothered to look at her as she thanked him whilst collecting her music.

And still the pigeons awkwardly plodded along the barren park path; Carol's eyes listlessly followed them, but didn't really see them. Now she was the one who was auditioning, and somehow the pigeons knew that they weren't going to find what they were looking for here.

The thought of what she had done, the shame of which still stalked every thought and quiet moment, to earn her audition caused her to wryly smile. A small, dying laugh exhaled from her mouth as she blew out the cigarette smoke.

In her mind, a props manager entered and started to stack the recent memories of unsuccessful auditions against the stage wall of her consciousness. From stage right new thoughts, new scenarios checked their costumes, drew their breath in and stood poised, ready to emerge and take their positions.

A fresh cast had been assembled. Doubts. Damaged self-esteem. An overwhelming and bitter sense of failure. Hopes, dreams, fantasies preciously nursed from childhood now finally immolated. Was this really it? On this bench? In this vast, grey depressing city? Amongst these faceless mannequins that were arranged around her? Was this where her hoped-for life ended?

She threw the cigarette stub in front of her. A pigeon comically ran away to avoid it.

What to tell Denis? What to say to a man who thought her faultless? He thought she was going to be somebody. Someone. And now she had to admit, "I'm like you Denis Dunne. As normal. As talentless. As equal."

Equal? And with that realisation a gulp of sorrow burst violently from her chest, causing her spittle and snot to speckle her coat.

A young couple standing near, alarmed at her distress, moved stealthily away. A man who had stopped to take in the view pretended to look at his watch and departed with the self-conscious awkwardness of an amateur actor. Still Carol sobbed. Within a very short time she found herself entirely alone.

Most of the pigeons had also taken flight when the first emotional cry had left her. One pigeon remained. It's cold, disinterested eye opening and shutting like the lens of a camera.

20

The walk from the bus terminus to the bar where the party was to be held was pleasant enough. Above the Victorian gables of the pollution-blasted Town Hall, Hope could see the last flecks of spun cloud up-lit by the sun. A dying breath of warmth was still present in the evening air, tainted with the heavy scent of bus diesel.

But the pleasantness couldn't lessen the anxiety she felt about what might lie ahead. After a lifetime of negotiating with her Father about going out to the various discos and parties that occasionally swerved into her path, this one had been won at a heavy price.

She'd always managed to wheedle an agreement from him before; this time he was set firm against her going. Instead, time passed and neither spoke again about her request. Six long weeks had been a sufficient buffer for him to forget the conversation and, earlier in the evening, she'd told him that she and Christine Baron were going to revise and so she might stay the night at her house.

"I thought your exams were done now."

"Except for General Studies, Dad."

"How can you revise for General Studies?"

"One minute you're criticising me for not revising enough, now you're telling me not to bother revising."

"I'm not telling you anything. Just don't see what you're going to revise about."

He lowered his newspaper and looked at Hope over his glasses.

"And where d'you say you'll be?"

"Christine's house. *All night.*"

She smiled to stress the last two words. He returned to his paper and Hope knew – through his silence – she'd won his grudging consent to her going. But she'd lied more than she'd ever lied to him before and felt desperately uneasy about it. There were no rules, no morals, about lying to other people. Everyone did it. But lying to someone you cared about and trusted so much pulled her up short.

And now she wondered if she could go through with it, having to walk into The Black Penny bar on her own. She was underage, but had been reassured that, as it was largely a private party, she needn't worry. She remembered, when she had originally asked her father, the fact that this event was to be held in a busy bar was the one insurmountable obstacle.

She walked on robotically: her limbs carrying her ever closer but her mind willing her to turn back to the Bus Station.

"Hope!"

The voice behind her was Lesley Flaherty. Hope despised Lesley but was, in the circumstances, reluctantly glad to see her.

"Hi, Lesley. What time is it?"

"Time we were at Michael Petrenko's party! Are you looking forward to it? Should be a laugh."

"Course."

Hope now received her first shock of the evening. As she took Lesley in properly she was astounded to see how much trouble she'd gone to. No longer the thin burgundy cardigans and pleated grey school skirts that both had lived in for the last five years or so; here was a very different Lesley. She was wearing an apple green trouser suit – Hope guessed Polyester – and looked very different with the flicks in her hair, testament to an early evening spent with a pair of tongs.

"Not sure if I have the time to go, actually. I was just…"

"Come on, Hope. It'll be a laugh."

That was the second time that Lesley had used that expression and Hope wasn't sure it would be anything of the kind. She also, now, felt much underdressed. After looking and re-looking through her wardrobe, she had eventually decided on a matching tank top and blouse, but now those clothes seemed so horribly 'casual' next to Lesley's crisp suit and new platforms.

"Well, just come in for one drink. One's not gonna hurt. They'll serve you, you know."

They were now yards away from the entrance to The Black Penny and Hope knew that it was now or never. Her face froze in a failed smile as she turned to Lesley.

"You go first."

"How'd your mocks go?" Lesley threw back as she swung the entrance door open.

"Oh, not very good."

As Hope entered, the next surprise was the sheer loudness of the music. Before, at the various school and church discos, the music had been loud, but she was always able to talk over it. Here the music was deafening and all conversation reduced to alternately shouting short, alcohol-breathed sentences into your neighbour's straining ear.

To Hope's rising horror, she felt utterly out of place. Everyone looked grown up! They'd left School on Friday looking, as most sixth formers often look, as if on the cusp of adulthood. But here the transformation, in Hope's eyes, had been complete. Here they *were* adults, whilst Hope felt lesser, younger, humiliated. It was always the same pattern that she had first noticed in Primary school. Life was a party that she had never been given the invitation to, so she constantly found herself in the same position of onlooker. Always the outsider. Always the wrong side of any window.

Maria Brady walked past holding two half-pint glasses high above her, trying to ease between the backs of adjacent groups of people. She looked across at Hope and took her in.

Without even acknowledging her presence she squeezed onwards, one high elbow tapping the shoulder of Frances Chivers whom she slyly implored to look back at Hope. Frances did so before brazenly sniggering with Maria Brady. A confused shame rose in Hope's breast and she looked in panic for the exit. She was so miserably out of her depth. What had she been thinking of? She had lied to be here and now could only anticipate being crushed down by her own overwhelming sense of inadequacy. Where was the way out?

She momentarily flinched as someone hollered into her ear: "Hello, Sunshine Girl!"

It was Neil Dowling

21

Martina Grabowska had no humour. Or, come to think of it, no sense of irony either. Perhaps, Hope mused, it was because *all* Polish people had no sense of humour or irony. Martina always looked sour. Hope imagined a cut lime on her bony shoulders, its pale fillets of flesh bisected by a white goal line of pith.

The conversation that had prompted this thought in Hope's mind had taken place only minutes before. Martina, had been slowly chewing her lunch (without betraying any discernible pleasure in her food) whilst devouring all of the titillating text *The Sun*. She consumed a newspaper in the same way that she consumed food: methodically and slowly.

She looked up from her reading. "Trains are on strike again. It says here that they are walking out on Thursday. No trains on Thursday, it looks like."

Hope had known about the strike. It had been on the news as she had driven in that morning.

"Well, they're due their annual holiday." Hope sneered, pleased with the acidity of her satire.

Martina flinched a little and looked at Hope with a faintly superior smile.

"It's not a Holiday, Hope. It's a strike. It's not a Holiday."

Hope was irritated by Martina's patronising response; an irritation further exacerbated by her habit of always repeating information in case you lacked the intelligence to absorb what she'd said the first time round.

"Joke, Martina; joke."

"Joke? Did I miss something? Did I miss the joke?"

Hope considered momentarily whether she should explain but quickly thought better of it and turned her eyes back to the computer screen.

Martina looked once again at the paper. "It's not a joke, it's true."

She might speak the language, thought Hope, but that's about it. Didn't someone cover the word 'irony' in Poland with Martina, once they knew she was coming to England? The Poles, the Americans, in fact nearly all cultures seemed to completely fail to appreciate the unique British sense of irony. There should be workshops in it, concluded Hope. The first thing these immigrants should get, once they'd brazened their way through the UK's incontinent customs, would be to immediately attend a British humour workshop. 'What makes Brits laugh'; yes, she concluded, that would be a good title.

Hope could now feel herself slipping down into a mire of resentment about Martina, becoming further needled when she remembered how easily Martina laughed whenever a Company Director was present. Even their weakest of attempts at humour had her laughing with a deeply annoying giggle that rattled from the back of her throat. Martina didn't struggle to see the funny side then, not when there were senior male managers to drape herself over.

"Robin, really. That's too much! Don't…"

Witnessing the effect Martina had on men made Hope wince inwardly in embarrassment. Even the severest of directors were unable to resist Martina's easy manner; Hope thought about how they stood there, to a man, secretly considering whether something special between them and Martina might be slowly developing at that moment. It made Hope wish that she had videoed each one of them so that she could play it back to them all. Video excerpt after video excerpt of the same technique, the same laugh, the same physical closeness that rendered each man helpless before this Polish siren.

"Steve, really. That's too much! Don't…"

Men defenceless because all they have wrapped around them is the indomitable belief that – early middle age or late middle age – their attractiveness is abundant still.

"Ray, really. That's too much! Don't…"

With her high Slavic cheekbones and fathomless eyes, Martina carried the insouciance of a young woman secure in the knowledge that every casual gesture – carefully rehearsed - was irresistible to this weak, pathetic species.

"Keith, really. That's too much! Don't…"

With these men, Hope felt invisible. Whenever any director or senior manager stood by her, they would talk with the same warmth and passion as they would as if addressing their own faded wives. Hope was 'one of the boys' one had once told her. Not even a woman; certainly not young. Not like Martina.

"Trains are on strike again. It says here that they are walking out on Thursday. No trains on Thursday, it looks like."

"Well, they're due their annual holiday."

"Hope, really. That's too much! Don't…"

Fucking Polack Bitch.

22

"I'm up here!"

Carol Dunne slid the scarf from her neck and let it fall to the floor in one slow, snake-like slither.

"How'd it go?" The far-away question made her pinch the bridge of her nose with tiredness.

Denis Dunne's heavy footsteps padded down the stairs.

"Well, love?"

"Well what?"

"You know well what. Good news or bad?"

"What d'yer think. What other news is there?"

Denis sucked in his cheeks, not sure whether to comfort Carol with a touch or not. He awkwardly raised his hand towards her.

"Don't. I just need some time to myself…"

With pride bruised, he walked into the kitchen and snatched the kettle from the hob. The dimness of the day outside leached its greyness over the kitchen walls; Denis flicked the light on.

"Let me make tea. Then you can…"

"I don't want tea."

Denis turned the tap off for a moment, went to say something but decided against it. He proceeded to finish filling the kettle and, in an attempt to lighten the mood, added cheerily, "Not good, eh? Sure there'll be others now."

"There won't be any others. I'm not going through that again."

"Come on, love. It was never going to be easy. We'd always…"

"For God's sake I know it's not easy! It's never going to happen! Can't you see it? Because I can see it. You don't stand there looking like a... like a... eejit. Like a fecking eejit while some half-wit doesn't even have the... the courtesy to…"

"Love, love. Let's not talk about it. Let's leave it be for a bit. Forget it."

"Oh, you're right there, 'cos I *am* going to forget it." Carol struggled to extract her arm from the sleeve of her coat.

"Now that's not right. You've had your disappointments before and look how you've…."

"Look how I've what? Look how I've what? Look how I've come back to this hole every time and said 'Oh, they didn't think I was experienced enough'. Tall enough. Good enough. Well I'm not. I'm not good enough and you keep telling me all the time how fucking wonderful I am – well that makes it worse. You're living a lie. Now, for the love of Mary, help me by not talking about it." The coat was thrown in anger against the wall.

On that wintry, late Tuesday afternoon, Carol Maguire left Denis. All that remained from that day forward was Carol Dunne. An outer shell that used to house the precious woman he had first fallen for – in a small church dance - in Athlone in 1955.

At first, at friends' houses, he tried to get her to do a 'turn' just like she used to. But each time her rebuff was a steely and unflinching "I don't think so". After a few attempts over the months and years, he left off encouraging her to sing again.

"Such a lovely voice", he'd tell people. "The voice of a blessed angel."

He'd recall the early days, when he'd hear her in a neighbouring room singing '*God Bless the Child*'; he'd lay his paper down and allow himself a few unashamed tears as her voice, lonely and sweet, would lie on the air.

Them that's got shall get
Them that's not shall lose
So the Bible said and it still is news…

Denis had loved her so profoundly in those early, tender days of marriage. Struggling to establish themselves in a dilapidated set of small rooms in Kilburn, he knew he'd found himself a woman like no other. His little caged bird, pouring out her prison song.

Yes, the strong gets more
While the weak ones fade…

But she never sang again. Not even when she thought she was alone. He tried to broach the subject once when they were having a quiet drink in a pub, before going on to see Joe Lynch at the Bamba Club on the High Road, but she swept past the subject with another angry, dismissive, "Not that again. Not now."

And, over the succeeding years, it was as if she had never sung.

Mama may have, Papa may have
But God bless the child that's got his own
That's got his own.

23

"Is there a special someone in your life?"

Hope smiled and tried to look enigmatic. It was only Barry Bufton asking so why should she reply? She was still masking her disappointment that, after all the male company that had thronged the hotel reception rooms earlier, she should be left to enjoy her last drinks of the evening with this buffoon of a man.

"I thought so. Nice woman like you."

They were sitting in a corner of the hotel's main lounge; the clock had showed them that it was now well past 2am and all of the other conference guests had long since drifted away. The barman leaned forward over his bar in a posture that conveyed to

Hope and Barry that any further requests for drinks would be a severe inconvenience at such a late hour.

Hope went out so seldom these days that she seized on any social opportunity she could, wringing the last minutes from this occasion regardless that in five short hours she was expected to be helping with the organisation of meaningless team activities on the conference's final day.

"And you? Is there a lucky Mrs Bufton and a gaggle of little Buftonettes?"

"There was. Well there still is, but, well, that's not very interesting."

Hope centred her wine glass exactly in the middle of the scallop-edged, wafery table mat.

"I'm interested. In Mrs Bufton, I mean."

Barry looked bothered. It was the first time that Hope had seen him like this and she wasn't sure how to react. Gone was the endless stream of aphorisms and upbeat, life-enhancing mottos. Here was a different Barry, a vulnerable Barry who was uncomfortably disarmed.

"I, um… it just ended. Just another marriage statistic."

"You don't have to tell me. I don't want to pry." Hope lied.

"No, you're not prying, let's just say it ended and now I am a proud MacDonald's Daddy every Saturday. Mind you, at least we're past the Happy Meal phase. Bloody rip-offs, eh?"

He smiled into his glass, Hope felt he was buying time to reorganise his thoughts, maybe even reach for some old saw about 'Everything in life being a learning opportunity' or something feeble like that. Hope wondered if his brain was, at that very moment, desperately reaching for a soothing sentence plucked from some inspirational internet website.

Hope took pity. "Well, for me, no children so no MacDonald's. I did have a burger there once but I don't remember enjoying it. It's not real is it? Burgers and things. It's not even a proper meal."

Barry said nothing but looked back at her after she'd finished speaking.

A full minute passed during which Hope pretended to find the neighbouring reception area fascinating, just to avoid Barry's stare.

"Sorry, miles away. So who is he?" suddenly came Barry's question as he pulled himself back into the conversation.

"Who's who?"

"You know, the special one in your life. Does he work for us?"

"That's very forward of you. There might not be anyone special in my life."

Barry persisted and leaned into her, warming to his task.

"I'm sure that there's someone. Lovely lady like yourself. Got to be. Would I know him?"

Hope was enjoying being the centre of attention. Earlier, there had been conversations passing before her amongst the almost entirely male group that seemed to ignore the fact that there was a woman present. Would their wives have allowed them to speak in front of *them* like that? Hope thought they probably wouldn't have.

"You might know him."

Barry looked a little incredulous before asking, "Are you having an affair?"

"Barry, really!"

"No, tell me. Are you?"

Hope suddenly felt at a loss for what to say. Her first thought was to be dramatic and play for Barry's sympathy. Then she decided that this might be regretted once the effects of the drink had deserted her in the morning.

"Oh, I think it's over. I'm, or we're, not sure."

"So it is an affair? Is it Gavin? Tell me..." Barry leant conspiratorially towards her, "... it's Gavin isn't it?"

She didn't like the uncomfortable way that the focus of the conversation had suddenly turned and decided that she'd have to make an exit immediately.

"Sorry, Barry, I can't finish that drink. I didn't realise the time."

"I won't tell anyone. Your secret's safe with me Miss Dunne!"

She looked back at Barry with a forced smile, "I have no secrets. I'm afraid I'm not very interesting, really. Goodnight!"

"Bloody hell!" Barry thought to himself. "Hope and bloody Gavin."

He immediately thought about who he could tell.

24

"A Daddy Long Legs should do it."

Denis whipped the rod and took up a little of the slack line with his left hand. The artificial fly fell softly on the surface. The wind had now dropped completely and the still, glassy lough stretched smoothly away before him.

"Daddy thinks you'd be better trolling. Bigger fish he says."

"I've got my big fish." He looked back at Carol, lying with eyes closed on some flattened grass; he registered the soft bare flesh of her white calves.

"Besides, you get some good trout in the shallows. I've had some beauties."

"Would they feed a family, your fine trout? Mammy's gutted some monsters."

Denis felt the competitive urge rising; he was certainly a better fisherman than her father, but how to say it? He decided to leave it.

"I'm sure she has now. I'm sure she has."

Carol sat up and folded her arms around her knees. She looked at the discarded bicycle which she had earlier pushed against the knoll.

"What about me puncture? I'm not walking back to town."

"I'll fix it sure enough. It's nothing."

The westering sun had dipped below the horizon and a slim, peach streak now began to uncurl itself across the dimming sky.

Denis considered packing up. He'd landed two fair fish that would do for a bit of supper. Then he felt Carol's two arms slowly encircle his waist and the pressure of her head settle lovingly between his shoulder blades. Fishing, this woman, this lough and this sky… It was all too perfect. Could even Audie Murphy want for more?

"Dunney."

"Yes, Miss Lombard."

"When I'm famous, will you be jealous? Will you be so mad with jealousy that you'll follow me around everywhere making sure that all those movie stars don't come on to me?"

"I might. Depends."

"Depends on what?"

"Depends if you're my wife or not. If you were my wife then I'd be OK, I suppose."

"And if we weren't wed? What if we weren't?"

"Then I'd carry my priest and cosh the lot of them. As a signal, like."

"I'd like you to cosh them. You promise me you'll cosh them?"

He went to reply but the jerk of the rod told him that a fish had taken and the line spun out of his reel at a dizzying speed.

"Cripes! Cripes, Carol!"

Carol held her hands to her mouth before pulling them away to release an excited burst of laughter.

"He's a big one all right. He's a…"

"Hold on to him Dunney! Hold on to him!"

"Get me the net! Over there, the net!"

She ran and snatched up the landing net, expertly wielding it round to the lake's edge, ready.

Denis could feel the thrilling, tugging pull of the line as the trout lurched and lunged combatively. He let some of the line out, conscious that some adjacent reeds would be the first place the powerful fish would make for. He quickly adjusted his stance, moving round to compensate for the angles the trout's random surges took.

"Cripes! Cripes!" He repeated, losing all sense of time and moment, entirely given up to the urgent battle against the fish.

"Hold on, Dunney!" Carol jumped up and down in excitement. "Hold on!"

He reeled in a little more, hoping that the fish would be tiring by now. But still the pull felt desperately powerful and full.

"Come on you beauty, come on…" Denis whispered in secret conversation to his desperate foe.

Just as he thought, the trout made for the reed bed to Denis's right, but its power was now weakening and Denis skilfully reeled in more line whilst the rod top continued to pull, arch and quiver, a needle wickedly flickering with the electricity of the tussle. The trout's last bolt for life was in vain and, some minutes later, the dead prize lay before them: speckled with water and its mouth and gills streaked in dark blood. They both stared at the fish, its flanks still sheened with the fading lustre of life; blades of grass sticking to its pale underbelly.

Eventually, Carol's voice broke in with the question, "Fifteen pounds?"

Denis nodded. "At least, I'd say. But it's a beautiful thing. To think I'd almost given up."

"Ach, you should never give up, Dunney." Carol playfully thumped his back before turning away, picking up and shaking out her coat.

Denis became suddenly conscious of an overwhelming sense of profound satisfaction. He stood at the water's edge with hands planted confidently on his hips and stared across Lough Ree. He felt he wanted to offer a prayer to the vast, broad lake in a humble supplication; to thank this huge body of water for yielding up a prize that had been the final, flawless jewel in the crown of a perfect day.

He carefully dismantled his cane rod and gathered up the three limp trophies, placing each gently in his fishing bag. Then he thought again and took out the trout he'd just caught and wrapped it separately in some of the newspaper Carol had been reading earlier.

"That's for your Mam."

"I can't take that. Me Father wouldn't like it for a start."

"I know", Denis winked at her, "Now let's have a look at that puncture."

25

"Good morning, Jupiter Rent-A-Car, Hope speaking, how may I help you?"

"Oh, hi Hope. Is Gavin there?"

Hope instantly realised that it was Thuong, Gavin's wife.

"I'm sorry, he's away from his desk at the moment. Can I ask who's calling?"

"It's Thuong, Hope. Is he really away from his desk? I need to speak with him."

"Oh, hello Thuong, I didn't recognise you. He really is away from his desk. Shall I leave a message?"

"Can you tell him it's very urgent?"

Hope drew a row of swastikas on her memo pad.

"Of course. Are you at home?"

"Yes, but I'll try his mobile as well."

"I'll tell him you called."

"Thanks, Hope. Bye."

"Bye, Thuong."

Slitty, slitty, slitty-eyed cow.

Hope considered the swastikas for a moment. Had she drawn them all the right way round?

A mobile trilled in the next office.

"Gavin… Oh, hullo Babe."

26

John Maguire had had an argument with his wife and was now doing the only thing that was assured to settle his volcanic temper: standing in the Donkey Field at the back of his cottage, practising the casting of his newly-tied artificial fly. Denis Dunne entered the field unperturbed by the incongruous sight of a seemingly sane man fishing in the grass.

"Mr Maguire."

"Denis." Mr Maguire continued to stare ahead at where the fly repeatedly fell.

Denis enjoyed the lift of a warm breeze sweeping across him, pausing to watch fat, inflated clouds crawl imperiously across the sky.

"Fine Day."

"It is, so."

"I'd say that wind's got rain on it, Mr Maguire."

"It has, so."

Across the fields, Denis could see the Galway train smoothing between the banks and hedges. John Maguire preferred to keep his eye on the rod tip, flexing the line forward and back as if bringing an imaginary lion to order.

"A nymph, Sir?"

"My own. Just made it. It's small but it's a winner."

"I prefer the smaller ones myself, Mr Maguire."

"Trouble is, Mr Dunne, people open up their bag and go for the biggest. I see a lot of men do it now. With a smaller one you can kiss the water."

"Too right."

"Your Father's well?"

"He's grand."

"And your Mother?"

"She's grand."

"Have you tried the Inny of late? I hear there's good fishing."

Denis stepped sideward to lessen the space between himself and Mr Maguire. He felt this was the moment, but couldn't think of the earlier line he'd rehearsed to open with.

"That's a... that's a fine rod you have there, Mr Maguire," he stammered.

"It is. Had it a good long while now, but it will see me out. I hear you had great sport the other day?"

"Ah, someone up there was looking after me. I was just ready to pack up and everything before she took."

"The answer's 'yes', Mr Dunne. What you've come here to ask me, and I respect you for it, the answer's 'yes'."

Denis was stunned. He suddenly became conscious that he had been constantly circling his cap in his hands since entering the field. He eventually recovered a small degree of composure, asserting, "I've not asked you yet, Mr Maguire. Do me the favour of letting me ask you first."

"You've nothing going for you, Mr Dunne. There's no future in dairy. Your family are not...are not... well, never mind what they're not. But you're decent enough. And, God knows, you're the only hope that girl has."

"What do you mean the only hope?"

"For Carol. You're the only hope. She's a head full of films. Chock full of Hollywood and musicals and whatnot. She holds a good tune and moves well enough. But there are plenty like that. Better looking too."

Denis wanted to take issue, "Well, she's as fine a girl as… as…"

Unmoved by Dunne's keen advocacy of Carol, Maguire steadily retrieved his fly, arched the rod backwards before propelling the bait once more towards the small vest he'd placed earlier as a target. This time the fly fell well short.

"Ker-rist!"

Denis, momentarily motioned towards him to make a suggestion about the amount of line he was feeding through, but checked himself with the thought that it might appear impertinent.

"Mr Maguire, Carol told me that she wants to go to England."

Maguire said nothing, but Denis noticed how – even side on – his features set firm.

"My cousin's got something in London for me. Cable work. I'm to go over, make a start and then come back. I want to come back for her. For Carol, that is. Then, of course, going back with her as my wife."

Mr Maguire, who hadn't looked once at Denis during the entire conversation stared forward, as if expecting a trout to rise at any moment through the surface of the grass to take his new nymph to the muddy soil below.

Denis continued, "So I'm away soon to London to get things ready. When I think I've got it sorted then I'll be back. But not until…"

"Mr Dunne." Still John Maguire peered solemnly at the small, distant, white square of cloth before him. Denis didn't know how to respond, but reasoned that deference was probably the safest course to steer.

"Yes, Mr Maguire?"

Maguire released his right hand from the barrel of the rod's handle and held it open towards Denis, ready for the expectant handshake. But still his stare was resolutely eyeing the turf for that emerging trout.

Denis placed his large hand in Maguire's, feeling his broad span enveloped by a strong and decisive grasp. Their hands remained firmly clasped. Then Maguire withdrew and placed it back on the rod.

"Thank you, sir. I'll get on now."

Denis walked backwards for the gate, wanting to wait until he'd reached a respectful distance before he showed Maguire his back.

"Mr Dunne!"

Denis stopped and Maguire turned his fierce eyes towards him. Then his features relaxed as if an awful pain had just left him.

"I love my daughter very much."

Denis was, at first, unsettled by this rare display of tenderness. Gathering himself, he placed his cap on his head and smiled.

"That's two of us, Sir."

27

"So what's this I hear? So what's this I hear about you wanting..."

Father Kirwan suddenly became aware of an unfortunate pleat in his cassock.

"Wanting to pursue a vocation at the Convent of the Holy..."

Hope wasn't sure about the right way that she should express her response. If she smiled then that wouldn't seem right. She looked down and thought about how the beads on her Rosary were centred to the right of her lap. She began to count each bead to confirm that the cross was at the centre.

The Priest sprang out of his chair and moved to the window. He'd been asked to talk to Hope by Mr Terrance, her House Master, concerned about the religious zeal that had recently emerged in her. Not only was it affecting her A levels, her behaviour had started to become a distraction within the wider school and, only this week, Mr Terrance had been approached by two teachers who were troubled by her manner. Hope's latest pronouncement was that she intended to renounce her studies and take the vow to become a nun.

"It's a big, big..."

He placed the flat of his palm on the window pane. Small veins rose on the back of his tense hand.

"It's a big what, Father?"

"Isn't it just! Isn't it just a big thing, now? You wanting to go off and whatever..."

Hope felt uncomfortable with the way that he was smiling at her. He drew up a chair, which he'd taken from an adjacent school desk and sat awkwardly on it.

He was still a comparatively young man with the beardless face and smoothed-back hair that Hope had never seen before on a priest. To Hope, all priests had been aged and distant. Father Kirwan was so different. He wasn't confident, he never seemed sure of what to say and that was what made him so very different from all of the priests she'd met before.

"Do you love God, Hope? Do you love God very much?"

"Yes."

Father Kirwan stood up and moved his child's chair to the side of Hope's. He sat slowly down on it and made sure that his arm rested against Hope's arm.

"How much? How much do you love God? I mean really love him?"

Hope felt afraid. These were questions she'd never faced before. Why would he be asking them? Her right hand reached down to pull down the hem of her skirt. After this she pushed her fingers into the stretched webbing of tight fabric behind her knee just for something to do. She slowly realised that she was shaking.

28

The smell emerging from Jamilla's scratched plastic lunchbox was spicy and fragrant. It was also turning Hope's stomach. Martina had finished her lunch and was staring intently at her newspaper.

"That's a very intense aroma, Jay. Is it Indian?"

Jamilla just nodded, her mouth full of the rice dish she'd prepared only that morning.

"It's amazing how much those aromas carry, isn't it, Jay? It makes you think of bazaars and Indian markets."

Jamilla swallowed. "We've forgotten how to smell. When you're in India, the first thing you notice is the smell. Beautiful smells: spices, dishes, cooking. In England nothing smells."

"Oh, I wouldn't say that."

Jamilla looked up from her food. "Is this food all right? It's not too strong is it? I can go and eat it in the canteen if you like. I don't mind."

"It's a nice smell, Jay. No, don't be silly. Once in a while doesn't hurt. Did you make it yourself?"

"I always make my own food. That stuff in the canteen – I remember eating in there when I first worked here – was too salty. Much too salty. I don't know how people can do that to themselves. It's like having a mouthful of salt with every forkful." She shivered to express her culinary disapproval.

Hope nodded her assent and decided that today was not going to be a salad day. She'd get a chicken and bacon sandwich from

Marks and Spencer when she went out to collect the printing from the stationer on the High Street.

"Oh, I never buy lunch, Jay. Too fatty. Never know what you're eating really. Or who's made it. You only have to watch how many people don't wash their hands after going to the loo to know that some people's standards…"

"Oh I do that!"

"Do what?"

"Notice how many people don't wash their hands. When they've been for a pee. Men are worse."

"How do you know men are worse?"

"It's obvious. When you stand outside waiting for your husband to come out of the toilet and some men come out seconds after they've gone in. Men who went in after my Gopi come out before him. I say to him, Gopi, why don't men wash their hands? It's disgusting! Men, quite respectable looking, not washing their hands after they've been fiddling with their thingy. Gopi, I say, why don't they wash their hands? Haven't you noticed, Hope?"

"Well, I don't wait outside men's toilets really."

"Oh no. I forgot. I suppose you wouldn't really."

Martina's mobile burbled into life and she hurried from the office. All Hope could catch was "Hi, hi, look, could you stop…" But to her frustration she couldn't make out any more of Martina's clandestine conversation.

"Hope, were you ever married?"

Hope steadied herself, momentarily shaken by the question. "Yes" she replied, coolly.

"How long?"

"About two years."

"Two years? Was he nice?"

"You could say that. He had his moment."

"His moment? Don't you mean moments?"

Hope smiled mysteriously, "His moment."

Jamilla cocked her head to one side and thought about what had just been said, showing in her face that Hope's sarcasm had not been missed. After a few brief moments she continued, "You never talk about things. You never talk about your past. You're such a lovely woman. Why aren't you with a nice man? I'll lend you my Gopi for the night!"

Jamilla though this hilarious and was soon cackling at what she'd just said, clapping her hands in a fervent applause. Hope noticed that a husk of rice had been vomited from Jamilla's merry throat onto the desk. It disgusted her and she found it difficult to switch from the revulsion she felt to adopting the false demeanour of laughing at Jay's suggestion.

"No, no. That's silly of me I know. But tell me, who this great man was who captured our mysterious Miss Dunne. I bet he was a handsome man. A looker. I bet you were a handsome couple."

Hope was still preoccupied with the liberated rice husk, shiny with saliva and completely unnoticed by Jamilla herself. Jamilla lazily reclined backwards from her finished meal, held the palm of her hand across her mouth and absently looked out at the view across the city. A small echo of a laugh escaped from behind her hand, still delighted with the conversation that had just taken place. She decided that, as she was enjoying this seam of humour so much, there was more to be mined.

"Yes, yes. I will lend you my Gopi. You will like him. He's a great man. Maybe not as good as your husband. But a great man."

"I wasn't married in that way."

"Hmm? 'In that way'? What other way is there?" Jamilla looked suddenly serious and her motherly frame leaned forward, eager for more. "You're either married or you're not married. What other way is there?"

"I was married, Jay. But he wasn't a man." Hope realised that there was pleasure to be had in this teasing of Jamilla. It also allowed her to turn away from the offensive husk that was coming to preoccupy her thoughts.

"Not a man? Is this a trick question? You're having me on."

"I can assure you I'm not."

Hey, it was a woman! You got married to a woman! No! And then you found out…"

Hope felt a twist of hunger and knew that she'd have to make for the chicken and bacon sandwich soon.

"It wasn't a woman." She stacked a sheaf of papers and slid them into a manila folder.

Jay hauled herself out of the chair and, intrigued, leant against the side of her desk and replaced the hand over her mouth. Then her eyes widened and she held both palms towards Hope, fingers splayed as if counting to ten. "It was illegal! The priest was a fraud! I've seen it in a play. He married people but he couldn't 'cos he was never a priest in the first place. And that's what happened to you!"

Hope reached for her keys and stood up. "Wrong again."

"Then just tell me. Stop teasing! Tell me who he was."

Hope held Jamilla's imploring stare and let the silence hang between them.

"So who was it? Who did you marry?"

"I married…God."

The door slammed open with such a force that the prefab walls visibly shook; Martina walking briskly back to her desk. She sat perfectly upright and stared at Jay. She then directed her glassy stare slowly towards Hope. Her face remained perfectly composed but tears coursed rapidly down her face.

29

"Would you like to see a film?"

"Not really."

Denis was feeling awkward standing in such an exposed spot as Church Street. People were passing on either side and seemed to convey in their glances that they could see right through him. Everyone acted as if they were fully aware that he'd been hanging around Flemmings waiting to – by chance – catch Carol as she came out from the Pharmacy for her lunch. This had been the second attempt this week and he knew every article in every shop window adjacent to where she worked.

"We could go for a walk, then?"

"We could."

"So you'll come out for a walk?"

"No. Not tonight."

Denis's senses were overwhelmed by the scent and the sight of Carol Maguire. She was a song. If she wasn't a song then he'd write her a song. She was perfect. Lovely. The loveliest woman in the world. He felt more confident of that than of any other fact he'd ever been confident of. He would love her forever. He wanted to look after her forever. He deeply, deeply wanted her to love him.

"Tomorrow then?"

"Can't. Confession."

He began to feel naïve and awkward in her presence. She was too good for him. He saw that now. What was he thinking? What could he offer? He was just another eejit with an uncertain future and a life that had been nothing but cows, pasture and milking yields. Where was the attraction for any girl in that? How could a woman like Carol Maguire fall for that? What was he thinking? He rubbed his large hands together and stepped backwards, accepting defeat.

"Well, let me know if you're ever free. I've to drop into Doyle's now."

He had walked only a few paces from her when, from behind, he caught her voice.

"Saturday. I've nothing to do on Saturday. But it'll have to be after work."

He turned and looked hard at her. Her face retained exactly the same expression as when, only a very few moments ago, he'd been asking her about the possibility of a second date.

"Six. I'll pick you up at six?"

"Seven. And smarten yourself up. You'll probably have to wait in the front room, so don't break Mammy's best china." Her eyes narrowed as she gently smiled.

Denis Dunne thought that he might expire at that very moment. Surely a man's body could not contain that amount of sweet elation?

30

Hope Dunne and Neil Dowling rested back-to-back on the grass leaning into each other. They had slipped into the Lido and now sat on a grass verge from where they could hear the distant shufflings and calls of the resting ducks and geese. It was nearly four in the morning and the dim, mauve streak of the coming day had edged on to the sky.

Neil reached for the Party Seven can he had stolen and refilled the two glasses, which they had also surreptitiously sneaked out from the earlier party.

He stood upright and held out a glass for Hope. "Madam, your wine." Neil bowed deep, momentarily losing his balance as he did so.

"Ah, and is it a good year?"

"But the best! 1975! A fine year. 'Tis the finest wine for the finest lady." He sat down once more with his back hard against hers.

"Mr Dowling, you are a gentleman and a scholar."

They could feel the quiet laughter almost ricochet from one spine to another. It wasn't even funny, but that didn't matter.

Hope breathed deeply and stared into the dark.

"What are you going to do, Sticky?"

"Apply to uni I suppose. If I get in."

"You'll get in. I won't. I've already failed the mocks. If I can't pass the mocks then I haven't got much chance with the real things."

"Do a resit. Lots of people do a resit."

"Nah. I'll go and work. Do three years at uni and I'll still have to go and get a job. Why wait?"

"'Cos you get a better job, that's why. You'll have a degree, Dumbo, that's why."

Hope wanted to stop talking about education. She knew she'd made the wrong subject choices and this conversation was a reminder of later ones she would have to have with her Dad.

"What'll you do after uni? If, cleverest clog of clogs, you get in. Which I know you will."

"Fuck knows. Become an astronaut. English degree would be the perfect qualification."

"It makes you want to be an astronaut, doesn't it?"

"What does?"

"This big, big sky." Hope waved her glass slowly across the heavens. It had been a clear night and the stars hung limpidly above them. Neil looked up and around, craning his neck to take in the entire purple dome.

"You cold, Dunney?"

"Nah."

"Sure?"

"Sure, sure. You?"

"Nah."

"Neil…" Hope couldn't stop herself burping with the gassy bitter, "I wish I was leaving Ruislip one day. I hate it. I'm going to become a Commie and I'm going to level the whole fucking suburb. If I don't, it will drown me. I'll die in fucking Ruislip. Me and Dad. Two up, two down..."

Neil started to laugh.

"What's so funny, moron?"

"Why can only Commies level suburbs? Is that what Commies do? Can't Capitalists do it? Is it a party-political thing?"

Hope giggled and rolled on her side shaking with laughter. Neil's giggles made him rock one way, then another, and ended with him falling on top of her. Hope's face was now inches from his. Both immediately stopped laughing.

"You're not going to kiss me are you, Sticky?"

"No. I'm not going to kiss you."

Hope suddenly recalled the practise she'd secretly carried out in the bathroom, passionately kissing the back of her passionless hand. Would it be the same? Even as the question raised itself in her mind their lips touched briefly, then she became conscious that his hand was interposing itself between the ground and the back of her head. Their lips came together again, their heads moved to find the position for their lips to properly meet. Suddenly, Neil jerked away from Hope, clutching his testicles, Hope's knee having jabbed sharply upwards between his legs.

"Fucking hell, Dunne!"

"Fucking hell yourself, pervert."

She pulled her jacket together, buttoned it up and triumphantly walked down towards the water's edge. Someone, something was calling her. She was certain that, if she could only turn her head to listen, she would catch a sad, inarticulate voice folded inside the wind. She looped her hair back behind her ear and turned her head slightly to try and hear.

Someone was calling her. Someone was softly crying. There was a whisper too faint to discern amongst the summer night breezes smoothing across the Lido surface. It was a young boy's voice. Or was it? Was it her voice? Yes, it might even be her voice.

31

Gavin led Hope towards the small meeting room. Something was wrong, she could tell that. You can't be so intimately close to someone and not know when something is wrong. She remembered how, even when they lay together in the dark of her living room, exhausted and naked, she could still sense his mood. But today was very obvious. He was pacing through the corridor always a metre ahead of her, not walking alongside her idly chatting as was his normal style. The door to the meeting room was brusquely opened and he waited for her to enter.

"Like some water?"

"No thanks, Gavin. Can I get you some?"

"Not really."

Not really? What sort of answer was that? It didn't make sense, Hope thought. He probably didn't even hear what I said.

Gavin spoke immediately as he sat down.

"Hope, I have something which is difficult to talk about. It's best if I come straight to the point."

So something was wrong. Perhaps he was very ill? Perhaps he'd just received some dreadful news from his Doctor? Hope couldn't bear to think of life without him, even if their time together was just confined to work.

"Of course." That was weak, she thought.

"Lately, I sometimes find your behaviour a bit… bizarre. It's really difficult…"

"Bizarre?"

"Yes. I took a call from Thuong last week…"

"But that Thai bitch would say anything to spite me, Gavin!"

"…and she said…"

"Don't believe a fucking thing that evil cow says!"

"…you deliberately…"

"She's just a lying jealous slut."

"...told her I wasn't available for her call when I was."

"But I thought that you were on another call."

"Hope, you sit outside my office; my door was open. You could see – even if you couldn't hear – that I wasn't on a call. For Christ's sake I'm only a couple of metres away."

Hope steeled herself and steadied her voice. "I thought you told me that the job of an EA was to field unwanted calls."

"My wife is not an unwanted call! And Hope, this isn't the only time you've done it. I've found her emails in my deleted box and I haven't even read them. You must have been deleting them as well. Or are they 'unwanted' emails?"

"You told me to field your calls. I may have deleted the emails by mistake."

"How can you come into my office, go on my PC and delete Thuong's emails by mistake? And emails are not fielding calls."

"Gavin, if you would cast your mind back, you distinctly told me to field your unwanted communications."

Gavin looked aghast. "Unwanted communications? You're telling me I asked you to field my unwanted communications?"

"That's what I recall. So that's what I did. Next time you'll need to be more specific. You'll need to tell me which communications are wanted and which I should block."

"Hope, do not play word games with me. And do not create some sort of fictional conversation that we are supposed to have had. When you and I first sat down I agreed that part of your role was to keep cold callers and low priority queries away from me. My wife is neither a cold caller nor a low priority."

Hope raised her head. "Well – and I'm sorry to say this - but she is."

Gavin sat bolt upright in his chair, the features stiffening in shock on his face.

"I beg your pardon?" The words came slowly.

"She is both cold calling and, in the work place, a low priority. Not to you, of course, but to the business. You're asking me to override company procedure by encouraging personal calls. That's not a reasonable request of me."

"I can't believe I'm having this conversation. I find what you say to be utterly incredible. It's not only incredible but deeply insulting."

"It is not insulting; I wouldn't dream of saying this as an insult. I only wanted to ask for a better definition. Who do I let through to you and who don't I let through to you? After this conversation I will find it impossible to make the right decision."

"Well, let me make this perfectly clear to you then, Miss Dunne. My wife is both high priority and the sort of 'wanted call' I like receiving. If you ever block or misdirect one of her calls again – or an email – then I will look upon our next meeting as part of the disciplinary process. Is that clear?"

Hope said nothing, but just carried on staring back at him, unable to understand why this man who could love her so deeply, so passionately, could be so cruel in equal measure.

"Now I've got a four o'clock on the third floor." He rose quickly and stood next to Hope, his hand inches from hers on the table. "I mean it Hope. I've had enough of this."

After he'd left, Hope reflected for a few moments on what had just taken place. She was numbed by his callousness. Did their relationship count for nothing? Surely, every time Thuong (that fucking, fucking bitch) had phoned him in the office, she'd seen him glance through the window that separated them both?

Within minutes Hope was back at her desk. Luckily both Martina and Jay were out. She didn't want them to see just how shaken she was. She almost leapt from her chair in shock when the phone on her desk sounded. It was Thuong.

God is great, thought Hope.

"Hi Thuong. How are you? Good. Children well? I bet they're a real handful. Gavin's got their latest photo. Yes, haven't they grown? It's a lovely one of you as well. I love your hair shorter. It really suits you. Gavin? Certainly. Just putting you through."

She allowed herself a knowing smirk as the unanswered phone rang in Gavin's office. She then rose, calmly put on her coat and left.

32

"I have the most terrible doubt."

Carol Dunne stared almost wild-eyed across the rim of her rum and black, the glass held high up to her face.

Patsy, Carol's sister, unaware of Carol's sudden heartfelt cry, was starting to wave her arms around in a giddy, tipsy whirl to add emphasis to her story. "So, this enormous man sat on the bus beside me. He was a giant! Huge now! And I was reading my book…"

"If something doesn't go right soon..."

"So I tucked myself in like this and… oh, this glass is empty. Martin, it's our round now I'd say."

Martin Whelan, who was pretending to enjoy Patsy's monologue, was slim and carefully – perhaps too carefully – dressed. His suits were always impeccably pressed, his ties invariably highly coloured and he was a man never to be seen without cufflinks. He affected to sit forward at tables with hands clasped together and his elbows on the table; this allowed his cufflinks to emerge from the jacket sleeves so that the fake stones could catch the glints of light in them. He had the blue-black hair of Spanish conquistadors, swept back but invariably some strands falling forward when he became animated in conversation.

Patsy was determined to continue: "So I said to him, 'Excuse me Sir, would you mind moving out a little and letting me have some space to breathe here…'"

Carol turned away from Patsy, desperate for another conversation: "Denis, is James Quinn on in Kilburn? Can we go and see him soon?"

Denis placed his broad hand on her forearm, nodded quickly at her and carried on smiling at Patsy, eager for her to continue her story.

"Denis, I have the most terrible doubt."

He again looked briefly across at her. She couldn't read anything in his look. Was he irritated? Was he angry? Was he just perplexed at her words? Denis then fell back against his chair shaking with laughter. Carol felt horribly isolated, even amongst these people she knew so well.

"More drinks? Patsy, give me a hand here." Denis pushed back his chair and collected three empty glasses. The club was a wash of noise with the laughter and swirl of different Irish accents – from Donegal to Waterford – rising and falling, blending and blaring. A fug of smoke hung directly beneath the smoke-tanned ceiling, its vapour drifting and commingling around the room's small, grubby chandeliers.

A panic rose in Carol's mind at the thought of being left alone with Martin Whelan. She felt unsteady, almost drowning in the sea of sound and the constantly moving tableau of people pushing, drinking, smoking and laughing before her. She desperately tried to look composed, feeling that Martin – with his cold wolf eyes - was watching her.

"It's an impressive sight, Mrs Dunne."

She looked away, and added with as much disinterest as she could muster, "What's an impressive sight, Mr Whelan, now?"

He swept his hand in a dramatic arc in front of Carol. "Carol Dunne, Hollywood Star."

"I just see the roof of the club, Martin."

Martin Whelan nudged in beside her until she could smell his Palmolive aftershave. "But look harder, my lovely. Look harder, beyond and through the roof. You've only to push through the bricks and mortar with your imagination."

"I still only see a roof."

"Then I must teach you to see, my angel. I must teach you to see opportunity with an angel's eyes."

He then placed a impertinent hand upon her thigh. She wanted a knife to pinion it into her own flesh so that his agony would be her agony.

Martin Whelan had – over the short years Carol had come to know him as Patsy's boyfriend, fiancé and husband – become increasingly repulsive to her. Handsome, lean-limbed and so at ease with himself, he lounged around like a man born to the good things in life. He leant into her with a personal authority that so many men of that disposition feel: that women – and the enjoyment of women - are a natural right. Like game in Africa, they are simply there to be cornered and bagged.

"Your hand, Martin."

"My hand? What about my hand, Carol?"

"Please take it away."

Martin withdrew it from Carol's thigh and relaxed arrogantly in his chair, completely unaffected by her censure. He relighted his thin cigar; Carol felt him staring with a glare that bore into the side of her face.

She pulled her legs away from Martin's so that she could feel separate from him, avoiding the feeling she always had of being compromised or soiled when he insinuated himself beside her.

He watched her do this, smiled, and then placed his hand behind her neck. Carol froze, shuddering as Martin Whelan's thick fingers glanced and probed uninvitingly.

"Take your fucking hand off me."

"Now why should I do that, Mrs Dunne? It's a lovely place for a man's fingers to rest awhile."

"I mean it; take your grubby hands off me."

"The same grubby hands that have landed you a part in a new play? Are you talking about those grubby hands?"

"I don't give a fuck what new play you imagine you've got me."

"Oh, I think you give a very big fuck. A very big fuck indeed."

Carol took Martin's jacket sleeve and lifted it from her with the same cold, absence of passion that a crane hoists cargo across the quayside of a dock. She then sat up and strained to see where Denis and Patsy were. They were still waiting in a long queue at the bar, chatting amiably and quite ignorant to the events that were playing out on the other side of the large room.

Her curiosity overtook her and, still maintaining an irritated air, she looked at him.

"What part?"

"It's not a big part. Even Martin Whelan has his limits. But it's a start." He blew out a long, insolent line of cigar smoke.

Carol tried to penetrate Martin's grinning mask. Was it true? Or was it just some ploy to satisfy his lechery? But he was always impossible to read.

"How could a little insurance salesman land anyone a part?" She scoffed and looked resignedly away.

"I'm not just an insurance salesman. Of course, I'm probably the best insurance man for miles, but I have other talents as well. Certain talents – I have to say - that only a good and happy marriage prevents me from sharing."

Carol, exasperated at the preening self-regard of the man, reached for another cigarette.

But Martin continued, "And these talents, naturally, introduce me to other talented people. Brendan Donovan, no less. Theatre impresario. He showily stressed each syllable to add to the effect.

"Oh, Mr Brendan Donovan, right enough." Carol tried to invest the sentence with as much derision as she could muster.

"The very man. Oh, I don't affect to know him well. But I covered a little insurance arrangement for him – beneficial to both him and yours truly – and that left him on the debit side, shall we say, with the favours. So I called one in."

"What? Are you telling me the truth?"

"Now where are my lovely wife and your man with those drinks?"

"Martin, look at me, tell me straight now, is that true?"

"Is what true? What was I saying now?"

"You know well enough what you were saying! About Brendan Donovan. The producer."

"Would I lie to you? Can you spare me one of those for later? Mine must be on the kitchen table." Martin pointed to Carol's open cigarette packet.

"Did you really tell him about me?"

"I believe I did. But not just tell him. Asked him. Was there something he might find for you? Walk-on maid. That sort of thing."

"Walk-on maid! That's not a part!"

Martin's features became quickly irritated, "It's a part. And it's a fucking damn sight more than you've ever found yourself, Miss Audrey bloody Hepburn."

Carol, words escaping from her brain, struggled to speak. Eventually, she smiled and gushed, "Martin, I don't know what to say."

"You could start by saying 'Yes'."

33

"It's complicated. I'm complicated. God knows, if life hadn't begun so… oh, I'm just rattling on now."

"There's nothing complicated. So, I grant you, *you* might be complicated, but that doesn't mean that *we* have to be complicated."

Hope took her glass and pulled it across the table towards her. The perfectly sliced lime returned her stare like a frozen traffic light. Glancing at his hand she eyed his wedding ring, the gold band already worn away to a dull metallic patina; small nicks and scratches scythed across its lustreless surface.

"I don't know what's gone on in your life. But you know what's happened to me. You know I can be trusted."

Hope went to reply but it hung – insubstantial and weak – behind her lips. How could she begin to explain? She looked up and smiled, "When people say 'trust me', that's a very clear sign to me that they are not to be trusted."

"I'm not sure I agree with that. Sounds like a poor line from a very poor book. So what do you want me to do?"

She looked around the kitchen and into the room beyond. The house was a mausoleum to her, she thought. Is this man's memory also a mausoleum? Will he endlessly be comparing her to this other, perfect, woman? This Rebecca?

Hope leaned in towards him. "First, just believe me. Second, learn to trust me."

34

"Where's your Dad, Hope?"

"Out I think. Probably at the cemetery."

Martin Whelan had, as usual, let himself in through the kitchen door. Hope resolved immediately to lock and bolt it from now on when she got back from school.

"Is the kettle boiled? I'd love a cup of tea."

Hope reluctantly put her homework aside and went to the kitchen.

"Have you music?" shouted Martin after her.

"What sort?"

"Good music. Stick one of Denis's things on. A bit of your man will do."

Hope came out of the kitchen and looked quizzically at her Uncle. "What man will do?"

"Dino. Dean Martin. I love to hear that record. It's in there somewhere."

"Let me just get the pot ready and then I'll do it."

Martin Whelan sat as one who had achieved everything in life. The fact that his life was a model of increasing under-achievement never troubled him. He took the occasional triumphs and inflated them enormously. His many failures he skilfully stashed away beyond the view of those he worked with. His easy manner and effortless charm had allowed himself to rise unopposed in the international insurance company he worked for, using his position to satiate his appetites by the promise of promotions and the passing on of the more lucrative accounts to those who had 'accommodated' him.

He leaned back in the chair and regretted the sorry state of the Dunne's garden. There were flecks of brown spots on the patio window panes.... What were they? Certainly Patsy wouldn't have let those sorts of things appear on their windows. The thought of the bacteria involved with irrigating those blots of filth, those smudges of neglect, caused him to shudder inside his Hepworth suit.

"A biscuit, Uncle Martin?"

"Oh, no thanks."

Hope rested the tea cup beside him and then sat again by her essay.

Martin, still looking out through the dining room window, said "So what's that you're studying?"

"Hardy. I have to read him before I go back."

"Hardy who?"

"Thomas Hardy. Hardy is his second name."

"Oh, right so. And what's that you're reading?"

"The Return of the Native."

"Right. And who's it by?"

"I told you. Thomas Hardy."

Martin stood up and walked away to the front window, sipping his tea. He turned to Hope with, "Miss Dunne. Do you like the tie?"

Hope looked at the small amber flowers, each with a blue centre, militarily arranged across a brown background.

"No."

Martin ignored her and, turning the back of the tie towards him, he grandly read out, "Liberty of London by Berkley. What do you think of that now?"

"Wow," Hope said without expression. Martin Whelan smiled and turned his attention back to the garden.

"Is it a love story?"

Hope sighed, "Not really."

"So what is it then? If it's not a love story?

"It's a fucking novel, you complete and utter twat. It's a novel about characters caught up in a situation they can't extricate themselves from. But you won't recognise that. You won't recognise that because you're thick as pig shit. You're blessed with an inability to make sense of the things in the world that normal people make sense of. You are massively inadequate. You will always be massively inadequate from your inconvenient birth to the dissatisfying last words on your death bed."

"I like love stories. I know that sounds strange but I do. I love 'em. Brings a bit of… well, whatever they bring in a bit of."

Martin stood by the table, placed his feet a metre apart, and then sang:

"Love is a many splendored thing
It's the April rose that only grows in the early spring
Love is nature's way of giving
A reason to be living
The golden crown that makes a man a king."

Hope had heard that her Uncle Martin had a wonderful voice, but now she was witnessing it first-hand. Its deep tenor thrust disturbed her and she felt it go through her. How could such a feckless man produce something so beautiful?

Martin finished singing and, with a manufactured embarrassment, sat close beside her.

"So what's that you're studying, then?"

Hope felt revolted by his intimate presence, but she explained, calmly, what homework she'd been given. She was to read the book and write about whether Egdon Heath was as much a character in the novel as the people who walked upon it.

Her face quickly turned after she had gone through this – and found herself uncomfortably close to the face of her Uncle Martin. Martin moved uneasily back in his chair before springing up and affecting to look at his watch. It had been a strange, confusing moment.

"How's your Mam?" he quickly asked.

Martin's question brought Hope back to Earth. "She's good."

"Strange expression. Being your mother and everything. Anyway, tell your dad I called. When's he going to mow that lawn?"

"Don't know."

Martin looked inquisitively at Hope.

"Hope, how old are you now?"

"15, almost."

"Christ. Almost 15, eh? Well, I've got to go."

Hope slumped back in her chair but then was shocked to see Uncle Martin's head reappear around the side of the living room door.

"Mankind is at the mercy of an uncomprehending and hostile universe."

"Sorry?"

"Thomas Hardy. Return of the Native. Read it years ago. Stick it in your essay."

Martin winked and bounded out the house, leaving the kitchen door wide open behind him and an untouched cup of tea on the draining board.

35

Hope carefully watched the boy next to her. He was gripping the pencil carefully with his left hand, making deliberate and slow motions trying to keep to the feint-ruled line Mrs Ducker had prepared. Each 'a' he wrote was preceded by a short stroke and then the fat, round circle of the letter emerged followed by an identical sequence of characters across the page.

She looked again at her own still-blank page, resting her uncertain fist upon it. She glanced once more at Francis' looping a's and looked up again at the 'Marion Richardson School of Handwriting' poster. It was only then that she became aware of a movement she could see through the glass window in the classroom door. It was Miss Thorne, the deputy headmistress motioning for the attention of Mrs Ducker, Hope's teacher. Mrs Ducker eventually turned sideways and quickly moved across the floor to the door, which she opened silently and pulled too behind her.

Hope saw Mrs Ducker hold her hand to her mouth to stifle her shock. Mrs Ducker's hand then moved to her forehead and turned away so that no-one could see. The rest of the class worked on, looping and dropping circular and perpendicular lines across their respective sheets. But Hope knew something was wrong and, moreover, was certain that the commotion outside the classroom door was about her.

Hope expected an angry Mrs Ducker to re-enter the classroom, but it was Miss Thorne who did so. Smiling, as if ambling through a cornfield in the full, warming glare of a high sun, she crossed over to the collection of six desks at which Hope and the other children sat. She then affected to look at the children's work, still carrying a beatific glow that irradiated beams of goodness to those beneath her.

She stopped behind Hope and gently rested her hand on Hope's small shoulder. Looking at the blank page, she said, "Oh, Hope. That is very good. Shall we show the Headmistress?" Confused, Hope smiled and picked up the blank sheet, still carrying her pencil tight in her other hand.

When they had stepped out from the classroom, Miss Thorne stopped her and asked, "Where is your coat, Hope? Will you go and get it for me?"

Hope walked to the collection of hooks opposite and took down her coat.

"Have you got a bag or satchel?" Hope shook her head.

Mrs Ducker was sitting on the low cloakroom bench adjacent to the coats; although her eyes were glassy with tears, she forced a smile as she looked at Hope.

"Are you crying, Miss?"

"Of course not, Hope. Now you go with Miss Thorne and be a good girl."

"Come on now, Hope." Miss Thorne led Hope away and they walked through the eerily quiet school hall towards the administrative offices at the far end. The low hum of children's conversations as they were working could just be heard from the adjacent classrooms. As they turned into the long corridor, Miss Thorne motioned Hope to walk ahead.

The headmaster's door was ajar; Hope could see the easily recognisable figure of her Father, sitting side-on, slumped in a chair. Looking wearily down at the floor, he still hadn't seen her. As she got closer, she could hear the distinctive tones of the Headmaster, but couldn't quite catch what he was saying.

Then the door was opened wide and a Policewoman emerged; she crouched down and smiled as Hope approached her.

"You must be Hope."

36

Barry Bufton walked into the office with a wide, self-satisfied, grin on his face.

"Is Gavin there?" As he drew near to Hope's desk, Gavin Laing emerged from his office idly scrolling through texts on his mobile.

"Mr Bufton. You look pleased with yourself. Good news?"

Barry faked a laugh – something, Hope noticed, he often did without even realising it.

"I've been ideating, Mr Laing. And I've ideated an idea that gets at the nub of your little dilemma."

Gavin looked perplexed. "What little dilemma was that?"

"At the conference. You remember? We had a chat about taking responsibility and I promised that I would go away and think about it. And I 'thinked' about it and came up with the most brilliant solution."

Hope thought that, if someone really took hold of Barry Bufton, burned his clothes and then dressed him properly, he could almost pass for a member of the human race.

"Right," agreed Gavin, now remembering the conversation. "And..?"

"On the third day, once we've gone through the material, we ask them to sit by a train set."

"A train set?"

"Oh yes, one of those ones with the empty goods carriages on the back. You know the type. Some type of Hornby thing."

"A Hornby train set," repeated Gavin.

"And the train goes round and stops by each delegate – each of whom is a member of your team. I will then give each delegate – member of your team - a laminated card with the commitment that we have made during the workshop. Then they have to place the laminated card on to the train and declare to the others: 'I'm taking this commitment on board!'"

Gavin stared at Barry; Hope could see that he was desperately trying to think how he could ditch the idea without hurting his feelings.

"A train set. And you take the idea on board… Well, I… sorry, Barry, it's… It's crap."

Barry, so ebullient and upbeat moments before, looked utterly crestfallen. "You mean you don't like it."

"I, um… I appreciate the inventiveness, I just think… the team would find it patronising, Barry."

Like all of your workshops, thought Hope. She recalled the endless slew of positive psychology mantras and exercises she'd seen Barry's delegates subjected to.

"OK, well, perhaps if you give me a clearer idea of what you have in mind, Gav, and I'll run with it from there."

"Nice work, Barry. As I said, it's really different in its approach and would work for… well, you know what a hard-bitten lot salespeople can be."

Hope interrupted, "Gavin, you're on this interview panel in five minutes. Here are the questions."

Gavin looked relieved to have his attention diverted and slapped Barry hard on the bicep. "Think again, eh? Got to fly."

Barry looked at Hope and raised his eyebrows, acknowledging that the idea was all but a dead duck.

"It *was* a crap idea, Barry."

Barry corrected Hope, "No, Miss Dunne, it wasn't a crap idea. It was a great idea that has yet to find its place in the world. Reframe, Miss Dunne! Reframe!"

"If you say so."

Hope returned to her PC screen but slowly became aware that Barry was still standing at her desk.

"Was there something else?"

"I hope you don't mind me asking, but what you said at the conference. About you and Gavin. Was that true?"

Hope glanced very briefly up and then back at the document she'd just saved.

"I was having you on. I like being single and I certainly wouldn't waste my time on married men."

"Even once-married men?"

Hope shuddered at the flirtation.

"Was there something else, Barry?" she asked coldly.

Barry smiled and awkwardly withdrew. Two knockdowns were enough for one day.

37

It was such an abrupt, dislocating, change of mood. The Stylistics, slowly sashaying from foot to foot – with crotches that pushed menacingly at the zippers of their blue-mauve trousers – giving way to the ersatz, tinny pop of Sheila B. Devotion.

Hope had opened her eyes in resentment, aching for The Stylistics to soothe her once more with their fluty rendering of 'Wonderwoman', imagining their swaying thighs, stick-thin microphones held like peashooters, hair fizzed into ballooning marshmallows. A rolling, slinking, knowing movement as they moved their body weight from one bricked platform shoe to the other.

Then Noel Edmonds' jaunty, coiffured beard punctured her resentment, coolly announcing that Sheila B. Devotion was German. German? It was a fact that stood out of kilter with everything Hope knew about pop music. German? Surely she should look like every other German. She wasn't sure what that image would be, but knew that a spiked *Pikelhaube* would be worn for certain.

And what had she been singing? *Singing in the Rain.* A meaningless, pulsing rendition that twitched like the death throes of a newly-landed trout. Hope, sitting on the floor with her back to the settee, leaned over and wrapped her arms around Denis Dunne's knees.

"Did you ever sing, Dad?"

"Now and again."

"Did Grandad ever sing?"

"He'd a grand voice."

Hope turned her face up to him. "Sing me one."

Denis looked embarrassed. "I'm not the singer. Your Mam was the singer."

"Then sing now. Sing something for me now."

Denis Dunne sat slowly up, uncomfortable that he should show such vulnerability to his daughter. He affected a small cough.

"Now your Uncle Martin..."

"I've heard Uncle Martin. But I want to hear you."

"Right. Right now. A song..."

He hummed small sequences of notes at different points in the scale, trying to find the key that would bear him successfully through the ordeal. He looked down at Hope, then fixed his eyes on the artificial logs of the faux-gold and wood fireplace.

"When the golden sun sinks in the hills..."

Hope knew, at this very moment, that she could never love anyone like her father. He strained as he sang, left the home key for a neighbouring one, modulated into new keys obscurely remote from the original, but Hope followed his every syllable closely.

"There are two eyes that shine, just because they are mine..."

Denis Dunne's shyness clouded the expression of the words, but somehow you just knew this man *did* love his home, did remember with deep affection a *bohreen* along which his father's dairy farm lay, did remember lips he was longing to kiss.

"It's a corner of heaven itself, though it's only a tumble-down nest..."

Once this imperfect piece of musical perfection had ceased, he pulled his stare away from the fireplace and said, happily,

"Right now."

Hope said nothing. She turned towards the TV again and saw Brian and Michael, and a whole troupe of pre-pubescent girls swaying their heads to '*Matchstalk Men and Matchstalk Cats and Dogs.*'

Yes, she thought, she loved this man.

38

"What did you think of Barry's little idea yesterday?"

Hope settled primly into the chair opposite Gavin and checked that her pen was working by scribbling on the cover of her pad.

"I thought it was dreadful. It's exactly the pretentious stuff he's been peddling for years. I notice you never seem to grace any of his courses. You've no idea what he puts us all through."

Gavin laughed and looked out through the office partition window. "You have to admire him, though."

"Really?"

"Of course. He has such… such self-belief. He believes all that psycho mumbo-jumbo stuff, he really does. 'Take it on board'. Did he really think I'd let my team do that?"

"Other managers let him."

"You know something else he said?"

"Surprise me."

Gavin leaned forward. "He asked if you and I were…"

"Were what?"

Hope could feel her heart pounding and was sure that her face would be reddening as well.

"Having an affair! He thought we were seeing each other!"

"But we are, aren't we? Or we used to see each other."

"What put that idea in his head?"

"Can we start seeing each other again?"

"I put him right on that one, Hopey. Not you, not anyone I said. Bloody cheek!"

"How about one more evening? I'll make something for us. You like fish. I'll cook fish."

"Don't get me wrong, you're a lovely woman, but the idea."

"And that wine you brought. I'll get it this time. *Pouilly* whatever…"

“Anyway. Business. Who’s in and who’s out?”

“Just one last time where we can be together.”

“Did he now? When does he want to meet?”

“A last single night of love.”

“Do. And Ray as well. We’ll need the big guns on this one.”

“I just need to hold you. Please do that one thing again for me.”

“Let me just ask Martina.”

Gavin left the office to speak conspiratorially with Martina. Soon she was laughing with him. Hope smouldered with indignation. Should she go out and see what they were talking about?

Hope spat saliva on to her finger and smeared it around the rim of his cup. She thought about what she would need to wear. Something not too tarty. But at least it would have to be *arresting*. She wondered whether to go into town at the weekend and perhaps leave her Mum and Dad to their own devices.

She looked at her reflection on the glass of the file cupboard opposite. She looked all right. Still trim, she thought. Not too jowly. Eyes, could she do something about the eyes? Her blouse was neat. People always said she looked so smart. Are those blonde highlights coming out? Perhaps Gavin might prefer her a bit darker? Yes, once hers and Gavin’s meeting was through she’d call the hairdressers. See if Beverley had a space on Saturday.

She looked at the back of her hands. They were the hands of a 55 year-old woman, she thought. But not bad. Fingernails good. Skin not too loose. At least no dreaded liver spots yet. Gavin came in with the lope of a spring lamb.

“All done. We’re there and Martina says she’ll get her PowerPoint done by this afternoon. By the way”, Gavin changed to a serious and confidential tone, “Is Martina all right? She looks a bit pale.”

“Can’t say I’ve noticed. I’m sure she’s fine.”

What do I care about that fucking Polack, she thought.

"Well, she doesn't look fine to me."

"*C'est la vie.* When did you say you wanted Ray for?"

"Oh, work that out with his PA."

Gavin moved the pen so as to lie perfectly parallel to his phone. He then reached for his cup to drain its last shot of coffee.

"Hmm, got the hots for you, I'd say."

"Who has?"

"Barry Bufton. I'd watch yourself there."

39

"You look nice."

Hope couldn't think what to reply. The music was crashing in her ears and that seemed to disorientate her all the more.

She decided to giggle. That was stupid she thought.

"Would you like a drink?"

"Sorry?"

Neil leaned into her, his mouth warm against her ear. He repeated his question and she nodded, vigorously. She followed him through the crowd and stood proprietorially close behind him at the bar. He seemed so grown up. Hadn't she thought that earlier? Everyone was so grown up. She must stop saying it to herself, or try to think of something a bit more… Christ, she nearly thought it again!

A very drunk Michael Petrenko lurched in between them, face flushed with alcohol and his shirt now totally liberated from his high waistband Oxford bags. Hope thought she caught Neil saying something that had 'Birthday Boy' in it and decided to look around the bar. These people she thought she knew were now all quite unrecognisable. When did that happen? When did they all mature? Why hadn't anyone told her?

Michael Petrenko, clumsy with drink, lost his balance and careered into the back of a neighbouring drinker.

"Soz, mate!"

He then looked at Hope, belched, and smiled at her. "How about a Birthday kiss then…" But Neil intervened and guided him to a nearby crowd who soon enveloped him in a group clinch. Hope sighed with a deep relief. Neil returned and jerked his head in the direction of a free table away from the music speakers. He bowed ostentatiously, inviting her to take the corner seat.

Hope grinned and took her place gratefully. The music thudded its bass underlay, topped by the shrieks, shouts and laughter of the crowd. Michael Petrenko was slapping a girl's back with the gusto of an encouraging scrum half and she emptied the contents of her glass over her friend.

"He's having a good time."

Neil turned to see. "Who is?"

"Petrenko. Pissed."

"It's his Birthday. He's a right to be."

"S'pose. Thanks." Hope raised her glass in appreciation.

"Look, if you don't like it here, there's a party I know. Take about 10 minutes to walk to it. Could drink these and be there in no time. Be good to have a chat."

"What sort of party?"

"A party party. From my school. They're quite human you know. Well almost."

Hope shrugged her assent and swiftly despatched her drink. She realised that finishing it so quickly was probably not a wise thing to do, but tried not to let the unpleasantness of the gulp show.

Once they had stepped outside again, Hope much relieved to have left the party's hostile atmosphere, they were both surprised to find it still so light; the sun had almost set yet the light of the dying day seemed to be refusing to fade with it.

"Want to walk the long way round?"

"Not too long I hope?"

She enjoyed this strange turn in events. Neil had moved from her school in their third year, but they had occasionally seen each other at Mass. Close up, he seemed very tall, thought Hope, and his once painfully thin frame had filled out. It was one more change that had taken place when she wasn't looking. He still had the same sweep of dark brown hair that needed taming, constantly sweeping it back to hook it behind an ear.

It occurred to Hope that she quite liked this constant 'sweeping back' gesture. There was something rather winning about it. When does a once-attractive trait become your partner's irritating habit? When does the cunning of the kitten become the cruelty of the cat?

They continued to walk in silence for some time, but then Hope blurted out, "Are you seeing anyone?" She felt angry with herself, not only for asking the question, but for the desperate manner with which she asked it. What was she thinking? Why didn't she ask after Neil's Mum and Dad? She looked at the buildings on the opposite side of the road as an excuse to look away.

"No. You?"

"No."

"How's your Dad?"

"Good. Yours?

"He's good."

"And your Mum?"

"She's good."

It was an awkward exchange, but they both felt better.

"I'm glad you were at the party. I felt really out of place. Thanks." Hope added.

"Were you? I couldn't tell. Just glad to see you. Didn't really know a lot of people myself. Well, play rugger with a couple still, but once you've left it changes things. I thought that Frances Chivers' dress didn't leave much to the imagination."

"She's always shoved those big boobs in people's faces. She's probably glad for a chance to show 'em a bit more. Wait 'til she's dropped a couple of kids and they'll be banging against her knees."

Neil looked quizzically at her. "Where did that come from? I thought you were more of a convent girl?" He laughed.

Hope ignored him, "Well."

"See you're still going to Mass? See you with your Dad."

"It keeps me holy so that I can try and forgive Frances Chivers. Dad likes me going. It helps him."

"Petrenko told me that you're going to be a Nun. That's not true is it? The nun bit."

"Might do. Haven't made my mind up. Do you think I should?"

Neil Dowling kept his eyes on her. "No. I don't think it would suit you. You're no more nun material than I'm priest material. Besides…"

Hope let this hang for a while, but asked, "Besides what?"

"Besides you're too young. Have a life. See things. Then decide if you want to be a nun. But don't commit yourself before you've been out there."

Hope realised that she was enjoying this conversation. Yes, she had considered being a Nun, but wasn't sure in her own mind just how real a choice this was for her. There were reasons she'd begun to think about, genuine reasons of atonement that made a life of withdrawal from everything seem like an attractive one. But would she do it? She knew that she still hadn't made her mind up.

"Who's at the party?"

"School friends. Parents have gone away. Nothing special. It'll be a laugh."

Hope remembered that that was exactly what Lesley Flaherty had said before she'd entered The Penny Black.

Might be a good omen, perhaps?

40

"You're a bit lovely, Mrs Dunne."

"Let's get this over with."

Martin undid his tie. "No, let's take our time. I've earned this little treat. And it's not often I fall off the good Lord's path."

Carol Dunne said nothing; she hitched up her skirt, unhooked the stocking from its clip and rolled it perfunctorily down her leg.

"Hold on there! Christ, you might want it over with, but I don't. I'm not a man who rushes things."

Martin stood behind her and cupped each of her smooth shoulders in his broad hands. She could feel his breath on the nape of her neck and fought down the revulsion and nausea that rose from her stomach.

"I've been looking forward to this for a long time. Truth is I've been thinking about you a lot. He's a lucky man, is our Denis. You know I always thought I'd picked the wrong Maguire."

Carol closed her eyes. What was she doing this for? A chance of a part – she'd still not got much more from Martin about when or where – and was this worth it? She thought it would be quick, she thought it would be over in a matter of minutes. Now Martin was looking to stretch out the whole torment for her.

"Look, Martin. I don't want to talk about Patsy. We are doing something very wrong here. Betraying two people who trust us. For Christ's sake, let's get this done and over. It's more than I can stand."

Martin was now brushing his lips against her neck, his beery breath waving warm against her skin. She looked down at her opened blouse and noticed how rapidly her chest was rising and falling in panic. A hand moved quickly to her breast and cradled it roughly.

"No, no, no. It's no good. I can't go through with it." Carol had sprung from the small chair and, facing the stained hotel wall, was now buttoning up her blouse.

"Oh God, what am I doing?" She began to weep, covering her face with her two hands.

Martin sat slowly in the chair she'd just left. "Carol, Carol. Come on now. You're being a bit naïve. A bit innocent about all this."

Carol stifled the tears but said nothing. There was a weak, late afternoon light seeping through the unwashed net curtain, as if the day itself was shamefully withdrawing from what was passing in the hotel room. The bed was still unmade from where the previous occupants had hurriedly left only minutes before, passing Martin and Carol in the thin corridor outside, their allotted hour now spent.

"You don't understand that some favours are hard to win. I took a gamble with Donovan. I have the man's respect. I thought to myself, Carol's worth it. There's something very special about you, very talented. And I can do something to bring your talent to a wider world. I can put you up there, where you belong. Isn't that what you wanted?"

Carol merely nodded but would not face him.

"Can I tell you something? I would never say this to anyone, but it has a bearing on what I'm saying. I do love Patsy. You know I love Patsy. I'd die for Patsy! But, ever since the miscarriage, she just doesn't seem to love me. To want me. Can you imagine that? The feeling of not being wanted? The feeling of being unlovable."

Martin rose from the chair and parted the net curtain to look out of the window.

"It's a crushing thing. Oh, I said to myself, give her time. Give her some space, but it's two years on. That's a long time without love, without the closeness a man expects and needs from his wife. Perhaps that's why I'm saying about my feelings for you. Truth is, if the last two years had been normal, then maybe we wouldn't both be here now."

Carol murmured, "So what are you saying, Martin?"

"What I'm trying to say is, give me a break. Give me one afternoon with you and then let's forget it. Have some pity. Help me and help Patsy."

Carol gulped in derision. "This is helping Patsy?"

"Christ, yes. Don't go mocking me, Carol. Whatever you may think of me, I'm good to Patsy and I'm at the end of my fucking tether. One afternoon with you. Just one afternoon. Not quick. Not dirty. But one afternoon that I can remember and keep. And treasure. Something that'll carry me through until Patsy and I can..."

He turned towards her. "Is it really too much to ask?"

"And what about this Donovan? When do I get to see him?"

"All arranged, Miss Dunne."

He held a business card up in front of her.

"The man's expecting your call."

She reached for it, but Martin pulled it swiftly away.

"Fair's fair now, Carol."

41

Martina sullenly stared at her screen but didn't seem to see what was in front of her. The PC's glare accentuated the thin red lines that rimmed her eyes; the light they once had, that vivacious sparkle Hope had come to resent so intensely, seemed permanently extinguished.

Jamilla looked at Martina and then over at Hope. Hope smiled at Jamilla and carried on humming to herself.

"Martina," sang out Hope, as if her name was part of the melody she had just been quietly singing, "Gavin needs to finalise your holidays. Can you let me have them?"

There was no response.

"Martina?" This time each syllable was without any inflection whatsoever.

"Hmm?"

"Your holidays. Have you worked out when you'll be off?"

Martina still didn't pull her gaze away from the computer screen. "I might have to change them. I'll let you know."

"When will you let me know? I want to get this all sorted."

Martina now turned an angry glare at Hope, and spat out through tense, thin lips. "When I feel like letting you know, then I will let you know."

Hope felt the full, bitter loathing she had for Martina surge through her. To her horror, she realised that Jamilla had been looking at her reactions, perhaps had even read her mind and, having momentarily caught Hope's eye, pretended to reach down to a side drawer for some papers.

But the intensity of her resentment gnawed away still. Hope would get rid of Martina. She *will* get rid of Martina. That fucking foreign moron. She'd made a pact with herself and she wasn't going to break it. If she hadn't been in the office with the other two she would have shrieked out in anger. It worried her that the beating of animosity refused to ebb away.

Sensing the atmosphere, Martina petulantly pushed herself back from the desk and threw a loud, parting remark at Jamilla, "I'm going out to get some fresh air."

Jamilla looked at her as she went and rolled her eyes.

At last the force of emotion within Hope began to fade and she resumed her normal position at her PC.

"Have you noticed something about Martina, Hope?"

Oh, here we go, now Jamilla expects me to start saying I was wrong to ask a reasonable question. Now the immigrants are going to band together in combat.

"Can't say I did," Hope replied coolly, still keeping her eyes firmly on the screen.

"Haven't you noticed she's not been herself?"

"Not really. Too busy."

"Then shame on you."

This stung Hope and, when she looked at Jamilla she registered her shock at her remark.

"Sorry? Is it my job to watch the every move of our sales team? Will the sales team be taking notice of every change of mood I have? Hardly."

"I wonder about you sometimes. You're very brittle. Have you no compassion at all? No love?"

Hope didn't want to talk any more about Martina or herself. She couldn't think what to say in reply.

Jamilla back-tracked. "Sorry, that was rude. But you can be quite hard on people, you know."

Not to my own kind though, thought Hope.

"Maybe it's having children. It can make you more…" Jamilla thought about the right word, "…sensitive to things."

Hope could begin to feel herself rallying. "I come into work, I go home. I have problems but I keep them to myself. I don't expect people to care about my problems and I don't particularly care about the problems of other people. We're paid to work. We're not paid to care. That's the way I look at it. Probably a bit simple, but there it is. If Martina's got something wrong, then she'll get over it like we all have to. I dare say there are things you don't talk about. Well, that suits me too."

"Martina's pregnant."

Hope looked astonished. "Pregnant? Martina? She doesn't look pregnant."

"Well you don't at first! She's just found out."

"Well, what's she so upset about?"

"Because it's not her boyfriend's."

"How do you know? Course it's her boyfriend's."

"In Saudi? He's been on contract there for months."

Serves her right. Serves the little bitch right. Fantastic. The smug bitch is getting what she deserves.

Hope feigned interest, "Well, that's made it complicated. So who's the father?"

"I don't know. I just feel for her. She is so hurt."

Hope's thoughts turned immediately to dropping into Sainsbury's and treating herself to a bottle of wine. Maybe even Prosecco. Get Mum down for a drink perhaps. And an extra special treat for Pardew. One of those little foil trays he likes.

Martina pregnant and it's not her boyfriend's. That'll put the dampers on the Directors' ardour. Not quite the same flirting with a preggie Pole. *Schadenfreude*. Yes, that was the word: *Schadenfreude*. That was going to be her word for the month. It wasn't French, but this was a special occasion.

42

"So why did you move from, where was it?"

Hope placed the glass carefully on the floor so she wouldn't spill it. The warm, fizzing bitter was making her thoughts swim and she knew that she'd better slow down.

"Camden. Where I was born."

Both Neil and Hope were sitting in the living room side-by-side with their backs to the wall. The hard-edged chords of *Vicious* were growling in the background, and the braying voices of 17 and 18 year-old boys were just discernible from the garden. It wasn't Hope's idea of a party, more a gathering of school friends in a house empty of parents for a few days. But there was a kitchen sideboard groaning under bottles and cans of alcohol, more drink than Hope had ever seen before outside of a pub or bar.

The house that Neil had brought her to was, perhaps, the most beautiful she had ever been in. It was obviously Victorian: it's high coved ceilings, large bay windows and high fireplaces were all on a scale that she'd never seen before. And everything was so tasteful, from the fading Indian carpets draped over the rough, unvarnished floorboards to the enormous glass vases each billowing with fresh flowers and branches of foreign foliage.

Neil persisted, "So why'd you move?"

"Mum died. We needed to move away. Fresh start and all that."

"Course. What did she die of? Cancer?"

Hope looked at Neil in surprise. "How'd do you know? About it being cancer?"

"Unlucky guess. Had an Uncle who died of it."

"What sort?"

"What do you mean, what sort? Cancer cancer."

"No," Hope could hear her speech blurring as it left her, "Stomach cancer? Breast cancer? Brain cancer?"

Neil composed his face in thought, but shook his head. "Cancer. That's all I know."

Two other people entered the room from the garden; soon, a boy, face spattered with teenage spots, was enjoying the writhing of a slim girl on his thighs. It was impossible to make out what they were saying, but their eyes and smiles told you it was intimate and – in the morning – probably to be regretted. Hope hadn't realised that she was not the only girl here and didn't even remember this girl or boy arriving.

Hope was rather disappointed that they now had to share the room. She liked being like this, just her and Neil in a strange house sipping beer and being close.

"So you came to Ruislip?"

"Lucky Ruislip," Hope mocked.

"Dad still on the buses?"

"On the buses. Like Butler and Blakey."

They both giggled.

Hope turned to Neil and smiled, "I thought you were so clever. Did you know that? I remember…" (She couldn't believe how the word 'remember' elided so clumsily when she tried to say it) "…once when we were in Miss Fisher's class. And you always had your hand up first. Teacher's pet. She'd ask a question and up your hand went. Every time."

"Really? I don't remember that." (Why did he say it properly? Why couldn't she say it? He'd drunk far more than she had.) "I don't really remember Miss Fisher's class."

"I remember them all. Every class. Mrs Ducker…"

"I don't remember a Mrs Ducker?"

"Nor do I much. I wasn't in her class that long."

"In the Juniors? Mrs Ducker?"

"Camden. Last school in Camden."

"Right. D' you like Lou Reed?"

"Who's he?"

Neil motioned to the turntable. "That's Lou Reed. On now. You don't like it?"

"Bit frantic. Prefer something a bit smoochier."

"Oh yes? Would you like me to find something?"

Hope looked at Neil, closely studying his face from the side. The small ears and long, feminine eyelashes; smooth skin still lightly reddened from where he had shaved in readiness for the evening. At this moment she wanted to dance very close to him. To feel enfolded and safe within his frame. To be entirely smothered by him.

"No, not really. Mr Reed will do for now"

"Suit yourself."

The heat emanating from the couple opposite had quickly waned, not least due to the fact that – what had been a sexually promising clinch for him – had become a woozy hug for her and she was already gently slipping into a deep sleep.

Through the French Windows, Neil could just make out a small circular group drinking and passing around a cigarette.

"Fancy a walk?"

Hope sat up. "I do. Where shall we go?"

Hope narrowed her eyes. "Do you remember at my house? When I was going to teach you how to swim? Do you remember that?"

"Not really," Neil lied.

"So can you swim?"

"Not really."

"Not really or not at all?"

Neil took some time to reply. "Not at all."

"Want to learn?"

"What? Tonight?"

"Of course. Why not? Scared?"

Neil moved uncomfortably and now averted his eyes.

"You don't have to, Mr Dowling. Only if you want to."

"I haven't got anything to wear. My trunks and that."

Hope came around in front of him and, kneeling up, moved between Neil's two splayed legs. She rubbed the back of her hands along the top of his thighs.

"No one's there. There will only be you and I."

A delighted smirk spread across Neil's handsome face. "Well, I could be tempted to go *au naturel.*"

"French. I'm impressed. So what about it? Are you up for it?" Hope smirked with the sauciness of her *double entendre.*

"Where are we going to find a place to swim at this time?"

"What about the Lido? That never closes."

"I'll need some courage." Neil espied the unopened Party Seven just inside the kitchen door.

Hope followed his glance and saw the large can on the cluttered draining board. "That's a lot of courage."

"Well," said Neil, hauling himself up, "I'm scared."

"Dead scared?"

43

Denis slowly withdrew his hand from her breast and sat back against the uncomfortable, tussocky bank. He had never felt a woman's breast before. He thought that Carol might say something, but she calmly scrabbled in her bag and pulled out her cigarette packet.

Huge, he thought, Christ they were huge. She had kissed and scraped her teeth against the side of his neck and pushed her hand, urgently pushed her hand, inside his shirt. But then he froze. Oh, but how he remembered. How he remembered his large, splayed fingers enveloping the warm, fleshy mound in a tentative cup.

Denis had thought that it might be helpful to move his hand up and down. Perhaps it might convey experience? Maybe she'll think him skilled in the ways… the ways of what? His self-doubt repeatedly whispered that he was desperately out of his depth. He'd caught sight of a woman's breast only once before, when his neighbour Mrs McCarthy had, bending down to retrieve a dropped teaspoon, leant forward in front of him and let her summer dress fall forward to reveal her small, braless breasts.

The thought of the inviting droop in Mrs McCarthy's thin dress flooded his senses with that same intoxicating image that had aroused so many delicious erections and ejaculations. But shouldn't he have been doing more with Carol's breast? He'd sensed – and enjoyed - her breathing heavily against him, her confident, nibbling mouth hard against his cheek.

But he couldn't help but feel that a connection was missing. What the connection was he couldn't tell. It was just that, well.. Mrs McCarthy… so why wasn't he feeling it now?

Carol drew her legs up and pulled her thighs tight into her body. She flicked open the cigarette packet and took one out.

"Up there is a good place, I'm told." said Denis.

"Up there is a good place for what?"

"Perch. Not big, mind you. But three or four will do you breakfast."

Carol lit her cigarette and lazily leaned back. "That's a lot of fun to be had for a man. All those perch and that."

"Certainly is. They're buggers to bring in sometimes. Even perch. Put up a fight."

"Lucky perch."

A damp wind began to blow about them. Carol reached behind for her jacket and pulled it close about her. The large valley floor lay smooth beneath, except for the occasional wrinkle of river bank and field hillock. Carol pulled her breasts up with the flat of her hand and secured them in her bra before buttoning up her blouse.

Denis liked the way that she pulled deeply on her cigarette. He didn't smoke but took vicarious pleasure in the way that she smiled slightly in satisfaction with the release of nicotine.

"Mickey Dolan's a pig."

Denis' face darkened. "Why?"

Carol turned to Denis and laughed. "Why do you think? He doesn't know when to give up."

"Give up what?"

Carol shook her head. "Oh, stupid stuff. It's not important."

"What doesn't he give up?"

"I'm being stupid. I was just saying." Carol tapped her ash dismissively into the grass beside her.

"What doesn't he give up?" repeated Denis.

"What doesn't who give up?"

Denis affected to look at a neighbouring tree, but his voice was intense and urgent. "Mickey Dolan."

"Oh, him! It was nothing now."

"Give up what?"

Carol stared at the burning stem of her fag. "Sorry?"

"Give up what? What is it that Mickey doesn't know to give up?"

"Mickey? What about him?"

"Carol. You said that Mickey Dolan doesn't know when to give up. What doesn't he know when to give up?"

She looked at Denis and smiled teasingly. "Give up? Did I say 'give up'?"

Denis sat up and demanded, "You said that Mickey Dolan doesn't know when to give up. Give up what?"

Carol turned away, and calmly disagreed, "I think he doesn't know whether to give up. I don't believe I said when to give up. Is that Myra's farm down there? It's bigger than I thought."

"Don't try and change the subject. Is Mickey Dolan talking to you? I mean talking in a certain way?".

Carol held her head back and laughed. "A certain way? Talking to me in a certain way? I'm sure that is Myra's farm. How old do you think she is? I mean, she's older than Mammy and that's not young. Have you heard about her husband?"

Denis felt that he was being manipulated by Carol's conversational cul-de-sacs. "Never mind Myra, what about Dolan?"

Carol took in the greens and greys of the close-gathered fields, her eyes unblinking as if she didn't want to censor any of the images that flew up the valley side to occupy her. She could feel again that rain sodden wind that spoke of small, sharp showers and green-grass aromas. She closed her eyes, immersing herself in the sweet scents and breezes that bathed her.

"Are you happy, Denis? When you look at a view like this. Are you happy?"

"I'm happy enough. But this is all going off the point. You were saying about Mickey Dolan and… well, I don't mind saying that Mickey is a terrible…"

"Oh, but he's not, Mr Dunne. Mickey's not a terrible anything."

Denis found the words dry and shrivel in his throat. He knew he looked like a beached fish, his mouth gaping slowly for air.

"Sorry, Denis. Did I say something?"

Eventually he spluttered, "So Mickey's good is he?"

"Good at what, Denis?"

"Christ, Carol. You just said… I heard you just say that Mickey…"

Denis Dunne sprung up and angrily strode away. With arms folded high on his chest, he wrestled with his sense of inadequacy whilst staring hard ahead at nothing in particular.

Mickey Dolan was tall, dissolute, and strange. If Carol wanted him then she was welcome to him. Denis was going places. He had an opening in England. Something real. Something solid. Mickey Dolan had… well, what did he have? What did he *really* have? For all his ways and manners?

The wedding was so close. Only a matter of weeks. And now she was talking about that fucking (there, he'd said it now) Mickey Dolan who was nothing better than a...than a gowl. Denis felt he could walk away there and then, but he had a vision of Carol struggling alone on her bicycle and her father asking awkward questions. More than anything he wanted to leave her to the scraggly lanes and wind-whipped hedges but… but… something held him back. What was it? Decency perhaps? Dyes, perhaps it was decency…

Carol rubbed her hands across the tense blades of his shoulders.

"Jealous, Dunney?"

"Not at all."

She went on to her tiptoes and placed a tender kiss on the nape of his neck.

"Of course not. For what would you have to be jealous about, Mr Dunne?"

Denis felt the prick of a tear abrade the corner of an eye. He wanted to weep, but to do so would be to grant his fiancée an early victory.

"Sit here", said Carol. Denis reluctantly eased himself beside her. She reached for his right hand and guided it inside the cottony softness of her bra.

"I love you, Mr Dunne."

44

Mr Snipe had a dog. Every morning he would, vinegar-faced and resentful, take it out for a short walk to the nearby school playing field. Hope, having just turned the key to start the engine, looked on from her car, air-conditioning slowly lifting into life. She thought how much he resembled a man being led to the gallows by his indifferent hound. She remembered his nervy wife, taut as an over-tuned violin string, prematurely aged from the ceaseless anxiety of fretting about every small tension and imagined threat.

Rather than push the car into first gear to pull away, she watched his slightly bowed frame pace resignedly towards some imaginary gallows. Was this what it all came down to? The numbing existence of routine days that unfolded into numbing weeks. The years flashing by like the blur of a fast car. Inevitable oblivion receiving its prey with the same indifference that the bone-hard ground welcomes the splayed limbs of a suicidal parachutist.

Poor Mr Snipe. Him with the large, awkward thump of a son that disappointed at every turn. The very son that Mr Snipe would, with a zealousness only underachieving fathers could ever experience, turn up week in and week out to watch weak performances on the Rugby field. Here was marriage, thought Hope. The indifferent millwheel that snared its victims and then casually slaughtered them all beneath the crushing water.

Disappointment. Cold, bitter disappointment. Was Mrs Snipe at one time captivating? Seductive? Provocative? Was she lean-figured and quick of movement? Did she toss her head back to flick away the lock of hair that insistently covered her left eye? Did her gurgling laugh reveal small, perfect teeth? Was she pert? Or beautifully heavy? Could she hold you with an insolent stare? Did she touch your arm too much so that your resistance was cleverly outfoxed by this manipulative confusion of signals?

Now here she was: graceless and squat. Carrying a black recycling bin full of papers and wine bottles down to the front of her drive. Graceless and squat. An inelegant grunt left her body as she dropped it onto the apron of tarmac that glowed in the morning sun like a coal-polluted beach.

Graceless and squat.

Did she cup her hand around the back of your neck? Did she…

No, decided Hope. She could never have done that. Was she ever young? Was she ever carefree? Did she laugh with the sheer, deep pleasure of kicking up the rust-bitten leaves of autumn? Had she leant back and closed her eyes as her questing toes dug deep into the hot, liquid sand of a simmering beach?

Was it love at first sight when she initially met Jeremy Snipe? Or was it a calm acceptance of a limited choice that had fallen to her? Did he propose or did it arise awkwardly in a fudged conversation? Perhaps he had taken too much spirits or ale, or lager, before he felt ready to ask. Perhaps, seeing him unsteady and gauche, she had decided that this was how it was. It wasn't like *Jackie* or the other teen magazines she'd read. They told her how to practise her kissing and apply the free gaudy eye shadow. But they never covered swaying men with a compulsion to get a proposal of marriage over with.

So what was it that she had wanted? Happiness? The chance to live out the thin remainder of her life with a degree of control over what she did and what she still wanted?

Hope listened unconsciously to the subliminal patter of the engine, staring at the sad, black recycling box that lay still on the Snipe's drive. She thought that it would be good to cry now. To let free an emotional howl that resonated with sympathy for those that have fallen into the existential void of married life. But she just smiled and turned the air-conditioning off; she then opened the passenger window a little to allow the fresh morning breeze to fill the car.

"Look all around, there's nothing but blue skies,
Look straight ahead, nothing but blue skies..."

Hope lowered the sun visor and drew back the mirror's cover. Her eyes were bright and young today, she thought.

"Looking good, girl, looking good."

She slapped it back up into the roof of her car and eased away from the front drive.

Without looking she fumbled for the 'on' button of her radio. It was Grimmy's breakfast show. The music made her drive faster. She allowed herself to rock back and forward in her car seat in perfect synchrony with the pulse of the song. A wash of perfect recollection engulfed her. Gavin's lean, smooth hips thrusting so perfectly above her. The feel of his perspiring frame under her nails. His pleasure mixing...

And then her mobile rang.

Denis placed his large hands on Hope's small, bony shoulders and led her away towards where the other children were playing.

But Martin followed still. His usual sober swagger now corrupted into a yawing, lurching stagger that was testament to the volume of drink he had taken. Denis had smelled drink on him when he had arrived at the church. It was always Martin's way of dealing with a lot of the chaos and emotion life might throw at him: to take to the bottle.

"Come now, Mr Dunne. Have I offen… offended you. It wasn't…weren't meaning…"

"Not now Martin…" Denis motioned to move away to the other side of the school hall.

Denis took the hand of Mary McLaughlin in both of his and squeezed her thin, small, trapped fist with appreciation. "It was good of you to come over. It means a lot to me, Mary."

"I couldn't not be here, you silly man. You and Carol were always a lovely couple."

Denis winced. He then became uncomfortably aware that the shambling, drunken frame of Martin was bearing down on him again.

"But Christ! She's fuckin' loverly…" Martin raised his beer glass as if it were a champagne flute. "Here's to her. Here's to her now she can no longer be with us. Carol Dunne, and God bless all who sailed in…"

Martin didn't ever recall the powerful blow that caved in his wet, flabby mouth and caused him to reel so violently backward into an – thankfully – empty table. The beer glass had conspired to empty its entire contents onto his white shirt and pale blue trousered crotch. A dribble of blood quickly crept from his reddening lower lip.

Denis looked on horrified at what he had done. His hand still held high as if he feared that Martin might rise from his unconscious torpor and strike back. Slowly, his face changed from hate to confusion to remorse.

A hand, light and wizened, fell onto his shoulder. It was Mary McLaughlin. "Good man, yourself. I was hoping for the chance you might land him another."

Denis guffawed, realising that he'd been wanting to do that for a very long time. Why, on such a tragic occasion, had Martin been so insulting? So crass? So thoughtless?

As Denis' mind turned these matters over he looked at Martin's awkwardly limp limbs. How pathetic he looked. How stupid and ridiculous he was hunched forward like a discarded mannequin.

"To think that you… you moron... to think how you could ever let anything pass your lips about my darling wife."

At the end of the evening, Martin still hadn't stirred. Denis, genuinely apologetic, offered to make sure he got into a taxi home.

People who were there at the funeral could account for the swollen lip and bloodied nose. But they were unable to explain the broken cheekbone Martin seemed to have sustained later in the same day.

But Denis was very dismissive about their questions. "Perhaps he'd fallen over. People do you know."

46

"I need those..." Barry Bufton looked up from his notes, "over there."

Hope had backed into the door to open it, her arms laden with training folders, and wheeled round to deposit them on the desk at the front of the room.

"Merci, Mademoiselle Hope."

"Enchanté" replied Hope.

"You speak French?"

"Not really; it's my 'mot du jour.'"

"Your what?"

How do I explain this? How do I tell him that this word is what I have been using this week? At every opportunity, I have been flogging it in the same way that obviously put-upon waitresses have spat out 'No problem'.

"Anything else you need, Barry?"

"There is. But I guess that's not going to happen."

Hope was busy pushing in an unaligned table. "What's not going to happen," she asked absent-mindedly.

"You and I, Miss Dunne. We're not going to happen. Would that it were…"

Hope stiffened. "Would that it were what?"

Barry realised that he didn't know. He'd thought it was one of his witty phrases. Trouble was, until that moment of Hope's challenge, he realised that it was completely bereft of any wit.

The awkwardness was swept away by Gavin's sudden arrival in the room.

"All set?"

Barry recovered himself. "Think so."

Gavin rubbed his hands together. "The team are all up for it. Big Day. No turning back."

"I'm here for your team, Gavin. Today is about making sure that they are a) here for me, and b) here for each other."

"No doubt about that. It's the big one. The Rubicon. No turning back on this baby."

Gavin was appalled at how the pencils and A4 sheets of paper were out of alignment around the room. He immediately set about straightening them. This made Hope resentful. This was a task she particularly enjoyed.

"Opening exercise is all about letting go. I've a waste paper basket here and I'm going to ask them to write down their fears. Their anxieties. Then I'm going to ask them to come up to the front and announce that they are now letting go of that fear. They will then scrunch up that bit of paper and put it into my bin."

Gavin looked up, an unaligned pencil still in his hand.

"Won't that be embarrassing?"

"Embarrassing? I don't embarrass people, Gavin. I liberate them from what it is that embarrasses them. That's what today is about. It's not about learning. It's about unlearning. It's about emptying oneself so that one can accept the difficult and the new. It's about release…"

"It's about time we called them up from Reception." Hope had timed her intervention perfectly. The breath for Barry's next sentence was still in his throat.

"Send them up!" shouted Gavin, who had resumed his pencil and paper alignment.

Hope walked out to the 8th floor reception and told the petite temp, Bhavini who, she concluded, almost looked like a waiting schoolgirl who had chosen to sit in the receptionist's chair, that the delegates could now make their way upstairs.

"Where are they, Miss Dunne?"

"They're downstairs on the second floor. It's the sales team and they are going to attend a course."

"So is the training on the second floor?"

"Wrong! The training is on this floor which is why you sign in the delegates as you have been all fucking week, you sad Paki bitch."

"Oh, right, I'm sorry…"

"Isn't there a corner shop vacancy you ought to be applying for? Is this all just a bit much for your teeny Mumbai mind?"

"Of course, that was stupid of me. Be back soon!"

"Yes, that was."

Hope strode haughtily back towards the training room. Gavin had now gone and she was once more in the room again, alone, with Barry.

"Would you like to fuck me, Barry?"

"I think so. Just the video to set up."

"Where? Would you like to fuck here or at the back of the room?"

"No. The resolution of the projector keeps upsetting it. Let's stay as we are."

"So we'll fuck right here?"

"Is that focus sharp to you? What if I adjust it like this?"

"I've just realised why you can't fuck, Barry. Of course…"

47

It was for the best. If Hope went out into the back garden then she wouldn't have to listen to Uncle Martin and the others. Stephen embarrassed her. He not only embarrassed her but he had a way of always getting everyone's attention. Spastics can do that. Play up to ordinary people. With an airy "I'm going out for a minute" she ran for the door before anyone could say something that would keep her in the room.

She sat on the lawn uncaring whether it would leave grass stains on her dress. Hope pulled at the short grass and casually tossed it into a small heap. Yes, she could hear their voices, their laughter, but she chose to screen it out. The grass, the slow, methodical pulling of the grass, was what mattered and they didn't.

Why did the laughter of other people always sound so much more genuine when you weren't a part of it? Hope knew that, if she had gone back into the house, the same overwhelming dullness would have cast its net again over the group. She told herself that they were still engulfed in a boring, pointless conversation. She tried to convince herself of it.

She suddenly wanted to be an only child, realising - quite unemotionally - that it was because she hated her brother so much.

"Miss Dunne!" Martin was strolling down the lawn. He stopped, took a drink from his flat beer, and then continued towards her.

"Ah, grass. That's a good pastime. I'm a bit fond of grass pulling myself. Are you arranging the sward here?"

Hope, not knowing what 'sward' meant, calmly looked back at him.

"Here now, let me see. You've a lovely little bundle there. What if we make two? What if we start another one here?"

He sat down awkwardly beside her and placed his beer glass on a nearby drain cover. He pulled quickly at the grass and started to create another mound of grass next to Hope's.

"There, now. That's a fine little hill. Are they even? It's good if they are. Look closer. Are they level? Tell me Miss Dunne: are those two small mounds level?"

Hope, quickly and reluctantly, looked at both and nodded.

"Stay there now."

Martin hauled himself up and went to Denis' allotment at the bottom of the garden. Within minutes he came back with two cabbage leaves.

"That should do it. That should do it now."

Martin placed each cabbage leaf over the small mounds of grass. "Perfect. Isn't that perfect?"

Hope, bemused, could think of nothing to say. Martin looked hard at Hope, the playful smile having temporarily fled from his face.

"Must go in and entertain the troops. Don't spend too long out here, my lovely."

Casually, dismissively, he patted down the cabbage leaves. Hope never understood the exchange between them but, and she didn't know why, she also never forgot it.

48

Martina's sniffles were beginning to irritate. Her head was supported by a closed fist that pushed up her hairline. Her red eyes looked wearily at the screen as she paged down the document.

Wasn't this supposed to be a happy event? It disturbed Hope that there wasn't even the faintest whiff of nuptials to give the child a decent upbringing but, Hope thought, maybe that's a Polack thing. So often Catholic countries go to the dogs once they start to put the state before the Church. Look at Ireland. Even they were considering abortion! 'Thin end of wedge if you ask me,' she decided, but no-one took the trouble to ask her.

Maybe it was time for the next French word? But all Hope could remember was 'fatigué' and that – if she took herself back to interminable French lessons with Mademoiselle Sauvigny – came in some sort of sentence. Perhaps there was another she could use? Ah, she had it.

"Martina, if you don't mind me saying, you're looking a little 'triste'?"

Jamilla looked sharply at Hope; Martina continued to stare at the screen.

"I don't know what 'triste' means," Martina replied.

"It's French."

"I thought it might be. I speak four languages. French isn't one of them."

Hope doubted whether it was worth continuing or not.

"Martina, you look a little sad."

"That is because I am sad. If you were in my situation you would be sad. There's nothing wrong with being sad."

Hope noticed that Martina, always usually dressed in well-fitting clothes that were always snug against her trim body, was wearing a rumpled, creamy smock that seemed one size too large.

Hope glanced over Martina's shoulder at Jamilla, seated on the desk behind. Jamilla, with a serious and steady glare, shook her head very slowly at Hope.

The room was eerily silent. The faint hum of the computer terminals punctuated only by the rhythmic punch of Martina's finger stabbing the 'PgDn' button. After two or three minutes, Martina pushed herself back from her desk and tiredly walked out of the office.

What a fucking Prima Donna, concluded Hope. Walks around like she's the only one with a care in the world. Well, and this may come as a shock to her, but people have had babies before her. And they will go on having babies long after her. If she and that half-wit of a boyfriend can't be bothered to take precautions then they deserve everything that's coming to them. Fuck the pair of them. No doubt they'll have the baby in a British hospital, educate it in a British school, send it to a British university (finding some EU loophole that means that we'll pick up the fees of course) and then they'll take their fortune back to Poland. Typical.

"Jamilla, I'm really worried about Martina. Is she all right?"

Jamilla raised her eyebrows and gave Hope a look that told her she didn't really know.

"It's probably all a bit of a shock for her. I don't think it was expected."

Hope pursed her lips and nodded an affected, weary assent.

"Life can be cruel sometimes. Thank God she's here where she can deal with it without people endlessly passing judgement on her. Has she got any friends?"

"Oh, I think she has lots of friends. But what can they say? Even worse, what can they do?"

"How old is the baby?"

"No idea. Weeks I guess. Like I say, what can she do?"

"Well…." at this point Hope drew in a large breath and left the sentence hanging in the air, hoping that Jamilla would sense what she had left unspoken.

"No. That's not the answer. That's never the answer. We make mistakes and we have to deal with them. You can't run away from a little baby. You can't kill a little baby because it's not convenient in your life."

Hope couldn't imagine Jamilla ever having made a mistake. To her, Jamilla's life had run as smoothly and unwaveringly as if it had been following the course of a railway line. Nice parents. Good upbringing. Then a degree. Arranged marriage. Adoring children. Where were the opportunities for mistakes in that? Jamilla's life had never been shunted into sidings. Derailed by tragedy. Held up by life's leaves being strewn across her track.

Mind you, Hope, mused with a wicked glee, she wasn't that attractive. A lot of fat people are normally very attractive. Would be more so if most of them lost a bit of weight. But not Jamilla, with her round face and Play-Doh nose. Good job the marriage was arranged. Probably the only way that she'd ever have bagged a husband really. Maybe she was thinner in those days.

"You're so right about us all having made mistakes. I know I have. Have you made mistakes? Your life always seems so happy to me."

Jamilla rocked in her chair, as she always did, when laughing. She then turned mock-serious: "Why no! Never!"

Jamilla then burst out laughing again. "Of course. God help me! But you know the secret, eh? The secret is, you don't let people know you make mistakes."

Hope smiled, but only because she felt it was what was expected of her. She came around the front of her desk to pick up a paper cup she'd inadvertently knocked on to the floor.

Jamila watched her. Hope knew that she was about to field a question.

"The answer's 'Yes', Mrs Quereshi. Lots. Including men."

Jamilla roared her approval and clapped her pudgy hands together in appreciation.

The opening door heralded Martina's return. She walked listlessly back to her seat.

"Having fun?"

"Not really," Jamilla sighed.

49

Carol felt herself drifting back to consciousness. A strange presentiment told her that there was someone beside her bed. No, not just the baby, someone else. Without opening her eyes she said, "Denis?"

"Almost right. Better looking."

Horrified, she opened her eyes and saw Martin sitting back, casually smoking with a small bouquet of flowers across his lap.

"What are you doing here? Where's Denis?"

"Taking a stroll. Probably gone to spend a penny. Before he goes back to work."

Martin stubbed out the cigarette in an adjacent ashtray.

"How long you been waiting?"

"Long enough to drink in the sleeping beauty. You're as beautiful when you're asleep as…"

"Shut it! Take your flowers and leave me alone!"

"I'm hurt. No, I seriously am very hurt. I take a break from my labours to visit my sweet sister-in-law and what am I met with? It's enough to drive a…"

"Martin, you saw the baby yesterday. You saw me yesterday. I take it you've seen Denis yesterday and today. Now go away."

"Will do no such thing. Might even ask the nurse for a cup of tea." He sprang up and, noticing a nurse nearby, instantly changed his gait to that of a prowling tiger, and walked imperiously towards her.

Carol couldn't hear the conversation, and was glad she couldn't. It would be the same patter he always brought out coupled with the smiling eyes and a fixed look that would make the poor, defenceless girl think she was the only person in the universe.

Sure enough, he was soon walking back with a cup brim-full with tea, which was already spilling out and streaking its faux-china bowl and saucer.

"Now there's a darling girl for you. Made me feel very welcome. Oh yes. Very welcome. Have you a pen?"

"What do you want a pen for?"

"Oh… just something I need to jot down before I forget."

Carol replied with a sarcastic, "I didn't think you'd ever forget your own phone number."

"Now that's libellous. If you weren't in a post-natal state I'd slap a writ on you here and now." He held the cup to his lips and took a long, satisfying draught of his tea.

"Don't you ever give up, Martin?"

"Never. I thought you'd know that. You see, I love a chase. And do you know what? Sometimes, when you've trapped your prey the easy thing to do would be to kill it right there. But I'm a sporting man and ending it there and then is too easy. So, like a cat now, I like to let the prey wander a bit. Move around. Delude it into thinking there's a chance of escape. But, of course, what you know and I know is: there isn't any escape."

"So I'm your prey now, am I?" Martin detected venom in her voice and smiled at her before returning to his lukewarm tea. He inspected the dregs as thoughtfully as if they held the secret of all knowledge within their streaky runes.

"Well, put it like this, Mrs Dunne. You're going nowhere now. Not without my say so."

"Don't for a moment ever think..."

But Martin was rising from his chair a second time, ready to greet a returning Denis with an excited Hope leaving his side to run to her Mother.

"Hello Mum!"

Carol leaned as far out of the bed as she could, encircled Hope with her right arm and kissed her tenderly on the top of her head.

"Hello darling."

"Hello Uncle Martin." Hope reluctantly allowed herself to be hugged by him.

"My God, what have we here? Only the prettiest girl in the whole land! They're going to have to lock you up my girl. There isn't a lad in the land who won't be begging you to marry him. Is that not so, Denis?"

But Denis had walked around the other side of the hospital bed and taken Carol's hand between both of his.

"How are you, Carol? Rested?"

"I'm good. Tired but good. Where's Stephen?" There was a rising panic in her voice. From her prone position in the bed she couldn't see if he was in his cot or not.

"Don't worry. He's there. He's fast asleep now. He's had a rough time of it you know. As have you."

Carol allowed her head to sink slowly back on to the pillow. "At least he's stopped crying. The Doctor was here earlier. They just needed to do some tests they said. Routine ones. I fell asleep waiting for them to bring him back."

Carol couldn't help noticing that Denis had become uncomfortable. What was it? Was he hiding something?

With an oddly dramatic timing, a Doctor turned the corner to enter their small ward and strode quickly up to Martin.

"Good afternoon, are you the father?"

"I wish I was now, but the lucky man you want is there." He nodded towards Denis.

The Doctor recovered himself from his thoughtless error and smiled awkwardly before rapidly resuming his authoritative air again.

"Mr Dunne, I was wondering if I might have a quiet word with you and your wife? 10 minutes should do it."

Carol looked from the Doctor to Denis, confused and fearful.

Martin took his cue and, with the hammy flourish of a Shakespearian actor, extended an open hand to Hope. "Miss Dunne, could I prevail on you to escort me around this lovely building whilst the good Doctor talks with your Mam and Dad? It's medical, now, and you and I wouldn't understand."

Hope glanced quickly at Carol.

But it was Denis who said encouragingly, "We won't be long, love. Go with your Uncle Martin for a little while."

She took Martin's hand and let herself be led from the ward. She gave one last look at her mother's bed. The Doctor - speaking so low that she couldn't make out what he was saying - had started to awkwardly tug the stiff white curtains across to hide the bed.

50

"Have you remembered the folders?"

Hope placed her bag on the back seat of Gavin's car and slammed the door shut. "Of course. And a spare copy of your presentation is on your laptop and..." she held up a small orange flash drive, "this memory stick."

"What would I do without you?"

Gavin sat in the driver's seat and immediately jumped out again to take off his suit jacket. Hope made herself comfortable, not sure about how the seat belt was sitting across her breasts. She looked behind and adjusted it upwards. She resentfully remembered that it was probably set this low for his little Vietcong doll.

She'd been looking forward to this day or, more specifically, this journey for many weeks. The conference was being held in some bland, magnolia painted conference hotel in Bristol. Gavin had suggested that Hope went with him; she now had two delicious hours of Gavin to herself. The world, safely isolated outside the steel and upholstered confines of Gavin's Audi, could go hang itself.

"Like some music, Hopey?"

"Of course."

"So what would you like?"

"You know what I like. You listen to it often enough at home."

"Hmm I don't think I have any of that stuff. Tell you what, have a listen to this."

He tapped the music system into life and soon the rapid plucking of – Hope couldn't make the instrument out, was it some sort of guitar perhaps? – started to fill the car. Hope groaned inwardly. It was probably Thuong's music and her heart sank that she would have to probably sit through its slurs, whines and microtonal cacophony for the rest of the journey.

"Like it?"

"It's really lovely. What is it? Vietnamese?"

"Yes. Classical Vietnamese music. Her name is Nguyen Thanh Thuy. She's playing the Dan Tranh. A bit like a sitar thing that goes on your lap. I love it. Thuong got me into it."

"And you're so shallow that you'll like anything as long as Thuong tells you it's good. Even though your ears, trained since you were born in the western classical tradition, are not attuned to listening to this twangy crap."

"Yes, I do listen to other Vietnamese stuff. Some I find harder to get on with, but I really love this. Glad you like it too."

"It's a foreign pile of musical shit."

"You're right, very atmospheric."

Gavin's Audi began to eat up the miles and Hope resigned herself to listening to whoever Gavin said it was and staring out of the window. She nearly wept with frustration when, without Gavin appearing to notice, the CD returned to the first track and started to replay once more.

"Mind if I listen to the news?"

Hope could barely conceal her ecstasy. "That would be great." She then wondered if going to the conference with Gavin was going to be quite the heavenly ride she'd anticipated.

Once the news was over Hope was delighted that he hadn't put the music back on. She thought about how to start the conversation, but it was Gavin, after a quick glance in his rear-view mirror, who started things going.

"Been to Bristol before?"

"I don't think so, not that I remember." Hope knew she'd never been anywhere near Bristol, but her answer sounded more 'travelled', as if she was so busy with the life that she couldn't even recall for certain where she'd been to or where she hadn't.

"I like it. Buzzing place. Lots going on. Couple of big contacts there. Hope to see them if poss".

If poss? If poss? What sort of word shortening is that? Hope wanted to say, 'Do you mean if possible?' but thought better of it. Don't want to turn things sour now that we were talking. Besides, he might stick that bloody awful music on if conversation went pear-shaped.

"Yes, I hear it has a real '*joie de vivre*'. She purred inwardly with the skilfully applied French interjection. Hopefully Gavin was also impressed with her faultless pronunciation.

"Certainly has. Though I guess we won't have much time for that. It's going to be a busy couple of days or so for you me both."

"It'll make a difference working somewhere else. Good to meet the team again. Is Malcolm coming down?"

"Yes. Be a tad late. Hopefully with the good news that Shell have signed up for a couple more years. Touch and go last night but he seemed more positive this morning."

Hope turned away and yawned. It had been an early start. Mum and Dad's breakfast. Feeding Pardew. Getting all her bags and things into the car. Dad looked very lonely last night, she recalled. "It's only until Friday," she had reassured him. But he still looked worried. She'd noticed how old he'd become. Diminished and old.

Gavin's voice interrupted, "Fancy a bite?"

"I've made us some sandwiches. If you'd like one."

"No, you keep 'em. Have them later. I fancy a bit of Sushi. What about you?"

"Sounds lovely!" Hope put aside the disappointment that she had packed a thoroughly nutritious lunch for them both. Sandwiches, a decent Pork Pie, salad with her own dressing and a half bottle of grassy Sauvignon Blanc in a wine cooler. But then what was she thinking? That they would sit in the large, open area of the service station and spread out a chequered blanket as if they were at Glyndebourne? Secretly, she wanted to take advantage of the soft summer day and find a stretch of grass that they could lazily sit back on.

"I love Sushi." She hoped she would like it.

Thankfully, when Gavin returned from the small Marks and Spencer outlet he carried only sandwiches and crisps.

"No sushi, I'm afraid. Sold out. Took the initiative. Hope you like something."

"That's a real shame." Hope grabbed the chicken salad sandwiches and tried to fathom how to open the triangular box.

"Here." Gavin quickly unzipped the cardboard and opened the packet up for her. "When you're on the road you can open them up on your lap whilst driving on the M62 and drinking your coffee. All sales people can."

Hope enjoyed her crisps. She liked to tell Martina and Jamilla that she never ate them, which always meant that she had to make sure they were finished before she got back to the office during her lunch hour. Best of all, she liked Marks and Spencer's crisps.

Neither spoke. Gavin was preoccupied and Hope wanted them both to go back to the secure intimacy of the car. She realised that, to all of the families, business people, scruffy children, insolent teenagers, sloppily dressed holidaymakers and coach crews traipsing by, they would think that Gavin and her would be together. Their lack of conversation, Hope thought, would *prove* they were a married couple.

Gavin scrunched up his crisp packet as a final flourish that the small lunch was finished. He picked up his car keys as a signal to Hope that he was eager to go.

"You're going to have to excuse me first. Need to make a quick call to the bathroom."

"Sure", said Gavin. "I'll just phone Rhona and get the latest on the MOD business."

Hope used the private moments in the toilet to sharpen up her make-up. The walk from the car to the service station had blown her hair about a good deal. She teased strands slowly and skilfully back into place. She then checked her teeth to make sure there weren't any pieces of crisps or sesame seeds unknowingly lodged in a crevice that might need winkling out. If Gavin was to get too close to her, she needed to be ready.

He had his back to her as she returned to his car. As she drew closer she began to make out the occasional words that Gavin was speaking, then complete sentences. "Had to rush… can't… next time… miss you too. Let's talk about that later. Tonight. Let's talk about it tonight. Love you."

"Do you say that to all your sales staff?"

Gavin, for the first time ever, looked caught out and flustered. "What?"

"Rhona. Sounds like you're very close?"

"Oh, that wasn't Rhona. Hmm, just called home."

Hope knew he was lying. And she could feel her whole world plunging towards the ground and shattering at her feet.

51

They are waiting for our petitions
Silent and calm.
Their lips no prayer can utter,
No suppliant psalm;
We have made them all too weary
With long delay,
For the souls in their still agony,
Good Christian pray.

Requiescant in pace,
Requiescant in pace.

Hope resented the hymn. Not resented it; hated it. The tune was stilted; the words were meaningless. Who was waiting for what petitions? Normal petitions? Were dead people waiting for sheaves of signatures?

No, it was a ridiculous hymn. Who wrote these hymns? Which outcast, empty of any human, normal interaction would spend time writing these obtuse lines? Were they designed to lift her soul up before the almighty? Was she supposed to experience a suffusing of grace through her physical being?

The dead can't be waiting for our petitions. Logically, that very sentence was a nonsense. Hope stopped singing. Was anybody looking? Did anyone suspect that her moving lips were producing no words? Scanning the teachers seemed to prove that no-one had realised that she was opening and closing her mouth, like a goldfish considering a castle feature that it was sure wasn't there 30 seconds ago; but still, she could never be sure.

Hope lowered the Banda machined hymn sheet and internally wrestled with school assemblies, school masses and school retreats.

This was all such a huge charade. Hundreds of children. Teachers lining the side of the school hall like Nazi soldiers still waiting for their promised first rifles. Row upon row upon row bemoaning the fact – in song - that the dead were enthusiastically waiting for them to petition God.

"Hello God, I'd like to recommend someone to you. They were great, really. When you got to know them. Good people. So my Mum said anyway. To be honest, I didn't really know them. Anyway, here's a petition I put together myself. It's probably not very good."

The Deputy Head, Miss Standing, shuffled up to the lectern, rattling a few throaty coughs to clear her smoker's throat, before she solemnly parted pages of the School Bible.

Having momentarily turned her head away to drag out the last viscous phlegm before, in all probability, swallowing it again, she now adopted her serious, profound pose. She allowed her left hand to rest on the lectern whilst her right hand, waiting for the final lines of the hymn, raised itself before providing, with its slowly falling gesture, a visual symbol that she was bringing the hymn to a close.

She swallowed again, before her reedy oboe of a voice scratched itself onto the silence.

"And in the sixth month the angel Gabriel was sent from God unto a city of Galilee, named Nazareth…"

Hope noticed that the teachers started to look tetchy, as if reluctantly stirred from their nomadic upright slumber. Mr Jacques, the Head Teacher dramatically sat up, as if struck by the deepness of Miss Standing's first utterance.

The sense of muted discomfort was now palpable. Why it should be so, Hope couldn't understand. All she knew was that the Head and his teachers were, to various degrees believers (Mr Simpson, the biology teacher was the exception, whom Hope knew to be firmly and scientifically agnostic and stood as someone quite immune to faith). But she knew that none of them believed this particular school hall charade. It was something to be got through. It was the endurance test of Monday morning and, once surmounted, the rest of the week was downhill all the way.

Oh, the smell! Oh, the smell of the polished parquet tiles! It lifted in brown thermals from the floor and surrounded Hope with a warming molasses calm that penetrated her clothing, from her slate-grey socks to the lapels of her school blazer. A soft, soft breathy geyser of buffed polish that eased and insinuated itself like…

…like Martin.

52

"Anybody home?"

Martin heard nothing, but the back door was open and that was invitation enough.

He strolled to the front of the house and stood and leaned against the bottom of the bannister.

"Hello!" He looked up and waited for someone to reply.

A toilet flushed and, after a slush of tap water followed, Hope emerged and walked slowly down the stairs.

She whispered, "Mum's asleep."

Rather than make way for Hope to pass him, he boldly watched her descent until she realised she couldn't go any further. Stopping three steps above him she smiled and asked, "Can I get past, Uncle Martin?"

Martin had his right elbow resting on the finial and relaxed his frame before her. "I wouldn't think so. Some things a man can let pass. But some things are too good to let through. Much too good to let through."

Hope didn't respond. She broadened her grin and remained composed on the step, her heel brushing slowly against the carpet of the riser. Martin was searching. She noticed he was greying; his eyes were now seamed with the scratches and folds of middle age, but he was still so handsome and she could see it. And she felt he knew it.

"Get out of the fucking way, *Uncle* Martin." She deliberately stressed the word 'Uncle' so that it was freighted with an intense derision. The effect on Martin was immediate. She had never seen him so discomforted. He braced with the shock and his elbow slipped awkwardly from the stair post.

"I beg your pardon?"

Hope smiled once more. "Get out of the fucking way, Mr *Uncle* fucking Martin."

"I can't believe you've just said that. Did your father teach you to speak like that?"

"Are you going to give my father lessons on fatherhood, Uncle Martin? Why don't you give me lessons on how I should speak to my father at the same time? He has a lot of trouble trusting the things people say to him."

"You little bitch…"

Hope quickly walked backwards up the stair. "Would you like a cup of tea, Uncle Martin?" Her smile was suddenly gone. The voice was steady and cold.

Martin, still trying to comprehend and accommodate Hope's unflinching manner, took a pace back and turned to enter the front room. For the first time in her life, she felt she had the upper hand with Uncle Martin. Composed, self-confident Uncle Martin. The man with an answer for everyone and everything. Witty Uncle

Martin. The endless-store-of-stories-and-jokes-Uncle-Martin. She had him. She knew she had him. She knew things about him.

Hope remained on the stairs, just as Martin had left her. She liked the feeling. What feeling? She couldn't answer. There were sounds coming from the front room. Martin sounds. His thick, knowing fingers flipping papers in the rack. Confident fingers. Pushing fingers. Squeezing fingers. Unbuttoning fingers. Hurtful fingers. Nicotine fingers. Casual fingers.

Hope reached out for the finial that Martin had deserted. It had been poorly painted; even Hope could see that. There were tears of dried white paint weeping at the edge. White tears. Frozen white tears. Her hand dropped over the crown of the finial and she felt a charge of calm repose. A moment of complete order. A moment of mastery.

She walked down the hall into the narrow kitchen. The kettle stirred slowly into action as Hope arranged the cups on the work surface. Her Mum's cup; her cup; Uncle Martin's cup. She made sure all three handles fell along a line that only her imagination could see.

Should she respond to Martin? Dare she respond to Martin? She thought Martin utterly repellent. But handsome. There was business to be resolved. A control to be exerted. A skirmish – not a battle – that she would triumph in.

She took her Mother's tea up first. She knew she probably wouldn't drink it and she'd be emptying the cold contents of the cup into the sink in about an hour or so. She slipped into her own bedroom and removed her school cardigan, shirt and bra before putting only her school shirt back on again. She tucked it tight into the waist of her skirt, billowed out the yoke and upper panels of the shirt and, with a glance at the mirror to assure herself that the right effect was achieved, ran her hand through her hair and closed the bedroom door behind her.

Then slowly, carefully, she descended the stairs, went into the kitchen and took hers and Martin's cups into the front room.

"Thank you, now." Martin had slumped unattractively into the armchair, reading the previous day's Daily Mirror. Hope stood against the window and fingered the edge of the net curtain, pretending to be watching the street outside.

Nothing was said between them before Martin, still with eyes steadily fixed on the paper, commented, "One day we won't have a car industry. The unions will see to that."

"Aren't they just looking after the working man?"

"Since when? I don't remember the Tolpuddle Martyrs working on a British Leyland assembly line. It's a class thing now. Managers against workers. What most people seem to forget, is that most managers were workers once. But all workers were never managers. That's the truth."

Hope pushed back the net curtain a little more whilst turning her figure side on for the light to pass through the thin shirt fabric.

"I might go into politics. Dad says I should."

Martin put down the open paper on his lap and looked straight at her. Hope made sure that she kept her position against the window; she held the cup a little way from her chest.

"On which side?" Martin enquired. Hope felt he must have noticed. She turned only her face from the window and fully met his gaze.

"Which side what?"

"Which side will you be on when you're the fine lady politician? Left or right?"

"Left of course. What would you expect?"

Martin's stare remained unblinking. Hope was sure he must have noticed. School shirts were cottony thin and she became aware of a delicious, sinful sensation. She desperately wanted to see if her nipples were showing through the surface of her shirt.

"Right enough," Martin snorted dismissively and held the paper back up in front of him. "Everyone's got a right to their wrong opinion. Even little schoolgirls." He turned the page of his paper.

"Is an opinion wrong because it's not your opinion? Is an opinion wrong because it's a schoolgirl's?"

Martin folded the corner of the paper over to look at Hope again. He held her in his look for a few seconds, smiled and winked, then returned to the Daily Mirror.

Without looking at Hope, he immediately threw out, "Do you think 'The Old Codgers' in this paper are real? I mean, none of them ever seem to die. And if they're old codgers, one of them is bound to meet his maker every so often."

Now Hope noticed, with Martin's eyes resolutely back on the newspaper, how the small, firm push of nipple was easily apparent through her school blouse. But Martin hadn't noticed or cared. She was reading the situation badly. There was no skirmish, no battle for control. He was sleazy and disinterested. Hope had thought she was about to engage Martin in some kind of sexual 'face-off', but he hadn't even noticed that she had discarded her bra.

She let the net curtain go, waited for a few seconds, and went back to the kitchen. Her own unwanted tea was emptied into the already-stained brown-white sink. She started to wash up and saw, from the corner of her eye, Martin amble up the hallway with his empty cup. He stood behind her and leaned across with his left hand and placed it carefully on the draining board. As his palm returned it brushed momentarily, but with an imperceptible pause, across Hope's chest.

"Bye, now!"

And he was gone.

53

It was a disappointing hotel. Relatives in Athlone had told Hope that it was 'wonderful'; that 'she'd be in luxury'. The truth was, it was as faceless and charmless as every other out-of-town hotel she'd ever stayed in. The room was fine enough. The bed seemed soft and was draped with clean cotton sheets; the bathroom, if one looked past the obvious scuffs and scrapes that most hotel bathroom doors wear like battle-weary 'badges of honour', was large enough. But it was the reception and bar that depressed most of all.

How inversely different to London, Hope mused. In London hotels, reception areas and foyers were often gold-tipped and grand but the unwelcoming bedrooms pinched with tiredness. In the McGarrett Spa and Hotel it was the opposite: tacky bars and faux dining rooms sat beneath bedrooms that appeared well-appointed and warm.

As Hope stared at the flat farmland that unrolled itself outside her window, she became slowly aware of the muffled speech of a neighbouring room. Occasionally, small uncertain bars of music would be displaced by the sound of people who, Hope was certain, must be talking into the fleshy palm of their hands.

Why hadn't Gavin appeared at Dublin airport like he promised? Why was she left to wait watching the passengers appear in the arrivals hall, straining to see if he would emerge at any moment half-hidden behind a bickering couple that were unknowingly shielding him? She strained to catch sight of all those with 'LHR' bag stickers, just to assure herself that the Heathrow flight was still disgorging its passengers.

Perhaps he'd lost his bag? Maybe a customs official had ushered him into… where did Customs Officials usher you into? She remembered that Barry Bufton had spoken once of having to be shown into a small anteroom to… to what? Why had they shown him into a small room and why did Barry's face turn red with the recollection? She must ask him. He never did tell her why.

Anyway, that was neither here or there. With a silent and slow-drip seething, she waited for Gavin. And waited. And waited.

And he never showed. Passengers from later flights started to appear. Bags braceleted with the LHR initials never appeared again. Hope moved aside to camouflage and cosset her disappointment. Disappointment gave way to despair. Despair curdled into a simmering anger. Stupidly, she wandered up to the monitor pretending to scrutinise the layers of text that rolled down its screen. Why? Why was she doing this? Was she trying to convince the other people in the arrivals hall that she'd just noticed an administrative error and needed to hurry away to tell someone? Even as she stood before the monitor she could sense the eyes of her fellow-waiters tunnelling into her back like acid-tipped arrows.

"She's been stood up."

"She's been let down and is now staring at that screen in the vague hope that the flight has been incorrectly captured on the screen."

"She's over-committed herself to a feckless man who has duped her into thinking that they had a future together."

Hope suddenly realised that this wasn't someone behind her speaking these sentences. This was her own conscience speaking to her.

Cold with humiliation, she nodded at the screen – as if fully expecting the information it gave her - and made her way to a revolving bookstand outside the airport newsagent. She feigned to read the carousel of titles that spun in front of her, before checking her wristwatch and walking smartly away.

She didn't cry. Even though her gut was twisted and wrung like some Dali-esque figure of torture, she didn't cry. She whispered, 'Fuck him!' She whispered, 'Fuck him!' again. She repeated the two words every twenty steps or so, turning away from on-comers who might hear the sequence of curses that she was releasing. Outside, the wind rounded the terminal building and blew a spiteful dust across her face.

She sat in her car and calmly placed her face into the warm, comforting palms of her hands. From her chest she could feel a small ball of bile rise towards her throat. She would master it. She would control it. It mutated into a tearful catch of breath that she forced back down into herself. The stifled emotion spread and suffused her shoulders and lungs. She had her agony under control.

It was whilst she was coasting along the N4 that an alien howl erupted from within her. A cry of pain so raw that she instantly pulled over to the side of the road, a car's horn angrily berating the sudden lurch of her driving as it floated past.

Hope's shoulders retched and rose with each stab of tears. Her hand desperately tried to stem the flow of snot and sorrow that leached into her hand. After 20 minutes or so she lifted her head up and stared at the long, grey road unwinding in front. Without looking down she felt for her bag and drew it into her lap; her fingers soon found the Kleenex tissues; she took two and dabbed and wiped her damp face and eyes. Eventually, her sniffles sounded clearer and she felt her senses settle. In the ditch that ran by the side of the road, the wind was gently tossing the meadowsweet and yellowing ears of grasses. Trees above were tenderly releasing their browning leaves.

Swearing wasn't the answer, she thought. There was no use swearing any more.

Was it the sound of the muffled chatter in the adjoining hotel room that made her think of the airport? How like the indistinct articulations of the dim tannoy that she struggled to understand as she walked towards the arrivals hall.

But that was this morning.

She listlessly picked up the magazine from the small table beside her. 'Not to be taken from the room' was hand-written on an adhesive square on its cover. Hope lifted the bottle of wine – which she had ordered in advance to greet her and Gavin when they had reached their room - from the warm ice bucket and read the sodden label. The lid clicked as she unscrewed it; she poured some of the wine into each glass and, taking one in each hand she held them up to the window, chinked them to release a hollow ring and said, "Cheers."

She gulped the contents of each and poured out two more slugs of wine. There was a quick knocking at the hotel door that came just as Hope had reached for the first glass. Gavin? Was that Gavin? Had he come by a later flight? Was there a later flight? Was this long-weekend about to transform into an unbelievably joyous, life-affirming experience? Had she been mistaken about him all along?

All these questions fell over each other in her mind. Composing herself, she quietly placed the glass down and made quick, awkward adjustments to her hair. A quick check that her make-up was still presentable preceded a repeat of the door knocking. Should she steady herself with a gulp of wine? No, it was too late for that.

Hope took a large intake of breath and reached out for the door handle.

54

"Have you been crying, Hope?"

Hope felt a soothing presence as Aunty Patsy sat slowly on the single bed. In the dark she felt Patsy's hand push Hope's teary hair back from her eyes. The smell of Patsy's scent mixed with the night odours that were seeping into her bedroom from the sash window by her bed.

"Have you been crying?" She repeated.

Hope slowly nodded her answer.

"Can I help? What will make it better?"

"Where's Mummy gone?" The words slipped from Hope's mouth slowly and awkwardly. Patsy's thumb began to rub slowly across Hope's left cheek, trying to smear away the hurt.

Patsy struggled herself and felt her thin lips press together as if to prevent the pain wrapping itself around what she wanted to say. Eventually she sighed, "Oh, she's just having a little break for a while. She'll be back before you know it."

"Where's Stephen? Why isn't he here?"

Thank God it's so dark in here, thought Patsy. Especially now that she became aware of her own silent tears itching and inching down her cheeks.

"I've got such a cold you know. Listen to me! I sound like an old bloodhound with my sniffling, don't you think?" She tried to laugh.

"Where's Stephen?"

Patsy stared out of the window and could just discern the dim gables of the opposite houses.

"Has Mummy ever explained about Stephen, Hope? Has she ever talked to you about his not being right. Like other boys and girls."

"Mummy told me."

"When children aren't well, like Stephen wasn't well, then they can get very sick. And… you see, Stephen became very sick and God… God, because he loved him so much, said, 'I love Stephen so much that I want to look after him. And do you know what he did? He said to Gabriel, one of his favourite angels, he said to Gabriel, 'Bring Stephen here so I can sit him right here, next to me, and keep him with me forever.' That's what he said. Now isn't that grand?"

Patsy put her hand across her mouth to prevent herself crying in front of Hope.

"Is he dead? Has he gone to heaven?"

"Yes. He's gone to heaven. And Mummy is so upset, even though she knows Stephen's with God, that she's had to go away. That's only right isn't it? A holiday. To help her get better."

"Has Daddy gone with her? On her holiday"

"Of course. And you're to stay with your Uncle Martin and Aunty Patsy until they, or… well, until it's over. That's good, isn't it?"

Hope said nothing for a few moments, slowly taking in all Patsy had revealed to her in the darkness.

"But why didn't they take me? Why can't I go on holiday?"

"Why? Because you've got to go to school, of course! You'll get your holiday right enough. But they can't take you with them when you have to go to school."

"Patsy."

"Yes, my darling?"

"I'm glad Stephen's dead."

55

She took the ticket out and proudly held it up.

"I can't see it over there. Bring it here."

"It's about time you got those gammy monacles seen to."

He took the ticket, held it inches from his face and peered closely at it. "Crikes. So how much did it cost you?"

Bridie O'Coffey affected a secretive smile and merely responded by enigmatically sipping her tea.

"Oh, come on now, Bridie. A fortune, I'm sure."

"Money well spent, and something to make up for all that's happened."

"£24 I heard the Reverend has paid. What I'd give to be as poor as a Church of Ireland Priest now. Stop with your playing and tell me. How much?"

"Seven pounds and fifteen shillings."

The amount had the desired effect. Johnny Coleman whistled slowly in admiration and stabbed his walking stick hard on the stone floor. "Jaysus. God forgive the swearing. Seven pounds and how many shillings?"

"Fifteen shillings."

"You, an Athlone girl going to America? Who'd have thought it? But why now? Isn't your man O'Brien doing great things? Your sons will be able to have their own land. Their own cottage. I can't understand why you're leaving. Haven't your sons already lost a parent?"

"I still have a life. Just because I have children doesn't mean my own life has to end. I should have gone years ago. When I first said I was going. If it hadn't been for my father I would have gone soon enough. I've always been bitter about that. He kept telling me I was a dreamer. But he didn't give me the chance to show what I could do."

"But you always seemed so happy, you and Joe, God rest his soul. Maybe I'm getting old, but I thought marriage was forever."

Bridie turned on her stool, opened the small door to the range and checked the turf.

"So did I. But it's not. Joe's buried and I'm left to carry on. The boys are fine. They've good futures and I've made sure about young Mary. And I'm still going."

"What have you done about Mary?"

I've seen the Maguires. She'll work for them and they'll give her a home. They're a good family and Mr Maguire is a great man and he has fine sons. Please God, Mary will be in clover there. She's happy enough about it. She's always taken a shine to that young John Maguire. Who knows? Maybe it'll come to something one day."

"Who knows indeed? So when are you going?"

"April. April 11th. God willing. I've a cousin in Queenstown. She'll be putting me up now. Next stop: New York."

"First class of course?" Johnny winked.

"Away with you", she laughed.

"I hear Eugene Daly's going as well. Him and a cousin. And one of the Mulvihill girls."

Bridie took the teapot and refilled Johnny's cup and then pushed the small jug of milk across the table towards him.

"There now, Johnny."

"Well, I'll miss you. Athlone's no match for New York sure enough. What I'd give to be going with you. Big ship like that. The paper says it's unsinkable."

56

With the full glare of the sun bouncing from the car in front directly into his eyes, Gavin reached up and lowered his visor.

"You OK?" inquired Hope.

"Hmm? Oh yes. Lots to think about. Be glad when this conference is over."

Hope let another couple of minutes pass, before asking, "Happy with your speech?"

Gavin took in a shallow breath before nodding, "I think so."

Hope couldn't let go of the phone call. There was something about it that worried her. It was even more frustrating that she couldn't quite pin down what it was. That wasn't Rhona he was talking to. Or was it? No, she reassured herself; Rhona might be only in her late 20s but her big personality was matched by a big arse and a lack of dress sense to hide it. Surely Gavin wouldn't pass her over for Rhona? No, she concluded unequivocally: it wasn't Rhona he'd been talking to.

So was it Thuong? He'd told her it was. But he didn't have the usual fawning music to his voice. It just didn't sound like the way he would normally speak. He was agitated. Worried. She'd never seen the smooth veneer of his manner so cracked. Maybe Thuong was telling him some terrible news. What was it she'd caught as she approached him unawares? 'Have to rush…' She remembered that. But that could be easily explained. You must have to say that, even to your wife. But what about 'Next time?' No, that didn't seem right. You're always going to see your wife again. You don't need to talk about a next time. Gavin was talking about something that didn't happen often. Something, the frequency of which, that had to be stated.

"So what did Rhona have to say? Did she get my email?"

"Oh… I didn't ask. I'm sure she did."

Hope began to let the resentment fester and build in her own mind. I bet you didn't ask her. I bet you didn't ask the fat-arsed Scottish cow. It's bad enough pretending to others that we don't have a relationship, but now you want to lie about the other relationships you're having. Fucking hypocrite. I have to live with your fucking married saintliness – knowing what we are to each other – and you can't even limit your prick to that. You're sticking it into everything that moves now. Who knows who that was on your fucking mobile?

Hang on. His mobile. The number will be on his mobile. All she had to do was to contrive a way of getting hold of his mobile. When did they leave the service station? A little after half past twelve. Did she call him or had he called her? What did it matter? It'll still be listed as a call.

She could see the phone in the small loose change receptacle next to the gearstick. She could reach for it now. But on what pretext? The only time that she'd ever touched his phone was when he asked her to pass it to him. No, it would look too obvious. She'd play this one for time. She didn't want him suspecting. She took a fleeting pleasure as she thought of Thuong pathetically grabbing his phone at every opportunity. That's what betrayed wives did: became amateur thieves. All wives know if their men are seeing someone else. That's their secret, mused Hope, and their punishment.

It could wait. She just needed the right moment.

But as mile passed upon tarmacked mile, Rhona's sneering face wouldn't go away. That mass of nut-brown hair that she always pushed back from her face with both hands with a showy gesture. The overpowering perfume that lingered like a scented miasma infecting the air long after she had departed. That affected, pretentious widening of the eyes when told something for the first time. Why did she do that? Why not raise her eyebrows like normal people?

Pushing Rhona underwater. A naked Rhona. Holding her by the scruff of her bottled-brown hair with one hand whilst a knee jerked into the small of her back. The huge fleshy, rump sinking; the tawny water washing over and drawing it down. The feeling of the cool water on her bare forearms as she pushed.

The lido. That night at the lido. That night with Neil. The voice that spoke to her. The whisper that came from somewhere far out on the water. The party seven. That long, slow kiss. Before the hurt. Or after the hurt? No, she thought, with Neil there was always hurt.

"Deep thoughts, Miss Dunne?"

She shook herself out of her daydream, realising that Gavin had been watching her.

"No. I just realised that we didn't kiss. I always thought we had."

"Whose 'we'?"

Hope laughed. "Oh, teenage stuff. Silly stuff."

"Teen romance?"

"Yes and no. Romance for one. I don't think it was romance for the other."

Gavin smiled at her. "So tell me all about it. Do you know I know nothing about you?"

"You know lots about me," Hope shrugged.

"You never got married. There was no one in your life. Certainly not before I met you at Jupiter. You've never mentioned anyone."

"Who wants to hear a middle-aged woman talk about her past? I certainly don't. It lacks a certain *Je ne sais quoi*".

"Well I want to know. Who was this long-lost love?"

"It doesn't end well. Is this our junction?"

"No. Stop avoiding the subject. Come on. Who was he?"

"His name was Neil 'Sticky' Dowling. I can't remember why he was called 'Sticky'. Probably some childish reason."

"So how old were you? When you kissed him."

Hope wasn't sure where she could safely draw a line under the subject. Where she could stop without saying too much. There was a certain danger of disclosure that she found herself enjoying, like one who steps gingerly towards the edge of a cliff, knowing that their fate – at that singular moment – rests entirely with them.

"We were sixteen or seventeen. He was nice. He liked Lou Reed and was very handsome. He liked to look after me."

"And?"

"And what?"

"And what happened next?"

"Nothing happened next. That was the problem. That became the problem."

"What do you mean 'Became the problem'?"

Hope had had enough.

"He went away."

"Broken heart, eh?" Gavin tapped the indicator stalk down, ready to overtake.

"Not really."

To Hope's relief, she could see that Gavin wasn't really listening anyway. Sales people are good at that. They can talk without ever really listening to what you're trying to say.

The image of Rhona's corpulent, naked body sinking into the water returned again. How can a corpse feel so warm? Why was she naked? Why wasn't there any blood? Why had Rhona not held her hands up to protect herself?

57

Carol knew that she was smoking too much. She hated Christmas. Oh. It was good seeing Patsy, but seeing Patsy meant seeing Martin. The dinner had been foul. Patsy was the cook in the family so why had she insisted on having Martin and Patsy over? Hours of peeling and boiling, washing and scraping, kneading and rubbing for twenty minutes of polite ingestion and feigned enjoyment. And the horror – she closed her eyes as the thought returned to her – of the dried out turkey. That poor bird, reared and slaughtered only to be served up as an unappetising, dehydrated crown of feather-dry flesh and sinew.

"Turkey's so hard to get right," Patsy had said, trying to assuage Carol's embarrassment as the stringy strands of the breast flesh flaked away when Denis' knife cut into the bird.

It was the pretence of it all. Pretending that they were all enjoying the day. Patsy dropping hints about Martin. Martin batting them away as fairy tales. Denis and Carol knowing the truth but playing along with the whole, sad charade. Or maybe only Carol knew. Poor Denis, Carol realised, was only aware of what she wanted him to be aware of. That Martin was a philanderer. That Patsy suspected. Her heart ached when she looked at Denis, red-faced with beer in the seat next to her, the child she'd always known he was.

Martin was giving out. He'd had too much to drink and now replaced the forced bonhomie of his sober self with the carping and cynical remarks that always swam beneath.

"Oh I tell you: everything has a price. All people have a price. And those that say they haven't have just thrown the tag away. But…"

Martin placed his glass on a small table, as if it might detract from the oration he was about to deliver.

"But," he repeated, "A few minutes conversation is all you need to calculate their asking price. Believe me."

His right index finger was held in the air to signify the gravity of his thinking.

"Well I don't believe you. Some people are not to be bought." Said Patsy.

Martin didn't turn to look at Patsy, in that way that certain men have when their wife's interjections are not even worth commenting on, but continued: "Everyone can be bought. I buy them all the time. Now, you've got a price, Carol, haven't you?"

Carol stared unblinkingly at him for a second, "Probably."

"Probably! Denis, you're on my side aren't you? Don't tell me you're in with these two eejits as well?"

Denis smiled at Patsy, the blurring effect of the beer delaying his calm response to Patsy's earlier remark, "I believe you, Patsy. Martin's got a very dark view of the world."

"A right view of the world! Whether that view is a dark one is up for debate, but that's not my point. We sell ourselves throughout our lives. We're all just packets of tea, going to the highest bidder at every stage."

Warming to his theme, Martin pulled himself to the edge of his chair.

"You get a job. What do you want? As much money as the boss man will give you. You get yourself a girl. Who will she be? The best girl a man with your looks can get. You go to work. What do you do? The least you can do for what they'll pay you. Early in your life, you decide what you're worth and then spend the rest of your life asking for it."

"That's nonsense" cried Carol.

"Oh, nonsense is it? What does a woman have? She has her honour. And what is it worth? Whatever she can get for the amount of honour she has. Even a fucking Nun...."

"Language, Martin!"

"Sorry, Denis, that was wrong of me. Even a fucking Nun has a price. Oh, they might be all dolled up in their Nunnery finery, but offer them the right price and they'll jump on you like a two-shilling call girl."

Denis, now irritated, interrupted, "Now Martin, that's offensive. Have your opinions but be careful in what company you share them. Anyway, Hope's upstairs and I don't want her waking up to language like that."

Looking temporarily chastened, Martin held up an acknowledging hand. "OK, OK. But what I'm trying to say is that, with the right man, at the right price, they'd..." Martin sat back letting the sentence hang enigmatically in the air.

Carol stared coldly at Martin.

"Are you trying to tell me that the same Nuns who have lost their lives for their vocation and beliefs (God rest their souls), sometimes lost their lives horribly, are the same Nuns that would jump at the chance – for the right price of course – to throw over everything for a sordid night with you?"

"That's about the size of it. Well I don't mean 'all Nuns'. I wasn't talking about the old ones. They're not interested anyhow. I meant the younger ones. The ones with a bit of life left in them."

Carol, exasperated, leaped up, telling Denis, "I'm going to see if Hope is all right."

Denis coolly drained his glass. "I think you're wrong, Martin. Very wrong. And what you've said offends every woman and man of the cloth. There are some things that have a value. I'm not sure 'price' is the right word. I acknowledge that. But a man's soul is not to be traded. Not a good man's soul. Or even a woman's for that matter. Another Rum and Pep, Patsy?"

"I will. Here let me get it. Where did you get your sideboard?"

"In a sideboard shop. Where do you think he got it?" growled Martin.

"Randalls. Off the Uxbridge High Street."

"I've always liked it."

"What's wrong with the one I bought you?"

Patsy turned and faced Martin, "Who said anything was wrong with it?"

"Well, if you're going around admiring other people's sideboards, it must be because you're bored of the one you've got. That's what it sounds like to me."

"Oh, is that what people do, Martin? Well, you live and learn."

Martin winced and reached for his glass. "Sometimes what you bought doesn't do what it's supposed to do. That's the truth now."

Unaware of what was passing, Denis leaned over and rubbed his finger against the sideboard edge.

"There, just there. The veneer's coming away."

58

"So what's this? 'Fleet Phospho-soda..'"

Barry snatched the box away from Hope and scrambled it into a side-drawer. Hope could see that he was embarrassed and wondered whether she should add to his discomfort or not.

"Laxatives?"

"Hardly," Barry said, still refusing to look up at Hope.

Hope let a few, sweetly excruciating moments pass. There was something very pleasurable about making people squirm. Especially self-satisfied people. People who walk around in a smug, self-possessed and knowing way. Barry always had that air. In the training room he remained unruffled, even when confronted by experience that contradicted the neat theory he wanted people to swallow. It wasn't that he was wrong, Barry had once said, it was only that other people had yet to move into a place of rightness. He looked at his delegates in the same, benign way a parent looks at their erring infant.

"Sorry, Hope, was there something you wanted?"

"'Fraid so. Gavin says the budget's run out so he needs you to do an exercise on the second day of the conference. We can't afford the external company."

"What! Now? There's less than a week to go. How am I going to get something together in that time? When did Gavin say this?"

"Not so cocky now, Bufton, are you?"

"So why has it taken so long to let me know?"

"Because it would only have taken the pleasure away of watching you mentally unravel if I'd told you any earlier."

"But he could have phoned me. Christ! That's all I need."

"Can't you cancel your holiday?"

"I can't, it's not a holiday."

"Oh," said Hope knowingly; "Well, maybe they can rearrange the interview…"

"It's not an interview."

Now it was Hope's turn to be confused.

Barry softened. "Look, I can't talk about it. It's a medical thing."

"That's OK. I respect your privacy."

Hope desperately tried to remember what she'd seen on the box Barry had taken offence over. What was it that had made her think it was a laxative? She'd read something about 'bowel cleansing'. It was probably all related to his smelly little secret. She decided she genuinely didn't want to know any more.

Barry pushed his hands through his hair, which pulled his drawn pale skin upwards in what was, Hope thought, a very unattractive way.

"Shall I tell him you can't do it, Barry?"

"I can't do it, but I'm going to have to. I've no choice have I?"

Hope wasn't sure whether Barry might burst into tears at any moment. She waited for a few moments to see if he would, but then gave up.

"You could always look upon it as a challenge. Or an opportunity? Isn't that what you tell us we have? Opportunities, not problems?"

"Ha, bloody, ha."

59

"It's Nellie's turn, now. Come on Nellie! Give us a song now."

After bellowing his beery encouragement, Martin stepped back and leaned against the wall of the living room.

Nellie sat up on the edge of the armchair and looked through the window, through the night air, through the suburbs of Ruislip, through the folds of the Welsh hills, skimmed across the angry twisting of the Irish Sea and settled herself on imagined, verdant hills sloping down to lonely farmsteads and burbling rivers.

Oh, father why are you so sad
On this bright Easter morn'
When Irish men are proud and glad

Of the land where they were born?
Oh, son, I see sad mem'ries view
Of far-off distant days
When, being just a boy like you
I joined the IRA.

She looked briefly at Martin to encourage him to join her. His deep baritone crept alongside her wavering soprano. On the pick-up notes of the chorus they sang:

Where are the lads that stood with me?
When history was made?

And the rest of the room fell in behind.

A ghrá mo chroí, I long to see
The boys of the old brigade.

Denis looked into his glass and pretended to be thinking of something very different. Martin sat on the arm of his chair.

"You're not singing, Denis. Do you not know the words?"

"I know the words right enough." He took a drink of the beer that was sitting on the bottom of the glass.

Martin looked up to the eager faces that filled the small front room.

"He knows the words right enough. That's what he said. He knows the words right enough. But I think he's choosing not to sing them. Denis, tell me now, did Nellie start too high? Is that not your key? Nellie, tell me, what was the key you were in?"

"As if I should know, Martin. I wouldn't know a key if it sat next to me in Mass."

"I'd say the key was B minor. I'm not a musical man, you'll all attest to that, but my limited understanding would say that you were in B minor. What say you Mr Dunne?"

Denis, depressed to be feeling quite alone amongst so much high spirits, pulled himself up and said, "It's not a minor key, Martin. You know that yourself. Why ask me?"

Martin slapped his forehead in a mock display of realisation. He then turned, grinning to the couples arrayed around the seats and floor of the room. "How stupid of me! To think I thought that lovely old song was in a minor key. Maybe the thirds weren't flattened enough for old Martin's ears? Is that so? Maybe the thirds were not flattened enough. Is that right, Denis?"

Martin cupped his left hand to the side of his mouth and shouted: "Was the key a melodic minor or a natural minor. Come on now Denis. Put the good people here out of their misery!"

The crowd soon started to laugh with Martin, and he could feel their irritation with Denis gathering behind him. Martin calmed the group down by holding up the palm of his hand.

Patsy, seeing how cruel Martin could be in his sadistic enjoyment of adding to Denis' burden of sadness, couldn't take any more.

"Martin. Have you no feelings? You're not even funny."

"Don't mock. Don't mock the poor afflicted. I tell you what. I'll personally take Denis to Lourdes, throw myself down at the statue of St. Bernadette and say, 'Have mercy on this poor Irish man. Yes, have mercy on this poor Irish man with a tin ear! He's good, Lord. He's a good man. But he's assailed. That's what he is. He's assailed. Assailed by a contempt for the flattened third. Unable to…"

"Martin", interjected Nellie. "Can I sing it again?"

Martin felt the alcohol pleasantly course through his frame and momentarily swayed with the effect.

"Let me start," he said. "Let me get you going."

He didn't look at the group assembled in front of him, but stared at the kitchen door, the other side of which Denis was now slowly pouring his beer.

"This one's for Carol, God bless her. May she soon be home."

Taking the centre of the floor, Martin looked dramatically at the faces that were watching and slowly began:

When boyhood's fire was in my blood
I read of ancient freemen,
For Greece and Rome who bravely stood,
Three hundred men and three men;
And then I prayed I yet might see
Our fetters rent in twain,
And Ireland, long a province, be.
A Nation once again!

A Nation once again,
A Nation once again,
And lreland, long a province, be
A Nation once again!

When the tumult of voices had died away, Nellie stood up and smiled regally. She let the silence hang for some moments, before taking a preparatory breath. A thin, fluting voice came from within her. Weak, tremulous, but piercing the silence all the same. The song lifted and escaped from her bony chest. Gradually, the muted sounds transmuted into words.

On Carrigdhoun, the heath is brown.
The clouds are dark o'er Ardnalee,
And many a stream comes rushing down
To swell the angry Owen na Buidhe.
The moaning blast is sweeping past

Through many a leafless tree,
And I'm alone, for he is gone,
My hawk has flown, ochone mo chroidhe.

Martin tried to look composed, but Hope, sitting in the alcove at the back of the room, could see how deeply troubled he had suddenly become. What was the song to him? He stared at the ground as Nellie moved slowly through the three verses. Despite his partially hidden face, the deepest agitation was crossing and re-crossing his features.

60

Her fingers pushed against her skin. She sighed and lifted her head. Yes, when she raised her head it was smoother. Gentle folds were pulled out and disappeared. Breathing in, she summoned her courage and drew her chin back in again. It was awful; the folds concertinaed back into position. The skin fell baggy and loose.

"Like an old hen. Like the scraggily neck of some old hen."

Hope pulled the cord of the light which lit the bathroom with a pornographic clarity. But even in the dark she could tell: however well her bone structure had preserved something of her youth, her neck was her body's stoolpigeon. It too easily confessed her age. Of course everyone must see it. The blouses would have to go. Scarves. Yes, scarves would help. This Saturday, John Lewis. Perhaps Marks. Anything to cover up the evidence.

She pushed Pardew away with her foot and turned her attention to her hair. Even without drying and combing it she thought it looked good. The blonde highlights, mattened by the shower, still sat neatly, attractively, around her face. That much was good. That much she could happily live with.

The towel? Should she go into her bedroom and, facing the full length mirror, drop her towel? How much of this self-inspection was healthy? How much could she accept – and cope with – in one day? No, that could wait. She knew herself to be slim. Yes, she was now in her mid-fifties, but she still… No, she didn't. She used to. Very recently she used to. But men didn't notice anymore. They noticed younger women. They said things. Things that seemed to assume that she wasn't there. Invisible. That was it, Hope realised, she had become invisible.

Invisible. As a woman, not existing. As an aging, uncomfortable presence, a reminder of mortality, she stood at the edge of conversational circles. Still capable of loving. Still full of needing. Still excited by the skin of another. Still able to feel the release of orgasm, the pleasure of a debauched afternoon, the delightful guilt of fucking someone who shouldn't be fucking you.

But not to the 'younger crew'. To these she knew she had no history. She was a PA, a set of muscle, brains and nerves that performed a duty in the same way that a coffee machine impersonally dispensed coffee. There was no history, no 'backstory', no life lived. To these men, Hope was peripheral, without feeling or past; without importance. Her childhood, teenage years, womanhood, all negated by the casual certainty of a man's indifference. She existed as light bulbs exist, necessary but rarely impinging on the consciousness of any males present.

Pardew returned and, purring like an electrical sub-station, passed the length of her furred flank against Hope's calf. She aggressively thrust away the cat with her ankle. Now was not the time for Pardew to be thinking of prandial pleasures, especially when Hope was finding her view of herself pulled up so short. She went back into her bedroom and sat on the end of her unmade bed. Should she go to Ireland? Gavin had told her the choice was hers. He needed someone to organise him, and would prefer her, but he could just as easily get someone from the Sligo office to 'fill in'.

She knew he was being deliberately distant. She was certain that it was because he really didn't want her to realise just how much he desperately wanted her to be there. This trip was going to yield the moment where he was going to make the final decision to dump Thuong and commit himself to her. She felt certain that it was going to happen. Even the way the trip had suddenly come together, the way everything so beautifully fell into place. The stars were moving in their heavens and influencing the lives of those below.

Hope smiled with the pleasure of the thought. Her and Gavin, in Ireland, desperately accepting the love of each other. Where might that happen? On a walk? In a meeting with the Irish sales team in a sudden glance across a polished meeting room table? Perhaps in tripping words over an after-dinner drink? Where do these things happen? In what moments do a woman and man bind together for life?

Pardew jumped on to Hope's towelled lap and began to pirouette the small cat circles that conveyed hunger. Hope, again, casually brushed her away with her arm and returned to the sweetness of her thoughts. An after-dinner drink. Gavin struggling all of a sudden to say something. The smoothness of his conversation being suddenly harpooned by awkward, difficult emotions. Hope feigning concern, but secretly bracing herself for the lines she'd craved to hear ever since first meeting him.

"Hopey, it's no good. There's something I really… well, there's something I guess I need to ask you."

Hope would thoughtfully put down her drink and lean slightly forward to listen. Gavin would then rub the back of his neck and, confused, look up again to meet her eyes.

"What is it you want to ask me, Gavin?"

"Well, Hope…"

Pardew's whole body retched with a single, coarse cough. She crouched quickly down before vomiting her half-digested breakfast onto the bedroom rug.

"For fuck's sake, Pardew… Oh, Christ!" The cat continued to haul in its flanks with the rhythm of each gastric palpitation, before scuttling out of Hope's bedroom on to the upstairs landing.

"What's wrong?" Hope heard her mother cry from her bedroom.

Hope pretended not to notice. Denis opened the door to ask, "What's with the noise?"

"The cat's been sick, that's all. Go back in now and I'll deal with it. Crisis over."

"Do you want me to help?"

Hope waved him away and returned to her room, shouting behind her, "All under control."

Denis pushed the bedroom door back in place. Pardew, having wrought his worst upon the warp and weft of the carpet, lightly went downstairs with his tail haughtily aloft.

Hope had grabbed a toilet roll and eyed the disgusting puddle that almost seemed to hover above the carpet.

Yes, she decided, Ireland must happen. It's our destiny.

61

"Where are you going?"

"Where do you think I'm going?" Neil put on his thin jacket and started to walk away.

"Neil!"

He hesitated but, deciding against staying, thought better of it and walked on.

"Neil!"

Neil stopped again and turned around, now a dim and somewhat distant shape in the unsteady light.

"Can I tell you something?"

Neil remained silent. He shrugged and looked away across the lido. Some seconds later he looked back again at Hope.

"Can I tell you something?" Hope repeated.

"Is it quick?"

Hope walked towards him and, still some yards away from him, knelt down.

"I'm really sorry. I'm really sorry about… Can I just talk to you?"

Neil refused to move. "I don't know. I'm fed up with all this…" He realised he couldn't quite nail what he was fed up with.

Hope placed her hands on her knees and looked behind to the Lido. The first small gasps of a chilled morning breeze were rising. She lifted her arms and wrapped them close around her.

"I'd like to talk. I don't deserve you as a friend. I never have. But I'd like to talk."

Neil remained where he was, careful to avoid looking at her.

"Could this wait? I don't think I'm in the right frame of mind…"

"Nor am I, Neil. And if I don't talk to someone… well, If I don't talk to you."

The creeping coldness now started to brush against him and he shivered. "Can we talk about this tomorrow?"

"That's what I'm trying to say. Here, finish this." Hope walked over to the place where they'd previously been talking and returned with Neil's unfinished drink.

Neil relented and slowly came forward, taking the drink from Hope. He slumped down and awkwardly fell backwards, spilling some of the bitter as he did so.

"Have you ever killed someone?"

Neil, taken aback by the surreal surprise of the question, waited some time before answering, "I don't think so."

"What would you say if you knew someone who had, a very long time ago, killed someone? Would you hate them?"

Again, silence followed Hope's question. Eventually, Neil's tense voice replied, "Have you killed someone?"

"I don't want to frighten you, but… but… I once did a terrible thing. I was very young. And it was..."

Neil sat up. "It was what?"

"I've never told anyone. I can't believe I'm telling you now. I'm probably going to hate myself in the morning."

"It is the morning."

Hope giggled through her tears. "Yes, course…"

"Did you really kill someone?"

"That's a stupid question. I've just said…"

"Hope? What are you saying?"

"I couldn't live with him."

"Couldn't live with whom?"

"My brother. I'd had enough. I hated him."

"You hated him? What brother?"

"Stephen. My brother Stephen. I hated him. He was a spastic. He wasn't happy, so I drowned him."

"Drowned him? Where…"

As soon as he'd said the word he realised where that awful event had taken place.

"You drowned him here, didn't you?"

Hope slowly nodded.

"Your brother? You killed your brother?"

Hope looked away and fixed her eyes on the noiseless body of water that brooded beside them. What secrets did it contain? What memories did it animate within her over and over again?

Neil stood up sharply. "For fuck's sake, Hope. You killed your brother?"

"You going then?"

"You killed your brother?"

Hope began to rub her palms against her thighs. "What do you think? What do you think I did? I wanted to tell you …"

"Your brother?"

"Stop saying 'your brother'! You didn't know him. He was ill. He was so fucking ill. You couldn't talk to him. He was a fucking vegetable. I hated him. I'm trying to speak to you. To tell you. I'm trying to fucking speak to you. Don't go away."

"Fuck's sake, Hope. You're telling me…"

"Oh, fuck off! Fuck off! I really wanted you to know! I really wanted you…"

"Fucking hell. I'm going home."

"Then fuck off, Neil!"

"You're telling me you killed your brother?"

Soon the shape of Neil was lost and Hope knew she was finally alone. She cast a quick, sidelong glance at the party seven, as she walked back slowly to the water's edge. Already the awful guilt of what she'd just told Neil was burrowing deep in her brain and beginning to taunt her. Why had she told him? What was she doing? This was a secret. A family secret. And now someone, outside of the family, shared that secret.

As she was staring at the surface of the lido she realised that dawn was leaking its first daubs of colour upon the water. She thought it would be good to cry at this point, but realised that this wasn't really an option. She'd never cried over Stephen. Perhaps she would one day. When might it happen? In a Doctor's surgery perhaps? A supermarket queue? Waiting for a ladies toilet to become free?

Poor Stephen. Right up to the end, he'd no idea.

62

"Is Gavin free?"

"Not really, Martina. Maybe later in the…"

"Don't worry," said Martina, who went back resignedly to her desk.

Hope carried on stapling the reports. Should she say something? She could try.

"Are you OK?"

"Of course," Martina said miserably. "Happy face today."

"Perhaps I could put some time in his diary for you?"

Martina glared at Hope as if she'd just insulted her.

Hope wondered just how attractive men would find her now, her face bread-white with exhaustion, and those oh-so-attractive Slavic cheekbones topped by the blue-black shadows of weariness under her eyes.

Not such a beauty queen after all, she surmised with some relish.

"So when is the happy day? I bet your boyfriend – sorry, your *partner* – is really looking forward to being a Dad."

"Don't talk about it. I don't want it."

Martina spoke with a calm indifference.

"Oh...." Hope said, weakly.

Martina's body stiffened in her chair. "Does that surprise you? Really? Do I look like a mother to you? Would you like this baby? No. Then that makes two of us."

"Well, serves you right for not being careful, you jumped-up Polack cow."

"I know you're all only trying to help, but it's not helping."

"Well fuck off back to Poland then and take your self-pity with you."

"I can't, I've got a teleconference with Sarah at four."

"Just don't take it out on me. You've got yourself into this hole and I'm enjoying every moment I watch you squirm."

"No I can't put it off. It's been set up for weeks."

"Well, you'd better get it done quick – otherwise you'll find the pricks that fawn over you a lot less attentive when your pencil-thin body is bloated like a Russian battleship."

"I'm sorry for snapping. I just didn't want all this."

Hope picked up her box of tissues, walked over to Martina's desk and pulled one free for her. Martina refused to weep, but the tears still fell into the dark crevices under her eyes and gathered as if contemplating their final slalom down her face. She sniffled and blew her nose.

"I would like to talk to my mother, but I can't. The only thing my Mother ever wants to hear me say is that I am pregnant. That I should marry my partner and come home."

Martina laughed with the irony. "Imagine that. 'Mother, not only am I not married, but I'm pregnant!' What do you think she would say to that? Papa, great news, we are to sink to new shame. We have new depths that our lovely daughter, whom we have raised in the faith of our Lord, will take us down to."

Hope suddenly realised that if she could suggest going home to have the baby, it would be one less health tourist birth that the NHS would have to take care of. One less little Polish baby living off British taxpayers.

"I don't think your Mother would say that for a moment. I'm a Catholic. We're not still in the dark ages."

"You might not be in the dark ages any longer but my Mother is. I promised her! I was only going to the UK to work. My future was in Poland. She didn't believe me and now she will tell me she was right when she didn't believe me."

Hope saw her chance. "Martina. Why don't you take a holiday? See your mother yourself? I'm sure she'd…"

"Are you mad? If I had this baby I would go home? Are you not listening?"

Hope sighed and walked back to her desk. One day the whole country would be overrun with Poles. The thought bit deep within and continued to irritate her.

"Hello!" shouted Jamilla, bustling in through the office door carrying armfuls of shopping bags.

And the Pakis. Pakis and Poles everywhere.

63

"What should I do first?"

Sister Benedict said nothing but smiled sorrowfully, creases tightening around her rheumy eyes. She leaned forward and placed her hand on Hope's arm.

"I'd pray first."

"But I have prayed. It doesn't help. I feel as if my mind is… unravelling."

"Then I'd keep praying."

Hope looked out onto the small green patch of sodden grass that lay like an unloved rug. She had called for this meeting with her Spiritual Director, Sister Benedict, because she knew she was in crisis. A crisis she knew she would always face because there was only so long one could live a lie.

"Why are you called Sister Benedict"? Why don't you have a woman's name like the others?"

Sister Benedict sat back and laughed.

"If I only had the choice! I'm afraid I was given my name. I hated it at first, but I've grown into it. I quite like it now."

"So why don't the others have men's names?"

Sister Benedict put her hand on the back of her chair to assist herself getting up, momentarily steadying her small frame before shuffling to the window.

"Vatican Two changed a lot of things. Some things for the better. One or two things for the worst. Is that a Goldfinch? It is and all."

Hope grew bored of twisting her rosary around her fingers and let it fall slowly into the lap of her long blue skirt. This is where an angry, heart-breaking conversation with her father had left her: a Postulant in a convent hidden amongst the hedges and hills of Gloucestershire. The unceasing prayer, rituals and rigours had all had a comforting rhythm about them when she'd first arrived. Now they were the jarring hammer blows of monotony that marked the passing of long, uneventful hours.

As if speaking to someone in the garden, Sister Benedict's voice cut across Hope's thoughts, "It's too obvious a metaphor, but a metaphor nonetheless."

Hope desperately tried to recall what a metaphor was and looked towards the wet lawn again as if it would yield up the answer.

"What is?" she eventually replied.

"That lovely Goldfinch. We tend not to get them in the garden here. Fields, yes. Amongst the thistles in the wood, often. But for some reason not in this garden. I've never understood why. They like other gardens. Often saw them when I was a little girl, out the kitchen window. But not here."

Hope leaned towards the window in the hope of catching sight of the subject of Sister Benedict's musings, but no life – bird or otherwise – was apparent.

"Why's it a metaphor?"

"Maybe my little Hope's a Goldfinch? Wouldn't you say so?"

Hope remained confused. If she could only remember what a metaphor was then she would be certain to decipher the riddles that Sister Benedict was talking in.

"When you have been silent, Hope, what did God tell you?"

Hope was relieved to be presented with a direct question, even if framed in a spiritual way.

"God hasn't spoken to me. I'm not sure that God ever spoke to me."

The kindly nun remained unperturbed by this reply to her question.

"And he still doesn't speak to you?"

Hope shook her head. Sister Benedict moved back to her chair and sat down carefully.

"When you were an Aspirant and we sent you home, why did we do that?"

"To think. To consider. To decide what I wanted to be."

"And what did you decide?"

Hope recalled her pleading father. His distressed eyes following her as she paced the room, afraid that she would disappear the moment he blinked or looked away. She remembered telling him that the religious life was the life she wanted, whilst feeling the shrinking of her heart with every lie. She didn't even know why she was doing it. Why did she do it? She wrenched herself away from the thoughts, unable to bear the anguish they carried with them.

Hope looked back at Sister Benedict, "I decided to return."

"To return and continue on the path to becoming a Sister - or just to return?"

With that one question Hope realised the sham of her ambitions. She'd once admonished Kathy, a Postulant like her who had started in the same week, for her graceless behaviour. Refusing at first to accept Kathy's offering of a secret gin bottle that she'd smuggled in, over time she gratefully accepted the offer of the emerald bottle and its magical properties for alleviating the tedium of her surroundings.

How high-handed she'd been, chiding Kathy that she would never become a nun because she couldn't let go of the world. And now here she was, calmly coming to grips with the fact that Kathy would probably go on towards becoming a novice, whereas she now contemplated something she knew secretly would always happen.

Two years previously, when she'd first looked upon the house and gardens that she had convinced herself would become a permanent – even a final - dwelling, she'd still felt a pang of incredulity. The calm outward expressions of her thoughts – in the excited conversation that she had with those that greeted her - bore no resemblance to the agitated conscience that whirled inside. These smiling Sisters were merely new characters in her play and, now she thought back, had probably realised that very thought themselves. Kathy's reception seemed more… how could she put it? Yes, more sincere.

"Am I the Goldfinch, Sister?"

Sister Benedict took Hope's slim young hands and enfolded them warmly in her own and leaned forward until her forehead touched Hope's, the fabric of her cornette feeling soft on Hope's brow.

"The others mustn't know," Sister Benedict whispered. "We'll keep it our secret. Be at seven o'clock Mass tomorrow and then stay behind with me. A couple of things to sign, that's all, and then my Goldfinch will fly away. Shall we call it our secret?"

Hope nodded and began to weep quietly.

"The trouble is, my angel, when God speaks to us, we may not have been listening."

64

Whichever way Hope held life up to look at it, it all looked very attractive. Martina's problems – problems which she'd brought on herself – felt good. Of course, Hope told herself, she hated to see anyone struggling with events, but not Martina. It had all the feeling of 'just desserts' about it. After all, fate was only dishing up the consequences of Martina's indiscretions.

Yes, a pregnant Martina was good. To see Martina upset, bewildered and unstable was really a seasoning that brought out the full savour of life's revenge.

Even the gear stick meshed beautifully as it directed the lowest gears to help Hope's car pull smoothly away. "C'est une belle jour" Hope declared out loud, "C'est une tres belle jour." And it *was* such a beautiful day. Hope had to pull down the visor to shield her eyes from the sun that emphatically pulled itself up across the Polish War Memorial bridge. A buttery sun that was clearing away the feathers and wisps of mist that sulked above the few grassed areas of Greenford.

Hope, happy Hope, flicked the radio switch from Grimmers' programme to Radio 2. She recognised the bouncy intro and was soon singing along to "I Can See Clearly Now" with an occasional attempt to sing the harmony above it.

She recalled that long ago year of 1972. She's striding towards school. Her heart is full of possibilities. What were those possibilities? Hope decided not to linger and moved into the outside lane of the A40. What was the Geography teacher's name? Temple? Temperington..?

As she hummed herself into the office, the feeling – the high, dizzying feeling – was still careening around her head. She smiled down at the hunched, almost foetal form of Martina who was writing a list to one side of her desk. Hope's bag swung rhythmically down and balanced perfectly on the back of her chair. She beamed beneficently and took in the whole length of the office: "Coffee?"

"Hope." It was Gavin. Gavin was actually in his office before she'd arrived. That was unusual.

"Oh, you're early."

"Yes. Have you got a minute?"

"Oh God", thought Hope. "This is too, too perfect. Gavin's about to tell me he's left the Vietcong. This is all too right. Too perfect."

Hope sat in the chair opposite Gavin's and suddenly, magically, her smile felt so wonderfully warm and genuine. She didn't need to make an effort. Her face fell naturally, comfortably, into an image of happy acquiescence.

Gavin's emotions didn't correspond in quite the same way. He looked older. Sterner. Hope noticed a tension and anxiety about his eyes. He got up and closed the door.

Must be serious, thought Hope.

"I've had an announcement."

So it was true. Thuong was leaving him. She's obviously heard about your carrying on with Rhona and now you've got to…

"Keith's left."

She was yanked back into a different set of thoughts. "Left? Keith? When?"

"Yesterday evening. I had a call at home from HR to let me know."

"That's a bit sudden."

"Par for the course in sales, I'm afraid. Whatever your position, VP, Director, manager, executive, it always hangs over you. They probably walked him out like they always do."

Gavin reached out for his mobile phone, noticing that it wasn't perfectly parallel with his keyboard.

Hope sensed Gavin's discomfort and asked, "I thought the sales figures were good. Aren't we supposed to be up on last year?"

He nodded, "A little bit, but obviously not enough. Expect a new broom with the next one."

"So who do you now report to?"

"Too early to say. But you and I are going to have to manage this. We've the conference in Ireland coming up. I need to get away. Create a little bit of headspace for myself. Where 's this Sales conference?"

"Athlone."

"Athlone? Where's that?"

"The West. Mum and Dad's bit of the country, actually."

Gavin's raised eyebrows and weak smile feigned interest.

"OK. Make the arrangements. Let's get a hotel and think about what we need to do next."

"Any preference about rooms?"

"No bed and breakfast. Something a bit nicer."

Hope stood up and went towards the door. "Where has Keith gone?"

Gavin stared at his mobile phone, as if expecting a call to come through at any minute.

"To the dogs, probably."

65

"Do you know what you're doing?"

Father Kirwan sprang out of his chair and returned to the window.

"I think I do know what I'm doing, Father."

Hope was fascinated by Father Kirwan's discomfort. Why was he so agitated? She was just an 18-year old girl that had discovered a wonderful vocation. He didn't seem so impressed.

"I had a calling when I was very young, Miss Dunne. I had made this chalice out of Lego and held it up, and then, suddenly, with my Lego chalice held high, I knew. Mad, eh?"

Hope couldn't quite take in the images that Father Kirwan was creating. "Not really. I'm sure it was a very important moment."

"Hope, do you know what this decision involves? Really involves? Have you thought it through?

"I think so. I've thought about it a lot."

Father Kirwan looked at Hope face on: "Don't do it, Hope."

"Don't do what, Father?"

"Don't sacrifice yourself, don't take your solemn vows, don't be a Nun!"

"It's not sacrificing myself. It's getting closer…"

"…to God? Who told you that?"

"Father Thirle. He said girls could only get closer to God through marrying God."

"Father Thirle?" Who's Father Thirle?"

"An old priest. He used to come into my Junior School."

Father Kirwan sat again on the small chair, "I'd like to pray. Will you pray with me? Come here and kneel beside me."

Hope knelt beside Father Kirwan and began to relax. She looked sideways at him and noticed his smooth, young face.

"Father, what do you pray for?"

Father Kirwan kept his eyes closed as he answered: "What do you mean, what do I pray for?"

"Is it something special? I mean, do you pray for something special or do you…include everyone?"

"I take something that is foremost in my mind and I support it with prayer."

Hope clasped her hands closer together, scrunching her eyelids tighter as if the almighty might perceive that this was part of a greater prayerfulness. After a few seconds her concentration began to give.

"What if you can't think of something? What if you can only think of 'me things'?"

"Me things?"

"Things to do with me. Selfish things."

Father Kirwan opened one eye and fixed it in Hope's direction.

"I think God knows how to deal with 'me things'."

Hope felt the nails from her touching middle fingers nuzzle against the edge of her nose. Pray for what? Peace? Weren't all prayers meant to be about other things? Good things?

"Should I pray for peace?"

"I think that would be a good start, Hope."

"Should I pray for your penis? Shall I pray for your sexual gratification?"

"He's always listening. Unfortunately, we aren't always listening to him."

"Don't you ever think about sex? Are you thinking about it now?"

"That's why we need to pray. To spend moments of eternity – those deeply felt moments – that bring us so close to God."

"How often do you masturbate, Father?"

"Several times a day. When I can of course. Sometimes, if I get very busy, I can't always find the time to pray as much as I'd like to."

"You must be exhausted."

"God's work is exhausting. But so rewarding."

"So why don't you want me to do it."

Father Kirwan sighed. "Because you're too young."

But, God, so was I, he thought.

66

It was awkward for Hope getting off the bus in her new shoes. Even though she could feel the hostility of those in the queue behind her who were also waiting to disembark, she still carefully placed her right foot down on to the pavement whilst clasping the bus pole behind.

She liked her new pointed shoes but decided that they would have to come off and she would walk home in her stockinged feet.

To her surprise, the pavement felt warm, the high sun having slowly heated the slabs during the course of the long day

"Zola Budd!" Shouted a sneering schoolboy from across the road. She walked on, deciding that it was best not to dignify his rudeness with any sort of response. In fact, she came to rather like the reference. Budd's collision with Mary Decker in the Olympics had been the talk of her workplace. Perhaps she might start a trend?

Before the interview she hadn't been too sure about the suit, but now she knew it had been perfect. The fact that it was a little too tight – and that this had been so quickly noticed by her interviewer, Mr Reynolds – had strangely played to her advantage. Asking his permission to take her jacket off had been an inspired moment. His initial questioning style had been hypothetical; at a certain point during the interview he had been talking in terms of 'when' she started, not 'if'.

But car rental? It wasn't very glamorous. It wasn't anything, really. Ideal for getting to, perhaps; from Ruislip the journey on the bus would be quick enough and she might be able to save up enough for a small car. That would be useful for running Dad around as well.

Denis was in the garden, hands deep in his pockets, carefully inspecting the unfurling flush of a rose. A pert, busying Blackbird insolently lifted and lowered its tail feathers only a few feet from where he stood.

"How'd it go at the unit?"

Denis hadn't noticed Hope walking into the garden. "Oh, hello, love. She's all right. Just the same now."

Hope knew that 'all right' and 'just the same' would form most of his answer. They always did.

"Someone called you. There's a number by the phone. Asked if you'd call him back."

It was Mr Reynolds! She knew it was Mr Reynolds. She hadn't expected a decision this soon and it could only mean that she'd got the job. No company phoned on the day of an interview to tell you that you'd been unsuccessful. That sorry task was left to the rejection letter.

"Who was it?"

"He didn't say. Just that you should call him back. How did the interview go?"

Hope tried to look calm. She'd suddenly thought that the phone call might be asking her back for a second interview. A cloud fell across her optimism.

"Oh, good, I think. Hard to say. Did he leave his name?"

"Who?"

"The man on the phone."

"No. Just asked for you that's all. I suppose I should have asked."

Hope smiled. She knew her father would have answered the call very reluctantly. She also knew that he would have wanted to end the call as soon as possible. Had he got the number right? He was terrible at those sorts of things like answering phones. What would Mr Reynolds think of her father's lack of telephone etiquette? Would it count against her?

No, she calmed herself, she was just being silly. If she had got the job it would mean the pleasurable task of telling Mrs Snaith, her loathsome boss, tomorrow.

"Have you had something to eat, Dad?"

"I had a little bit before I went out. I'm good. Where are your shoes?"

"Here." She held them up for him. "They were hurting my feet."

"Don't tell me you had an interview without your shoes on?"

"Course not. I took them off when I got off the bus. They pinch."

But Denis had become preoccupied with the roses again and didn't acknowledge her reply.

"I'll put the kettle on."

Hope instantly looked for the note beside the phone. In Denis' deliberate, firm hand he'd written 0171 054 1494. It was a central London number. If it had been Mr Reynolds at Jupiter Car Rental, phoning from drab and dreary Northolt, it would have begun with a '0181'. It wasn't just the shadow of a cloud moving across her optimism, but a long grey shelf of rain.

Her initial disappointment had prevented her from any kindling of curiosity of who the number might belong to and Hope dropped her shoes and bag and decided to make the tea.

She knew she really wanted the secretary job at Jupiter. The building was so much bigger than the small printers where she currently worked. Mrs Snaith, severe and humourless, was a leftover of typing pools and deferential manners. All the girls that Hope worked with were on Christian name terms, but not Mrs Snaith. A surname was, to her, a symbol of respect; a signifier of status and experience. Strangely, by the very tone that Mrs Snaith said "Miss Dunne", Hope could tell if the conversation was to be unpleasant or merely perfunctory. There was no warmth or consideration in Mrs Snaith's manner, just the conveyance of a request, criticism or order for something to be completed. To everyone she was 'the old bag' or 'witch', but Mrs Snaith sailed through the day oblivious to any mutterings or discontent she may have provoked.

They'd noticed that Mrs Snaith, despite the prefix, never mentioned her husband. Margaret heard that her husband had been killed in the war, but couldn't offer any credible source for this information. Perhaps that was what really had happened; that was why she carried herself resentfully through each working day.

'Lucky escape for him,' Hope had joked.

No, the prospect of continuing to work at Harbutts was a depressing one. Hope mulled how much longer the prison sentence of her current employment might continue, as she stirred the teaspoon in her father's mug.

Returning from the garden some minutes later she glanced again at the number. Maybe Jupiter had a central location and this was where she had to go next for another interview? If that was the case, then she'd better call them back right away. She placed the receiver into the crook of her neck and started to press the buttons of their two tone grey telephone.

"Dowling."

Hope, in surprise, let the receiver slither out from her shoulder and she panicked in her attempts to grasp it again.

"Hello?" The voice said.

"Neil?"

"Hope? Is that you? You got my message."

"Yes, my Dad told me."

"I wasn't sure if he was getting my number down properly."

"Oh, he's not very good with phones. Any technology really."

Why were they discussing Hope's Dad?

"Are you at work?" Hope asked.

"Yes, unfortunately. Was thinking about, you know, old times and wondered if you'd got married yet."

"No, but we've fixed a date."

"Oh…" Hope could detect a moment of disappointment hanging between them.

"So, who's the lucky man?"

"His name's Tony. Tony Lennon. And you?"

"Oh, resting, as an actor might say. Between relationships. You're still at home then?"

"Yes. Someone has to look after Dad. You're not, I imagine?"

"Not since leaving school. When was the last time we saw each other?"

Hope recalled the fateful evening at the Ruislip Lido when they'd argued.

"Can't remember. Probably Mass."

"Yes. That might have been it." Neil quickly changed the subject. "So you and Tony? When's the date?"

"June next year. Would you like to come? There's an evening thing."

Hope begun to wonder why he'd called. Was he expecting her to be unattached? Perhaps he'd just been ditched and was working his way through a grubby contacts book.

"I've actually just got a new job."

Why had she said that? She hadn't heard yet and now she was announcing her appointment as if it was cut and dried.

"Great. Where?"

"Jupiter. The car rental people in Northolt. Just found out actually."

"Are you celebrating?"

"Not yet. I was just about to call Tony and let him know. He really helped."

What was the feeling that hung just above Hope's stomach? An airy, pleasant sensation that was curling up and through her like the rising of wood smoke from a catching fire.

"Well, perhaps we could meet and catch up about everything. We could celebrate your news as well."

It was what Hope desperately wanted to hear.

"I don't think so. I'm not sure that would be right."

"Oh, I meant with Tony as well. Just catch up. Memory Lane and everything. He's got nothing to worry about. Anyway, we were never… an item."

But I wanted us to be.

"Why did you call, Neil? It's just so out of the blue."

"Oh, like I said, catching up, that's all."

Hope realised that the constant repetition of 'catching up' was gradually draining the meaning of the phrase every time Neil said it.

"Let me talk to Tony first. I'd like you to meet him. "

"You've got my number. It's easy for me to get over to Ruislip. I can stay with my Mum."

Later that evening Hope was quietly arranging the food tins in the cupboard so that all of the labels were properly facing forward. She'd been quite unable to think of anything else but Neil. The fact that she still hadn't heard from the car rental company about the job had even slipped entirely from her mind.

Her father shouted from the living room, "Did you call that number back?"

"I did. Just someone I was at school with. Nothing special."

Her next problem was to think of an excuse for not seeing Tony one night. There was an undeniable deliciousness to the deception. Hope indescribably felt alive again.

67

Hope couldn't bear the tension any longer. She'd just decided to open the hotel door when the three sharp raps were repeated. She tried to look relaxed as she swung the door back.

"Rhona!"

"Hiya sweetie!" Without being asked, Rhona swept past Hope into the room.

"Is there a drink in there for little me?"

Hope watched the short, dumpy figure half-run to the window table like a little girl desperately showing off. Hope spitefully chewed and gnawed on the phrase 'little me' in her mind.

"Of course. This is a surprise. I was expecting you to be...."

"Gavin? Oh, he's downstairs. He's... Oh, this wine's crap, Hopey (why had she called her 'Hopey'? Only Gavin called her

'Hopey')… downstairs in the bar. It was a horrible journey. They only had a tiny, tiny rental car and we had our knees up to our chests the whole way. Can I use your loo? I'm going to wet myself."

Rhona set down the empty glass and hurried to the toilet closing the door with a loud thump.

"Rhona. Fucking Rhona!" She inwardly screamed. "He came with that fucking Rhona." She closed her eyes and stood, incensed, by the window. So that was what was happening: he was seeing Rhona. It *was* her on the phone after all. Why? Why throw himself at that stupid cow? Couldn't he see through that squeaky girlish voice? Those pathetic mannerisms and gestures?

The sound of the flushing toilet gave Hope a little time to compose herself. Rhona emerged with both hands carefully shaping her hair back into a puckered, blood red scrunchie.

"I'm such a mess, Hopey" (she's said it again).

Without any invitation from Hope, she poured herself another glass of wine.

"Fancy some yourself?"

"No, I was just… celebrating."

Rhona became even more animated, "Celebrating? Is it your Birthday?"

"No. It's a personal thing."

"Oh, tell me. I love a secret. Are y'engaged?"

"You said you and Gavin came over together?"

Rhona was busy taking her next large gulp of wine, curiously holding out her left arm for balance as she did so. She vaguely nodded at Hope in acknowledgement as she swallowed.

"It was just I had arranged to pick him up from the airport," continued Hope.

"Oh yes, he mentioned that. He was supposed to phone you, I think. You know Gavin. Without you to organise him he's hopeless. There was a change of plan. I was seeing a client in

Belfast – Ulster Bank – and he thought it would be good to go there as well. On the way sort of thing."

Hope sucked her upper lip in, unsure how she should respond to Rhona. The fact that she was desperately trying to assimilate what Rhona was telling her whilst feigning a calm manner was almost proving too much for her. Add to this that the message was coming from Rhona, little fat fucking Rhona, and she felt that she might cry out in mental pain at any moment.

Having broken the bitter tidings to Hope, Rhona proceeded to top up her glass again, finishing what had been in the bottle.

"It's lovely you were able to do the trip with Gavin. Having some company always makes…" But Hope couldn't think how to finish the sentence and was happy enough to just let it tail off. Her thoughts turned back inwards. She could see that this business trip, so full of promise and anticipated pleasure, was careering like a Pamplona bull towards its own destruction. Rhona patted her chest before releasing a muffled belch.

Hope continued to look at Rhona, who now carelessly stared out of the hotel window, dressed in a grape-coloured suit that smothered and clung as if slowly intending to squeeze out her last breath. Probably two sizes too small, Hope sneered. Has no one told her about how to best dress for the 'fuller figure'? She secretly desired that no one ever would. A good nose, but it sat almost dead centre in a flat face that circumscribed it like a fleshy plinth. The small blue eyes, always over-eager, appeared to endlessly convey flashes of surprise, distress and emotion with the forced theatricality of some ageing silent actress.

And her hair! Over-washed, over-coloured and as brittle as spaghetti. Whole-wheat spaghetti. In twenty years' time Hope pictured her as a shrew, a harridan. Squat and sagging with spent breasts forlornly hanging like disused leather pouches. 'Witches' tits', Uncle Martin would have once called them.

Silently turning these comforting thoughts over caused Hope to rally her spirits. "In the bar is he? Shall we join him?"

"Of course. Let me just finish this. Hmm, that's better. Right, off to find my room first and I'll see you down there."

Hope followed her to the door with the enigmatic half-smile she often employed when wishing to convey nothing to others.

"Oh, the glass," blustered Rhona, pushing it into Hope's hand.

"Merci beaucoup."

"Merci pour tout, Mademoiselle Hopey. Je vous vois au bar plus tard!"

A raised hand accompanied Rhona's last words as she turned away and ran down the hotel corridor.

Hope considered the awful realisation that Rhona's French, though tossed away so effortlessly, was beautifully delivered. Worst of all, Hope hadn't understood a word of it. Just one more reason to utterly, utterly despise Rhona.

And she'd called her 'Hopey' again.

68

"Miss Lynch, sing me one of your beautiful songs."

Martin was lying back staring at the feathered drapery of clouds that were cutting fast across the sky.

"Are you going to pull your trousers up, Martin Whelan? The farmer or anybody could come."

Martin probed the discarded jacket to his left, eventually pulling out his cigarettes and lighter.

"I don't think so. Let them come. I've nothing to hide. Isn't that a beautiful sky?"

Maureen Lynch ignored the request to look up, preferring to methodically continue removing the stalks of grass from her creased skirt.

"So will you do it?"

"Will I do what?"

"Sing for Christ sakes."

Maureen lay beside him and took the cigarette from his hand, pulling hard and inhaling very slowly across his chest. She then carefully placed the cigarette back in his lips. The wind was spluttering with warm, uneven gusts, carrying the dying heat of the early evening sun across their faces.

"I was just thinking, Mr Whelan, I am going to really enjoy telling Deirdre that we're going to be married. Oh yes, I will really enjoy that. She forever lording it over me that she'd be up the aisle first."

Martin became alarmed. "You haven't told her yet, have you? I've got to ask your father first. In time of course."

"Course not. But when are you going to ask him? You keep saying…"

"Hey, hey, hey. All in God's good time. Don't go rushing in like that. Your father's more likely to say 'yes' if he knows I've a good job now. Come here, give me a.."

"Get off. You've had your fun. You won't find another woman in this town that lets you do what you do."

"You can't blame a man for not holding himself back when he's faced with the most beautiful girl in Ireland! I'm mortal after all. What man could show, could exercise, the self-control, he needs when close to you?"

"Say that to Patsy, do you?"

Martin sat up, immediately regretting having done so knowing that it had shown Maureen there was something in her question.

"Patsy who?" He tried to sound disinterested.

"You know Patsy who."

"Enlighten me, 'cos I haven't a feckin' clue what you're on about."

Martin threw the cigarette into the adjacent hedge.

"Just something someone told me. They'd seen you with Patsy Maguire. Said you were all over her like a rash."

"Who told you that? I'd like to slap…"

"Oh, so you don't deny it. You just want to shoot the messenger?"

"Course I deny it. I wouldn't sully my hands hitting the fraud who told you that. There's nothing to tell. And it surprises me that you'd even begin to believe it. I thought we were supposed to mean something to each other. We're practically engaged."

"But we're not engaged! There's no 'practically' in it. You have a way with words, Martin, but they're just so much fluff. We're not engaged and you've been seen around town with that slut Patsy Maguire!"

"Look, let's get this straight between us. I love you. I don't know what this person's talking about. I know Patsy. I *like* Patsy. We have a craic now and then. But she's not someone I like in the way you're implying."

Martin knelt in front of Maureen and took her firmly by her small shoulders.

"Look at me, Maureen." He held her jaw and twisted her face square with his own.

"I adore you. I have adored you from the moment you looked at me. In that room, my life, everything I was, changed. God had given me a gift of love so perfect that I have treasured and kept it close by me, inside me, ever since. And do you know what, Miss Lynch? The flower, no, the bud, of that flower has blossomed in a perfect way. It will always blossom. It will always be turned towards the sun and it is the love that will live forever. Don't insult me by believing the tittle-tattle of jealous people. Their lives are dull and pointless. When they see how perfect our love is, then they grow jealous and want you and me to be broken and bitter like them."

Maureen's eyes looked imploringly, tearfully into Martin's face, taking in his handsomeness, his smooth wind-tanned skin. The flick of hair that invariably escaped and fell forward.

Martin, sensing that he had almost convinced her, continued, "Now, do we let them destroy what we have? Do we let their dirty hands and minds ruin this perfection, this flower that we both hold in our hearts?"

Maureen reluctantly signalled her assent with a small nod.

Martin grazed his lips slowly across her forehead, punctuating their path with a series of small and tender kisses.

"Martin, I'd kill myself if you left me."

"Ah, don't be foolish, my love. Don't say things like that."

"I'm not being foolish. If I were to lose you, I'd have nothing to live for."

Martin quickly tried to change the subject, casually lying back with the mocking exclamation, "Well, there's no danger of that now, is there. So be gone silly thoughts and let's not trouble ourselves with their company any longer!"

Martin could sense that Maureen was serious. Did he really want to burden himself with some clinging nutcase like Maureen Lynch for the rest of his life? Feck, no. But if he got rid of her, he'd miss the sex. Patsy wasn't giving him any sex; not yet, anyhow. But he knew he'd wear her down. Pretty girl too.

"Would you still like me to sing for you?"

"More than anything in the world, my love."

Maureen was silent for a while, looking out over the small mounds and sad bleached-grey stones of the field.

On Carrigdhoun, the heath is brown.
The clouds are dark o'er Ardnalee,
And many a stream comes rushing down
To swell the angry Owen na Buidhe.
The moaning blast is sweeping past

Through many a leafless tree,
And I'm alone, for he is gone,
My hawk has flown, ochone mo chroidhe.

69

When Hope looked at the number of the incoming call she realised that it must be a mobile. She had first thought to ignore it but, seeing it wasn't Thuong's number, relented and answered.

"Hi Hope, it's Barry here."

"Oh, hi Barry, how can I help?"

"Could I ask a favour?"

"Of course." Her heart sank.

"I've left something under my desk. I need someone to get it for me. Would you mind?"

Hope tried to stifle the sigh she felt and repeated her earlier answer, "Of course. What is it?"

"It's a box of flip chart pens. They belong to me."

Hope tapped her mouse to disable the screen saver so that she could open an email that she remembered she had to answer before she went home.

"What would you like me to do with them, Barry?"

Gavin appeared at his office door and motioned to Hope that he'd like to speak with her when her call had finished.

"Well I'm outside the building at the moment in my car. I was wondering if you could bring them outside to me."

"Well I've got to go into a meeting with Gavin now, Barry. Could you pop in yourself and get them?"

"Not really."

Hope began to get annoyed. She was Gavin's EA. Why did everyone think that meant she was somehow everyone's EA? "Sorry Barry, but if you want them now you're going to have to get them yourself."

"I'd rather not."

There was something in his voice. She hadn't noticed it at first but it was easily discernible now. A discomfort that he was obviously feeling.

"Is something wrong?"

"Haven't you heard?"

Haven't I heard what?"

"They've made me redundant."

"Redundant? When?"

"This afternoon. There's a new broom and I'm the first to be swept away."

"What new broom? What are you talking about?"

"This Liz Slater. Keith's replacement. Says that training is not 'core'. So that's it. Walked into the building this morning with a job. Then walked out without one."

"Barry, I'm so sorry." Hope wasn't sure how sorry she really was, but it felt like the right thing to say.

"No, it's a new challenge. Success is always on the far side of failure, I must see it as a new opening."

But Hope's thoughts had turned abruptly away from Barry and were now focused on her own security. Was she 'core'? Why does Gavin want to see her? Oh God…

"So those pens? Any chance?"

"Look Barry, I'll call security now and ask them to get the pens for you. Whereabouts outside are you? Which car park?"

"I'm in a visitor space. They'll know."

"I'll do it now. Bye."

Was that a bit of an abrupt way to end the call? Well she hadn't time to think of it. She called Jerry the security guard and relayed Barry's request. He understood perfectly. It was Jerry himself who had watched Barry empty his desk before escorting him like a released prisoner off the premises.

Hope went into Gavin's office and apologised for being held up. Gavin said nothing but walked behind her and gently closed the door.

So this was it. First Barry, now her. Gavin seemed to have the gravitas of a funeral director.

"I've something to tell you."

So here it was. How long had she worked here? 29 years? Was almost three decades about to flash before her very eyes?

"Yes?"

"It's Barry. They've made him redundant."

"I thought they made the role redundant, not the person?"

"Of course. But it adds up to the same thing."

Hope relaxed. For now.

"That's awful. I mean he could be a bit pretentious and everything, but…"

Gavin leaned back and tapped the corner of his keyboard to align perfectly with his PC's monitor.

"No, Hopey, it's not easy is it? But he'll find something."

Hope didn't think Gavin sounded very convinced that Barry would find something.

"Is that it?"

Gavin held up the palms of his hands.

"That's it. You didn't seem very surprised."

Hope was going to explain about the call she'd just taken, but decided she really didn't want to.

She'd just opened the door to the office when Gavin interjected, "Oh, there is just one other thing."

"Yes?"

"Liz Slater. Keith's replacement would like to see you tomorrow at 9.30."

"Just me?"

"Just you."

"Did she say why?"

"Not really. We'd finished our meeting and she asked me to pass the message on."

"Am I next? Will I be following Barry out the door?"

"Well the usual protocol is that if anyone was going to tell you you'd lost your job, then it would be me. So I can't think it's that."

"Are all of us seeing her? What about Martina and Jamilla?"

Gavin remained tight-lipped for a few moments, before replying, "As I said, I don't think your meeting's anything to do with that."

Within fifteen minutes Hope's emotions had plummeted, rose and plummeted again. She thought she needed to get home.

For some reason her shoes were also hurting her.

70

The wing of the Hospital had just been painted. The smell hung most in the small rooms off the main corridor, the walls still bare waiting for the notice boards that would soon be mounted on them.

A small table had an opened sandwich carton with the remains of the filling gathered into one of its corners. Denis, sitting directly opposite the open door, had fastened his hands on to his knees waiting for the footsteps of someone 'official'. Hope sat beside him, constantly shifting from one position to another, quite unable to settle.

"Are you OK, Dad?"

Denis looked and smiled; a steely grimace that betrayed how much any hospital had become an ordeal to him.

A small commotion broke in as a bed was wheeled past their door. One nurse was walking alongside reassuring the patient with "not long to go now, my sweet" whilst the other was grimly positioning the bed for the ninety degree turn ahead into another corridor. The wallop and closing of the rubber double doors was the last noise they made before all became quiet once more.

The pattering of soft shoes announced the return of the nurse. She sat beside Denis and turned and bowed slightly to bring her head level with his.

Whatever happened, thought Hope as she took in the Indian nurse's slight figure and dyed black hair swept severely back from her forehead, to proper British nurses?.

"We can take you and your daughter in now. You said there was a Mrs Whelan. Have you been able to contact her?"

Hope interrupted, "We haven't. They were separated. We tried the last address we had for her but she'd moved on."

The nurse smiled benignly.

"When was the last time Mr Whelan saw his wife?"

"Not for some years, has he Dad?"

Denis, tight lipped, turned to the nurse and slightly shook his head, quickly looking away again.

"He's very poorly. The Doctor thinks he had a heart attack and was probably lying for some time before he was found. He may not be how you remember him last."

"Is he dying, nurse?"

The nurse, surprised by Hope's question, was temporarily lost for the right words.

"He's not very good." Another practised smile. She turned back to Denis, "I understand he's your brother-in-law?"

Again, Denis nodded, but this time kept looking out of the door.

The nurse waited to see if he would add to this gesture but, seeing that he didn't intend to, asked, "Would you like to go in and see him?"

The aroma of paint lessened as they stepped into the corridor, Hope quickly nipping back into the small room to retrieve Denis' scarf. Some yards on they passed another nurse at the small office area, her round, black, pleasing face lit from one side by the desktop lamp.

Were there any white nurses anymore? What happened to fierce matrons and blonde, busy nurses? Hope realised that her entire image of hospitals probably came courtesy of 1960s black and white pictures with a leering Kenneth Williams always about to burst in on the screen at any moment.

They turned into a ward comprising four beds; one bed was screened off with curtains. The nurse, smartly walking ahead, found the gap and held back one drape to let them through.

The lights had all been dimmed as it was so late, and it took Hope some time to accustom her eyes to the form of Martin, breathing hurriedly, lying quite still before her. She moved around between the bed and the window. Denis calmly looked down at Martin's face: pale, his closed eyes flickering as if small electrical charges were passing irregularly behind them.

How strange, surreal this all seemed to Hope. This man who had once been so significant in her life, who had negotiated every obstacle, difficulty and event seemingly without effort, now prostrate and agitated in his helplessness. She glanced down at his left hand. It was turned slightly upward, a mute pleading for reconciliation. She placed her hand near it on the soft blanket but found she couldn't touch him.

Denis lightly gripped Martin's upper arm. "Are you with me, Martin?"

To Hope's astonishment, Martin – almost imperceptibly - moved his head in response to Denis's kindly question; a rasp of sound, low and unintelligible, came from his throat.

"What's that now? What's that you're saying?"

Denis placed his ear by Martin's mouth. "France? What's that about France?"

Martin swallowed hard and tried to move his lips. A smile revealed itself slowly. A Martin smile that now seemed all the more grotesque on his blanched features.

He whispered to Denis: "I've been away, Denis."

"Sure you have, Martin. And we'll take you home when you're better."

But Martin didn't respond to Denis's remark. Again his voice sounded as if each word was dragging its form through gravel.

"I've been away to France to wear the fleur-de-lis."

"Fleur-de-lis?" Denis repeated.

Martin's eyes widened a little and Hope wasn't sure if they were moist through emotion or perspiration.

"I've been away."

"So you told me. And soon you'll be home, won't you? Do you remember home?"

Martin moved his head a little to Denis. Hope was desperate to leave. If she could have extricated herself from the side of the bed without being seen by Martin then she would have done so.

"…to wear the fleur-de-lis …"

Denis looked up at Hope, at a loss how to reply.

"Denis, tell her I'm back now."

"Tell who you're back? Patsy? She's coming to see you. You can tell her yourself."

"Not Patsy…."

"Tell who you're back?"

Martin's face froze as if suddenly confronted by some ghastly terror.

"Oh Christ.. Oh No.. Oh God please no… Look! She's drowning. Oh God no. Help them! They're drowning…"

Denis calmly stood up and withdrew a little from the bedside. Hope didn't understand what Martin was babbling about and looked across the bed into his face for some answer to the situation that was playing out in front of her.

Martin began to weep, tears falling down the side of his face onto the pillow. "Oh God, I can't do anything… they're drowning and I can't do anything…"

He closed his wet eyes and became calm. Soon he lost consciousness and his troubled breathing reasserted itself.

Martin didn't die; life simply left him. It withdrew so slowly that Denis, now alone with him after sending Hope home, had not even witnessed the final extinguishing of his ebbing spirit.

Through the window a vanguard of weak light was pushing up and into the night-wash of sodium sky. Denis looked down again at Martin, the hair now thinned and bearing the remains of poorly applied hair dye. In the relaxed repose of death the lines and crowfeet had smoothed out but the skin still bore the marks and blemishes of a man who had lived too much, hurt too much, and walked away from too much.

It was nearly 11am when Denis tiredly opened the door to home. Hope woke up from an uneasy sleep on the settee. "Dad?" she called.

"Hello." Denis quietly answered back.

She was still dressed from the night before, having returned from the hospital and resolving to have a small drink before going to bed. The glass of wine was still untouched on the nest of tables beside her. She realised that the smell of new paint from the hospital ward was still in her nostrils.

"Could you get hold of Patsy later? She might want to pay her respects."

So Martin was dead, thought Hope. No need to ask now.

"I'll try. I'll have to call into work. Are you going to tell Mum?"

"In time. Not for now."

"I'll make some tea."

Hope rose from her chair but turned back upon reaching the room door.

"What was he talking about? That 'drowning' thing. It was a bit strange."

"Not really. Not really."

"So..?" Hope pressed.

Denis turned and looked up at Hope, at first unsure what to say. Eventually he winked and said: "It was all a very long time ago. You know, I'd really love that cup of tea."

71

Hope tugged at the seam of her skirt and regretted that she hadn't gone for something a little more formal for her first day. It was a strange reception area. The receptionist was behind a glass screen as if you'd expected her to cash you a cheque rather than welcome you to a large car rental firm. Some small, grey seats were arranged facing two lifts, swallowing and spitting out an endless arrangement of body shapes and faces. So many people, she thought. Would she ever be able to remember everyone?

Hope eventually started to daydream. She'd been told that Leslie Reynolds would be down shortly, and was on edge at first ready to rise and greet him. But still he hadn't appeared. Again she took hold of the hem of her skirt and eased it over her thighs.

"Sorry I'm late!" Mr Reynolds had emerged from a crowded lift and caught Hope by surprise.

"Oh, hello." Hope's newspaper, which she'd bought at the last minute to make a good impression slithered from her lap as she stood up.

"Here let me." Mr Reynolds followed Hope's slim legs downward as he stopped to retrieve her paper.

"Do the crossword?"

Hope looked a little confused. "Sorry?"

"The crossword. The Telegraph?" He held the paper up in front of her. Hope could smell the heavy, citrusy aroma of Old

Spice Lime aftershave and wondered if she would need to hold her breath in the lift until she could get out.

"Oh, sometimes!"

"Cryptic?"

"Of course."

This was all going wrong. What crossword? What was he talking about?"

Mr Reynolds punched the lift button with his knuckles and, to Hope's relief, the doors immediately slid open ready to devour them both.

"After you." Hope moved to the back of the lift, not sure whether she should ask for the paper back or not.

"Always do them. Don't always get the time. Great for trains."

Hope had to get off this subject. "I'm really looking forward to working here. It's so different from Harbutts."

"And we love having you with us. You'll really brighten up our little office. We could quite do with a woman's touch."

"Oh, I thought you had a woman before?"

"Well yes, but she was quite a bit... you know. Up for retirement. Nice to have something a little younger."

Hope smiled but didn't really know why.

They got out at the fifth floor, Mr Reynolds's right arm (still holding the paper) guiding Hope out on to the landing.

They walked down a corridor with offices on either side. On the other sides of the glass she could see box files stacked against the window, wire baskets containing sheaves of paper and dark wooden desks arranged in groups of two or three. Two men, who had just been idly talking, immediately looked from within their office and watched Hope until she was gone.

"Here we are!" Again, with a dramatic flourish, a guiding arm held the door back. A middle-aged man slowly looked up from his desk at Mr Reynolds and the new arrival.

"Colin. Our lovely new girl. Do say hello."

Colin stood up and threw out his right hand towards Hope. The handshake was vigorous and manly.

"Very nice to meet you, Hope."

"And you, Colin."

Colin's 'white' shirt struck Hope as being the faintest of greys. His tie, which was dark, somewhere in colour between a royal and navy blue, was lightly mottled with something that Hope couldn't quite discern.

Leslie broke in, "Now, Hope. I bet you're gasping."

"Pardon?"

"For tea, of course! Whatever was she thinking, eh, Colin?"

"Tea would be lovely."

"Of course. Let me show you the kettle. What about you, old man?"

"No, fine thanks."

They passed out into the corridor again and Hope walked a little behind to escape the still pungent fragrance that Leslie had doubled his dose of only that morning.

At the end of the corridor was a small kitchen. Leslie pointed out the fridge, indicating which milk bottle belonged to whom, before swinging back the cupboard doors to reveal tea bags and assorted mugs.

"Now, let me leave you to it and then come and join us when you're ready."

"Would you like a cup of tea, Mr Reynolds?"

"Why, yes. Splendid. Hot, white and sweet. Like my women."

Mr Reynolds laughed at his quip with the fervour of a man who had said it for the first time. Hope suspected, though, that he hadn't.

Several minutes later, Hope re-entered the office.

"Oh, a tray! That's a new one! This little lady will be civilizing us all. Wait 'til Dougie gets in. He won't know what's hit him!"

Hope blushed. Had she done something wrong?

"I see we'll have to change our ways around here, Colin. Now we've got our new little lady."

But Colin smiled without lifting his head, calmly continuing to concentrate on the adjustments to the figures beneath his hovering biro.

"Come into my lair. Bring your tea."

Leslie Reynolds entered the small office and fell heavily into his leather chair. Hope began to realise that everything he did would probably be done with a theatrical gusto. She judged him as in his mid-fifties; a face that age was now gradually filling out with the slow ballooning of skin around his skull. Hair lined the top ridge of each ear and the creases of his forehead looked like they'd been slit deep by a scalpel. But the eyes were nervy and alert, like an edgy cat's, darting and noticing everything that was happening around him.

He picked up his mug of tea and, keeping eyes firmly fixed on Hope opposite, took a large noisy sip. He appeared to be, quite unashamedly, drinking Hope in.

"Sweet enough, Mr Reynolds?" asked Hope.

Leslie Reynolds said nothing, his face broadening into a large grin.

72

Hope looked at the clock in the corner of her screen. It was almost twenty past. She gathered the documents together that she'd been working from and placed them back in their wallet folder. Doing ordinary things calmed her nerves and, for a reason she didn't quite understand, she was very nervous about her imminent meeting with Liz Slater. There had been the reports of others who had already met her. Gavin, eternally positive Gavin, thought her to be 'probably just what was needed', but she always sensed how edgy he became whenever he went to any meeting with her.

She soon found herself with Nisha, Keith's old PA. She never liked Nisha. She always seemed very reticent when with Hope and, despite Hope's attempts to build some inroads with her, found she always was rebuffed with a lofty disinterest. Hope had always previously put it down to a clash of culture. There was no warmth to Nisha.

When Hope had entered Nisha looked up at her as if it was an everyday event. "Oh, hello Hope."

"Hi Nisha."

It felt strange to be waiting in the room. Nisha made no attempt to make small talk, so Hope found herself pretending to leaf through a magazine that she'd picked up from the small table beside her.

She listened hard for any noise through the door, but all was eerily quiet. Was this it? Was this the last meeting she was going to have, which was why Nisha was especially distant this morning? No need to be friendly with people you weren't going to see again. The thought gave her an uncomfortable reminder of her last conversation with Barry Bufton.

Nisha's phone rang. "Hi Liz. Of course."

Nisha looked at Hope and smiled, "Liz is ready for you now."

A panic began to surge in Hope's breast. How long had she worked here? 18 years? 19 years? Was this where it all ended? Would she be able to find work again? And what about Mum? What would it do to frail and fading Mum?

The first surprise for Hope was that Liz was not at her desk, but standing just in front of it. She was impeccably dressed wearing a jacket and suit that was a perfect fit for her petite, trim figure. Hope noticed her shoes next, that looked as if they'd been designed with only that outfit in mind, so cleverly did their colour complement the pale grey of her suit.

But it was when she was scanning Liz's face that she received the second – and all the greater – shock. She knew her. She was certain she knew her. And the realisation of this produced a sickening flow of sensations within her.

"Lovely to meet you again, Hope. Take a seat."

Liz motioned to the table and chairs on the right of her large office. Gone were Keith's sailing photographs, assorted memorabilia from previous conferences and his sales trophy cabinet. Instead there was a spartan, almost unlived in look about the office. No papers on the desk. Filing cabinets removed. Only two framed photographs on Liz's curving desk, their backs turned to Hope so she couldn't see who the photographs were of.

It was only when Hope had settled in her chair that she recalled the exact words that Liz had just spoken: "Lovely to meet you, *again*."

Hope watched Liz take up her seat beside her, trying to find the right time to scan her face closely. Had they worked together in the past? Was she someone's wife or partner that she'd been briefly introduced to? The mystery was maddening – Hope berating herself when her memory had always stood her in such good stead in the past.

The name: Slater. Did she know anyone else called Slater? No, she thought not. Perhaps she knew her before she was married. But again, nothing seemed to be coming.

"So how long have you been at Jupiter? I think Gavin said getting on for 20 years."

That voice. There was something in that voice. She knew she recognised it. But if that was the case, why couldn't she place it?

"Who are you?"

"Yes, it does fly by, doesn't it? I've only been here a matter of days, perhaps a couple of weeks, and it all seems like minutes."

"You're enjoying this aren't you? You're doing this deliberately."

"I'm sure it has. It's got a great pedigree and that's something I think we've stopped telling people. How long have you been Gavin's secretary?"

Liz's question snapped Hope out of her thoughts.

"I'm not his secretary, I'm his EA."

"Is there a difference? What's the difference?"

"It's a question of responsibilities. I don't do Gavin's typing. But I help organise his diary, in fact I probably organise everything around him and the department."

Liz looked calmly, unsmilingly at Hope. "That doesn't sound like a very good case for Gavin having an EA. Perhaps an Administrator might be more appropriate?"

Hope could feel the ground giving way beneath her. Here was a woman who now had her future in her hands - and Hope was playing her completely wrong. Where was Hope's guile? Where was the clever, plotting Hope of old who'd already put everyone, from Mr Reynolds to Gavin, back in their boxes?

"Liz, you said it was nice to meet again. And I know this sounds rude, but I just can't place you. Was it recently?"

"Not really."

"I'm afraid I just don't recognise your name. Perhaps I knew you before you were married?"

"Oh you did. You even knew me before people called me Liz."

Hope's mind feverishly pushed back, back into her adolescence. Not Liz… Elizabeth. Elizabeth… Elizabeth…

"Oh God. Elizabeth Clancy?"

She leaned towards Hope.

"Used to be. Elizabeth Clancy from 12a Partridge Close. I'm sure you'll remember it. It was very Council Housey. I do hope you and Mr Neil Dowling didn't catch anything."

"I don't follow, Liz."

"No, it was just a casual remark to you, I suppose. Just one of the throwaway cruel things children can say to each other. Once you've had your laugh, why would you want to commit it to memory?"

Get control, Hope pleaded with herself. You've lost all control.

"I don't really remember. Children say a lot of stupid things. I'm sure I was no different to anyone else."

"How long did you say you were Gavin's EA?" Liz sounded the last two letters with a sarcastic emphasis.

"Well, Gavin's only been here…"

Liz rose from the table and walked away as Hope was mid-sentence.

"Oh yes, he told me. Well thanks Hope. I enjoyed meeting you again."

Liz sat at her desk and slid open a drawer on her left, becoming preoccupied with sifting through some sheets within it.

Hope pushed her chair back and tried to remain calm, although she was still stinging from the arrogant manner with which the meeting had been concluded.

"Thanks for the tea," she shot back before pulling the door loudly behind her.

The emotional strands of anger, confusion, embarrassment and hatred twisted and pulled inside Hope as she found herself back in the corridor. Why Liz? Why had she come here? But something else was also pulling at her conscience: a realisation – hanging vaguely at the rim of her mind - that she was struggling to articulate. There was another reason why she wanted to be out of the building and drinking in the fresh air. Losing her job? No, that was now a racing certainty. It couldn't be that. Being outwitted by Liz? Yes, that hurt but somehow that didn't seem the reason either. And then it all too quickly revealed itself and, in doing so, appeared so formidable, so uncomfortable that Hope doubted whether she would ever be able to come to terms with it.

One day, maybe not even very long ago, life had suddenly passed her by.

73

"Carol? Are you home?"

Denis had just returned from work through the back door and put his lunchbox on the draining board. The back door had been open, which had surprised him as Carol had said only that morning she was hoping to go over to Hatch End to see Patsy and wouldn't be back until at least five o'clock or so.

"Carol?" Denis repeated. He walked into the living room and there found Carol sitting, staring at the TV, her legs pulled under her. The television wasn't on.

"Where's Stephen?"

"Asleep."

"I thought you were off to Patsy's?"

"It's not safe to go."

Denis sat beside her and breathed a sigh of disappointed recognition; he knew what was probably about to ensue.

"What do you mean not safe? She's your sister."

"It's not safe. Not now."

Denis leaned forward to try and catch her eye, but her unblinking stare remained focused on the television.

"What do you mean not now? What's changed, love?"

"They have a phone. They have a new phone."

This was new to Denis. He had grown used to the incessant, maddening conversation that suddenly broke off into an imperturbable silence. He had learned to humour Carol when she resurrected her desire to return to the stage – even though, other than the modest shows they had put on in Athlone, she had never been accepted once at the auditions she'd attended when they had first arrived in England. But this was new and he wasn't sure how to deal with it.

"Don't you like the new phone? Is there something wrong with it?"

"They're using it to spy on me. They think I don't know. But I know that's why they bought it."

"Who are spying on you? Martin and Patsy?"

"And others. They all just want to watch me. They'd like to catch me out."

"How are they going to do that with a phone?"

"Don't you see it's obvious? They want Stephen. They know he's ill and they want to take him." Now Carol suddenly turned to glare at Denis, her red-ringed eyes intense and afraid.

"Love, love, no-one's going to do that. No-one's going to take Stephen away. You know that. Lots of people have phones these days. The Sedgemoors have ordered one. You've used a telephone yourself. You weren't spying on anyone. Of course they're not for spying."

"Yes they are! You… you're in with them! You know they're using the phone! Even you…" Carol's voice trailed quickly off and she shook her head, tears running down her cheeks. Denis reached for her.

"No! Get off me!"

"I'm just trying to calm you, love…"

"Keep your feckin' hands off me!"

Denis withdrew a little. This was new and, this time, he wasn't sure that he knew how to deal with it. Since the birth of Stephen, occasional moments of odd behaviour had gradually increased until, over the last few months, they were a regular part of their lives. He'd tried to downplay it with Hope but, at this moment, he knew he'd have to get someone to help. But how could he do that without it appearing it was all part of the imaginary conspiracy

Carol was so convinced of? They had stopped going out. Other than Patsy, Carol had slowly withdrawn contact from everyone they had once known.

His mind wandered back to the chilling moment when the Doctor had asked to speak to them both in the maternity ward. He was a young man, Denis recalled. He was trying to think of the right phrase, the one that would soften the blow. But his words tumbled out before them in such an unformed way that both Denis and Carol had to stitch the dreadful meaning of what he was trying to say back together again.

"Of course, being premature…not always the case… but so premature… infection… intracranial haemorrhage… the brain bleeds… cerebral palsy… amazing what can be done these days… still, you must bear up…"

Denis closed his eyes. He could still see the Doctor's face, contorting and dipping as the sentence on little Stephen was passed. In the succeeding months and years, they had struggled to cope and, determined as they were that Hope wouldn't be affected, knew that she was suffering too.

And now this. This pain of having to watch Carol - this woman he loved so entirely that there were no words that might give form to the devotion he still felt - descend into a shadowy, shape-shifting hell was almost more than Denis could bear.

He opened his eyes again. She was still looking straight at him; as mute as stone. He rubbed his forehead and looked at the television himself. There they both were in the glass of the screen, frozen and helpless.

Denis said nothing, but slowly rose from the settee and walked back out into the garden. The air was fresh and caught silky traces of the pinks that were now in flower beside him. He noticed that he'd left out his hoe from last night's weeding and decided to take it down into the shed that sat, squat and sulking, at the far end of the lawn.

Locking the door behind him, his broad shoulders heaved and fell as he silently wept.

74

Hope thought it had been a mistake to have sat upstairs in the bus. The stench of cigarette smoke was very strong as she'd got to the top of the staircase but, with three people close behind her, she'd no choice but to scan the many passengers to find one who wasn't smoking. She'd not long sat down before the woman beside her was unclasping her bag and searching for her cigarettes.

Now back in the fresh air again she hoped that the smell might have worn off her clothes by the time she'd reached the pub.

Neil had promised to wait outside for her, so that she wouldn't have to go in by herself. The agreement was that they would meet at The Three Tuns, a large pub built in the late 1930s to service the large new housing estates that were mushrooming on the outer fringes of West London. She suddenly became aware that she was very nervous. Why? She knew Neil, there wasn't anything to worry about, even though it had been several years since they had last met.

Ah, several years since… that was it. What would he think of her now? Tony, her fiancé had called her the "best looking girl in West London" but, well, that was Tony being nice. But what would Neil think of her? She'd had to be very accommodating to Mr Reynolds lingering touches, and listen sympathetically as he told her that Mrs Reynolds "had moved their relationship beyond the physical stage" as he had so euphemistically phrased it. But her understanding had earned her what she had needed, the chance to slip away from work two hours early so that she would have the time to look her best for the evening.

Once she'd reassured herself that she didn't smell too much of cigarette smoke after all, she turned her attention to her new shoes. They were Stephane Kelian high heels sculpted in interlocking light brown leather that Martin had brought back for her from France. It embarrassed her that he still bought her such expensive presents but, when they were this perfect, she wasn't going to refuse.

As she neared the car park she saw a figure lazily leaning against a car. It was exactly the same pose that he'd adopted the day that she and Elizabeth Clancy had met him after school that steamingly hot summer day. 'Whatever became of her?' she mused. Neil hadn't yet seen Hope and then, looking around, instantly stood up. He seemed taller and had filled out across the chest. She took in his Gucci sweatshirt and the pastel jumper he'd loosely tied around his neck.

"Hello Neil."

"Hi. How are you?"

"I'm fine. You're taller."

How handsome he was. The face was still the Neil of old, but the features had all slightly adjusted into a more pleasing – very pleasing – shape. Could I love this man? Did I once love this man?

"When's Tony getting here?"

"Tony?"

"Your fiancé?"

"Oh, he wasn't able to come. He's at football practice."

She realised that she'd completely forgotten the fact that she'd told Neil that Tony would be coming as well.

"Right, I was looking forward to seeing him."

"He loves his football. Sometimes I think…" she stopped herself continuing. Telling Neil that she thought Tony was more interested in football than he was in her was too obvious. It also wasn't true.

"Is this your car?"

"The Ital? Yes, it's just a rebadged Marina but she's nice enough."

"Is it new? It looks new to me."

"A few months old. They've stopped making them so I got it for a great price."

A new car. Neil was driving a new car. She'd arranged to meet him at the Three Tuns because it was so easy to get to on the bus. At least now she'd be sure of a lift home.

"Tony's got a really nice Escort."

"What year?"

Hope needed to still play this right. "Not sure actually. It's pretty new." The image of Tony's thraped, faded red car rose up in her mind.

"Look, do you want to have a drink here, or ride out somewhere in the country."

Hope looked at the forbidding Three Tuns. She'd particularly chosen it as Tony would never have been seen dead in it. She had also told him that she was reluctantly meeting up with some people from work and, as she'd only just started there, was only going to help build relationships.

"Anywhere in mind?"

"Could go up to Marlow. Have a walk on the river maybe. Then get a drink."

"Fine."

Neil was obviously pleased that she'd accepted and hurried round to unlock the passenger door to let her in.

"Mind if I open the window?" asked Hope, conscious once more of the cigarette smoke.

"Course."

Once Neil had reversed out of the parking space, he suddenly turned to Hope, "Are you sure that Tony is OK with this?"

"Of course! I told him we're old friends from School. Don't worry; he knows he can trust me."

Hope realised that she didn't want to talk about Tony anymore, but might have to resign herself to the fact that conversation would probably keep turning back to him. Especially as she'd lied to Neil about the fact they were engaged.

The car was so smooth, she found herself glancing at the speedometer because the sensation she was feeling was that they were travelling so fast. Her father wouldn't have a car because, as a bus driver, he already enjoyed free travel with London Transport. The only other time she enjoyed sitting in a nice car was Martin's Jaguar, although he always complained about how badly built it was. She didn't care, a Jaguar was a Jaguar and she enjoyed its scented opulence of walnut and leather.

Hope watched mile after mile of the M40 sweep effortlessly by. She stole a surreptitious glance at Neil, who was talking about something technical to do with his job. What was it about him? He seemed so sure of himself; he'd always been so sure of himself. The spotty frog had turned into a prince and had wanted to see her. Yes, after all this time, he'd remembered her and called her up; called her completely out of the blue.

"So that's where we are. It's all very exciting. I tell you, it'll be completely different to the way we work today."

"What will?"

Neil turned to Hope. "You've not been listening to a word I said."

"Of course I was. I was just thinking about something."

Neil grinned and turned his eyes back to the motorway. "So what was I saying?"

"It'll be very different. See?"

"What will be very different?"

"Work will."

Neil relented, knowing that he'd probably been boring Hope.

"So what does Tony do?"

"He's a Service Manager, at Perry's."

"The Ford people? Which one?"

"Edgware. He's just moved there."

Why had she said Service Manager? Tony was a Parts Assistant, a job which he'd recently got so that "He didn't have to spend the rest of his life as a grease monkey", as he'd once told her. What if Neil should meet Tony? No, she realised, that was never going to happen.

"How's the new job going?"

"All right. Manager's a bit of a lech. If he's not staring at my chest he's making some double-meaning remark."

"What sort of remarks?"

"You know, 'How Hope puts the lead in our propelling pencils' and 'If I said you had…'"

"..A beautiful body would you hold it against me? Yeah, I know it…"

"He's all right, really. Long as you know how to play him."

"Sounds like a creep to me. Have you told someone?"

"Who can I tell? The Personnel Manager is as bad. His secretary can't even spell 'personnel'. On the log sheet for the photocopier she always writes 'personal'. Helps that she's all long legs and big shoulder pads."

Neil laughed. He still laughed the same way with a slight falsetto sound always sounding the first note.

"I could love you, Neil."

"How long? Since 1981. It's a company called Charters. Was at a place called Corbridge before, then applied for this."

"Why did we never hit it off?"

"Not always in this job. First job was as an assistant and then the manager left."

"Do you like me?"

"Bit strange at first, being the youngest. But no one seems to mention it now."

"Could you love me?"

"For the time being. With all this new stuff going on, it's a good place to be. Here we are."

Neil slowed the car down as he drove along the High Street, then saw a gap in a line of parked cars and manoeuvred the vehicle slowly into it.

"Want a bit of a walk, first? You can go down by the river."

A walk by the river seemed perfect. It all seemed perfect. The evening sky was the colour of cheap soap; a warm breeze blew eddies of dust and paper inside the doorway of an adjacent closed shop. Hope looked around at the large three-storied Georgian house that majestically spread it's frontage before her, like a swan spreading its vast wings.

Neil pointed. "The river's down there. Nice pub just before you reach it."

"Yeah. Great."

They walked a little uncertainly at first along the pavement. Hope became a disappointed when she realised that the High Street wasn't all old properties and that new buildings, bland and uninspired, disfigured many sections of the street.

"Can I ask you something?"

"Ask away, Mr Dowling."

"It's about your brother."

"Stephen?" Hope knew what was coming. She had hoped Neil had forgotten, but how could he have? How could anyone forget a conversation like that?

"There was a night, probably the last time I saw you."

"In the lido?"

"Yeah, and you told me…"

"I was drunk. I probably told you that I'd drowned him?"

"Well, yes, you did. So it's true?"

"Course not. I was upset and… probably wanted attention. I don't talk rubbish like I used to."

"Right. That's… that's all right then. I believed you. I couldn't believe that you…"

Hope was lost for anything else to say and hoped that Neil might move off the subject.

"So what happened to Stephen? You know, how did he..."

"Oh, he was very ill. He was born with a terminal... you know. I can't forgive myself for what I said that night."

Neil seemed relieved. He threw off the serious air and put his hands comfortably deep into his pockets.

"How's your Dad? Still on the buses?"

"Still on the buses. Got his hands full with Mum as well."

Neil stopped abruptly and looked confusedly at Hope.

"Your Mum? I thought your Mum was... I thought you told me she was dead."

"Who told you that?"

"You did. You'd told me she'd... she had cancer." A chilling emphasis fell on the last word.

Hope was utterly lost for what to say. The chords of *Vicious*, warm beer and a failure of a house party long ago during a summer evening in 1976, stood as guilty witnesses before her.

75

"Daydreaming, Miss Dunne?"

Hope was startled and quickly smiled at Jamilla. "'Fraid so."

"Anything nice?"

"Not really. I thought it was going to be nice but things don't always work out like you hoped they would."

"Tell me all!"

Hope laughed, "There's nothing to tell. Honest!"

"Oh, come on. You are always so mysterious. I bet you it was something romantic. See! You're blushing!"

Hope gathered up the pages on her desk, not because she needed to, but because it allowed her an excuse not to look at Jamilla.

"I'm waiting…" Jamilla teased.

"Well, it was an evening a long time ago and I thought it was going to be wonderful and then something happened."

"What happened?"

Hope couldn't decide how to answer. She was suddenly plunged back to a balmy summer evening when the low sun was throwing long, low shadows across a Marlow High Street and she was falling…

"Life happened. There. There's nothing more to tell. Now I must get on."

Jamilla relaxed into her seat and playfully mimicked the petulant face of a child to show her displeasure.

"There's nothing to tell. Believe me. My life was very dull. It still is."

"How can you say that when you have Martina and me to brighten up…"

"That's a point. Where is Martina?"

"Oh, she's helping Gavin put together some slides."

"Slides?"

"So they said."

Jamilla reached down inside a carrier bag and purposefully placed her Tupperware container on to her desk.

Oh God, thought Hope, not more fucking curry.

"I'm just nipping out. Promised to get some milk."

"OK. See you."

Hope looked in the shop windows of the small parade as if expecting to see something new, but it was the same windows with the same wares she always saw. Looking up she recognised the reflection of Barry Bufton, walking quickly across the road towards her.

"That's all I need," she whispered to herself.

She tried hard to smile and turned to acknowledge him, "Oh, hello Barry."

She took a short while to come to terms with the fact that he was dressed smartly. Barry Bufton looking smart!

"I like the whistle, Barry. I've never seen you in that before."

"Oh, it's for an interview. My new girlfriend..."

"New girlfriend? You *are* a quiet one. When did she come on the scene?" (Hope painfully recalled that the word 'come' was a favourite leering device for a certain Mr Reynolds, many years ago.)

"Couple of weeks back. Same week I got made redundant actually. One door closed and another one swung wide open."

Hope, watching his arms theatrically mimic the two doors he was referring to, concluded that Barry's confidence was beginning to ooze back into place.

"And I see she took your tailoring in hand."

"Oh this. Clothes maketh the man. Well, they are certainly maketh-ing this one."

"Where was the interview?"

"Not had it yet. Little bit nerve-wracking going through it all. Still, I always say let your nerves be your fuel. I like to tell my delegates on my Presentations course, 'We all get butterflies, the trick is making them fly in formation!'"

"Is that one of yours?"

"Wish it was. Just don't want anything bad to happen, that's all."

Hope sensed that Barry needed a confidant and turned her head sympathetically to one side to show him that she was that person.

"What sort of thing?"

"Well, do you remember when I was off a couple years ago? Told everyone it was a sabbatical?"

But Hope knew what he was going to say. The embarrassing rasps of wind that occasionally escaped from him. The laxative she'd spotted that she knew he could only have as preparation for some horrendous probing tube that was probably part of a follow-up procedure. And yes, the long break which everyone gossiped about, unable to determine exactly why he'd disappeared but knowing for certain it wasn't a sabbatical.

"I remember the sabbatical. Are you saying it wasn't one?"

Barry sighed and looked around, afraid that he might be overheard. Leaning his head conspiratorially forward he said in a low voice, "I had this operation."

Hope widened her eyes in mock disbelief.

"An operation? What sort of operation?"

"Well, I had cancer. Bowel cancer and they…"

"They what, Barry?"

"They... I have this bag."

Hope couldn't believe just how much she was enjoying Barry's discomfort. She might have been the first one he'd told since the operation. Except for his new bit of fluff, probably.

"What bag? I don't follow."

"This colostomy... you know? A colostomy bag."

"Oh, Barry, I had no idea. You've had a colostomy? So it wasn't a sabbatical?"

Again Barry looked quickly around.

"No, it was chemo and then the operation and then recovery. That's why I was off."

"Are there any after-effects? I mean, because of the operation?"

"One or two, but I'd rather not go into that…"

"Like the impotence, Barry?"

"Well, yes, there are a lot of tablets and what-not."

"So does your new woman know yet, or are you hoping she's not going to ask?"

"No, just once a year for a scan. Otherwise everything's back to normal."

"So not being able to make love again is back to normal is it?"

"You're right, losing the job hasn't helped. But with Becky's help..."

"Becky?"

"Oh, my new girlfriend, Becky. Or is it 'partner'? Feel a bit old to call her my girlfriend."

"I'm so pleased for you, Barry. I had no idea that all this was happening. And now you've got this interview?"

Conspiracy now over, Barry stepped back a little again. "Onwards and upwards! The lowest ebb is the turn of the tide and this is my job. It has Bufton's name written all over it."

Barry had brightened suddenly and then shrank back into himself again.

"Well it's my job as long as... as long as I don't..."

"As long as you don't what?"

"Oh, screw up the interview!"

"You meant as long as you don't fart, isn't that right, Barry?"

"Thanks for your reassurance, Hope. I'm really glad I saw you."

He walked off with Hope shouting after him, "Bonne chance!"

"Shouldn't that be 'Bon courage'?" A voice said behind her.

Unbelievable, thought Hope. It's Rhona.

76

"Denis."

"Martin."

Martin took out his cigarettes and offered them, but Denis shook his head.

"I hate feckin' funerals. They're so... black."

Denis glanced and nodded his agreement. Something was troubling Denis and Martin couldn't work out what it was. He decided to change the subject.

"Still thinking about moving to England? Carol said you'd both made your minds up."

The large empty hearse was now driving out from the small car park in front of the cemetery gates. Stones splintered and spat from beneath its broad tyres. The forecast had said there'd be showers drifting across the West of Ireland, but the morning had been dry, as if nature was refusing to bow to the grim meteorological clichés of a mid-morning funeral.

Denis turned to see where Carol and Patsy were and espied them in huddled, hunched conversations with other mourners. He took the opportunity to wriggle and loosen his tie, pulling it just clear enough so that he could undo the top button of his shirt.

"I'll have that cigarette," said Denis.

Martin reached back into his greatcoat pocket. "So you *do* smoke?"

"Not really."

Denis turned his head and blew the smoke out of the corner of his mouth, careful that it shouldn't drift into the paths of others who may have been standing nearby.

"Have the Lynch lot gone?"

Again, Denis just nodded.

"Someone told me it was suicide. That the Lynch's are trying to pass it off as an accident."

Denis studied his cigarette. "I heard that too."

"Did you get to the wake?"

"Carol and I went. Did you?"

"Ah, no. I, err... work and that. I heard it was some do they put on?"

"You busy then?"

"Cripes, yes. Too much if you ask me."

"You're in insurance now?"

"I certainly am. I hope it'll make my fortune one day. Are you covered yourself?"

"I've got to be honest, Martin. I'm a little surprised you're here."

Martin flinched and he pretended to look around for somewhere to throw his cigarette butt.

"Why do you say that? I've as much right as anyone here. Show my respects to her family."

Denis took another long drag from his cigarette. A few fat drops of rain fell, which Denis knew could either mean a heavy downpour or nothing at all.

"You and she were courting. I'd say the family might have something to say to you. Not today now. But her brother's out for your blood."

"Whatever Paddy Lynch says is a hat of shite. I wasn't very much to her. Of course, before I met Patsy, we had a bit of a thing. But it was just flirting. Nothing serious.

Denis continued to watch Martin closely.

"Not what I heard. Her sister Deirdre thought it might be a wedding and all. That's sounds pretty serious to me."

"Wedding? Maureen? God, no. It was never going to be that. Christ, Denis, you can't blame a little flirting for a woman drowning herself. Where'd we all be then? It's tragic right enough. But I was just part of her history."

"Very recent history Deirdre says. A few weeks ago even."

"She told you that? Well the girl's a… the girl's a fantasist. A couple of kisses after a dance and nothing else. I'd me eye on Patsy sure enough. That's just town talk. Feckin' Athlone's full of gossips."

"You're probably right. But she must have been in a bad way. Mixed up like. A broken heart and a baby."

"A baby?"

"So I heard. Probably just gossip. Town talk, you know."

Denis threw down the cigarette and extinguished it with the sole of his shoe. He redid the button on his shirt, pulled the tie back into place and walked off into the cemetery to talk with those still remaining by the newly dug grave.

Once Denis was gone, Martin Whelan reached like a drunkard for the wall behind him and fell back against it. When he'd heard of Maureen's drowning the memory of their time together - briefly - dimly lit a space in his conscience. But he soon reasoned that she'd have done away with herself at some stage in her life. If not because of him, then because of some other poor fella that she'd attached herself like a limpet to. And, feck knows, wasn't all fair in love and war?

But a baby. *His* baby? It would have to have been his baby. He couldn't stop thinking about what he'd lost. His child. She had killed his child. How could she do that? Why didn't she tell him? Give him a chance to put things right? What had she done to him for God's sake? Was that it – revenge? Her way of making him suffer by taking away something that was rightfully his?

The cigarette was nauseating and he threw it over the wall. His mind turned with a dizzying sensation of rage and hatred. That bitch. That feckin' whore had murdered my child.

When Carol, Patsy and Denis eventually stepped over the low breach in the white wall that led out on to the road from the cemetery, Martin was nowhere to be seen.

"I thought you said he was here?" Said Patsy.

"So he was. We were just talking. Perhaps he's gone ahead a bit."

77

Hope wondered if she should say something first. Neil was sitting forward on the bench, an elbow balanced on each knee and hands clasped so hard together that the skin turned pale at the tips of his fingers. The sulky Thames, barely moving, was tipped with the glints of pale yellows and mauves that it reflected from the evening sky.

Hope slumped back and studied her fingernails. What was she going to do about the nail on her right forefinger? It always broke so easily and she could feel a faint cleft already when she ran her thumbnail across it.

What was Neil going to do now? Speak? Or just get up and go back towards the car? Would he still give her a lift back? She wasn't even sure if Marlow had a train station.

Neil turned his head slightly to look downriver, disappointing Hope who thought that he would soon say something.

What could he say? Hope's unguarded answer to his question had brought a fantasy crashing down around them both. Lie after lie had meticulously been laid, one carefully resting on the other. She wasn't even sure why she had done it or where the whole deceit had started. But don't we all have layers of deceit around us? Perhaps she might say that to Neil. But, and she wasn't really sure why, she'd decided that Neil had to talk first.

She glanced again at her watch. Forty minutes had passed now. If she'd have been more careful then they would now be eating. This thought made Hope aware that she was hungry, which worried her a little. Her father always said that her being hungry always made her tetchy. "Just like your Mother," he'd invariably add.

Hope now recalled Neil's shocked face. Rather than show her the confusion and disgust he had felt when she failed to reply, he had turned and strode away, walking so fast that Hope was convinced that he would soon start running. She couldn't call after him. He might turn around and demand that she explain what she had said. She needed to think of something, something that would extricate her from this impossible position. She walked after him, but walked slowly, hoping that it might give her the time to think of a reason, of a way out.

At first she thought she'd lost sight of him. He'd turned down a small, twisting side road that soon swept him out of view; eventually the road gave way to a large public park. Hope carried on walking and, some two hundred meters ahead, there he sat on a riverside bench.

And this was how the evening was now playing out. She'd been so excited earlier at work, glancing at the office wall clock every few minutes, convinced that it was losing time until her wristwatch corroborated the fact that it was working. She'd imagined the conversations they would have, how she had so much to tell him since they'd last seen each other. She'd made herself promise to ask him all about his work, take an interest in what he did so that he would see how much she'd matured.

She could bear it no longer. She stood up and told Neil, "I'm going to get a train home." She feigned to be wiping something from her jacket, just to give him time to respond.

Neil didn't move at first and Hope now stopped the general sweeping action and pretended to be extracting a piece of grass, using her fingers as tweezers to do so.

"I'll take you home."

"No you won't! I'd rather drop dead first."

Now it was her turn to quickly walk away. After a few paces she stole a glance over her shoulder and was secretly gratified to see Neil walking after her.

"Hey! Hope! Don't…"

How quickly Hope's emotions could swing from remorse to hate. She hated Neil again. Hated him for exposing her, for making her feel so wretched. So she'd lied? Had he bothered to find out why?

"I'm not wasting any more of my evening with you," she cried back. She had wanted to say 'fucking' but felt it would have been just a little too coarse.

Neil said nothing now, but was walking a few yards behind, his feet scuffing the short summer grass.

"Why are you always lying?"

Hope turned and stared furiously at him.

"Wanna know? Really wanna know? No you don't. 'Cos you've got such a nice family. You come from such a nice family. What have you ever known about anything bad? Perfect parents. Perfect life. Perfect school. Perfect University. Perfect job. Know what I've had? Want to know what I've had? No you don't! And I wouldn't tell you. I wouldn't shatter your cosy fucking dream. I lied. There! I admit it. I lied. And if you knew what I knew then you'd lie too."

Hope walked on again, regretting that she'd sworn after all.

"You don't have to lie. Hope, stop walking off!"

But Hope strode away from him, carried forward by a sense of anger and vindication. In her outburst she had shown herself to be right. Yes, she lied, she created another life, but she needed to. Life was so awful. Life had been so awful. Why had she ever been excited about seeing Neil? He was nothing to her. Yes she had thought about him. Probably every day since their argument that night at the Lido. But he was just... he just...

Hope stopped suddenly. Neil, slightly breathless caught up and stood beside her, somewhat embarrassed by the events. She grabbed the back of his head and yanked him towards her, pressing her lips hard against his. Neil responded awkwardly at first, taken aback by the physical force of Hope's movements, but soon both bodies slowly relaxed and melted against each other. Neil pulled away and kissed Hope's neck, pulling her more closely towards him. Their lips met again and again, their kisses softened and Hope soon found her face buried against the folds of Neil's jumper.

"Oh God, Neil. We shouldn't have done this. We really shouldn't."

"You're not really going to marry him, are you?"

Hope briefly shook her head in answer. She was vaguely aware that someone with a dog was walking past them as they held on to each other on the pavement. She wanted to make love to Neil, such was the intensity of her desire for him. She breathed deeply in, taking in the scents of after shave and even the fabric softener of his sweatshirt.

"Still hungry?" Neil whispered.

"Not really. Are you?"

"I think so. Shall we try somewhere?"

Hope pulled away. "I must look terrible." She wiped a middle finger under her lower eyelid.

"You look wonderful, sunshine girl."

"I'll need to make a call."

"I thought he was football training or something?"

"He'll be back now. Have you a 10p?"

Hope found a call box on the High Street and Neil, tactfully, walked away and pretended to look in a Building Society shop window.

The money fell into the box and connected Hope's call.

"Hi Dad, it's Hope. I won't be back until tomorrow morning. Neil and I are in London and are probably going to a club later. Just wanted to let you know so you won't wait up."

78

Martin found Denis asleep in the front room and put down the paper he'd just bought for him. Rather than rouse him he opened the curtains and, even though the drizzling rain had deadened the day outside, the weak light crept quickly in and filled the room.

"Paper, Denis."

Denis looked startled as he came to. His foot knocked over an empty Mackeson's bottle and there was a metallic chink as it glanced the leg of the coffee table.

"Oh, Christ! What time is it?"

"Three o'clock. How long you been sitting there? The place is a tip."

Denis, sitting slowly up, closed his eyes again in an effort to control his headache.

Amongst the bottles lay several photographs that had fallen from Denis' lap. Martin took off his overcoat and stooped to pick them up.

"Memory lane, eh?" He then noticed that all of the photographs were of Stephen and cursed himself for his thoughtlessness.

"Three o'clock you say?"

"Gone three o'clock. Paper's there for you. If I'd known you were having a party I'd have come myself."

The watery slits of Denis' eyelids revealed veined, bloodshot eyes.

"How's Hope?"

"She's good. Patsy's taken her to some film now. Mary-I-don't-know-what. Mary Poppers? Yes, I think that's it."

Martin picked up some old newspapers from a chair and sat down.

"What have I done to deserve this, Martin? What did I do?"

"Ach, don't talk bollocks, Denis. She had a… I don't know. A turn or something. She's not herself. Not been herself for years. Not the Carol I knew anyhow. Not the Carol any of us knew."

"I'm just lost. I'm so lost. I really tried. And I… I wanted to make her so happy."

"For feck's sake, I know that. We all know that. It was nothing to do with you. She… just…"

Martin, grasping for something to say, could only let the words shrivel and fall in the air.

Denis panicked and looked around his chair. "There were photos…"

"Over there. On the table."

"I just can't come to terms with it. I can't make sense of it. I keep thinking it's a nightmare. The police. The funeral. The trial. I'm living this nightmare."

"Hey, Denis now. It's over. Where Carol is now, well, it's a better place for her. And Christ knows, I loved Stephen as if he were my own, it's a better place for the little man too."

"But murdering your own son…" A glassiness settled over Denis's eyes as he stared forward, not perceiving or feeling anything, his senses quite numbed by grieving.

Martin leaned forward, "Have you eaten? You've got to eat. For Hope as much as for yourself."

There was no response, so Martin tried again. "I know that this has all been hell for you, Denis. I know that. But you've got to make a new life for yourself. And who knows, one day Carol might be... well she might be released into your care sort of thing. So you've got to pull yourself together. Be strong for her. She's a sick woman; a very sick woman. So will you begin to help yourself? And help Carol? And help your daughter?"

Martin, exhausted of things to say, slumped back in his chair and looked out of the net-curtained window. Across the road, Martin could just see Dorothy Franks, Denis's neighbour from the opposite side of the street, returning home carrying a full tartan shopping bag.

Now that's a tin I'd love to rattle, thought Martin.

79

At first, as Hope looked around the long bar, she couldn't see Gavin at all. In fact, to her disappointment, it was Rhona whom she first noticed, moving her arms wildly to illustrate some story that was obviously giving her a great deal of enjoyment. Then Hope realised that the man she was regaling was Gavin, who had his back turned to her.

The hotel bar was dreary, not just because of the dim lighting, but also because the atmosphere hung leadenly within the huge open space. The khaki-coloured floorboards were burdened with tan leather sofas, small tables and abandoned chairs. Photographs of old Athlone were hung around the room in a desperate attempt to give the recently-built bar the gravitas of time. To Hope's left, a busying barman had placed down a beer mat and was now carefully placing a gin and tonic upon it. Some business men were stood at the bar, sharing depressingly racy stories whilst clocking anything remotely female that might drift into their line of sight.

Rhona noticed Hope and waved her arms frantically in the air, as if there was every chance that Hope would never be able to see her amongst the scattered groups of business drinkers. Hope chose what she thought was the right sort of smile and put it on. Not too enthusiastic, but sufficient to cover up the grimace that her face really wanted to adopt.

"Bon soir, Hope! Venez donc prendre une verre avec nous. Qu'est-ce que je vous offre?"

Gavin turned and seemed genuinely pleased to see Hope. He stood up and put an arm around her as she walked next to them.

"Can I get you a drink?"

Hope was still trying to translate what Rhona had just hollered at her, but gave up and looked up into Gavin's face with her widest eyes.

"White wine?"

"No," Rhona said, putting the flat of her hand against Gavin's chest, "Let me. My call."

"I'm sorry about the plane and everything. Something came up, I'm afraid."

Something came up. Who was it that used to say that? And then she shuddered with the seedy memory of Mr Reynolds and his battery of innuendos and *Carry On* jokes. "Sorry I'm late", he would announce to the small office, "Something came up." Nobody ever laughed but that never worried him. He seemed strangely impervious to any disdain about his manner.

"Yes, Rhona told me. Well, at least you were able to get here. That's all I was worried about. All set for tomorrow?"

Gavin took the drinks from Rhona and passed on the under-chilled white wine to Hope. Hope almost thanked Gavin with a throwaway 'Merci beaucoup' but, fearing another Gallic broadside from Rhona, offered a meek 'thanks' instead.

Gavin returned to Hope's question: "I think I've got everything. Have you brought the memory stick, just in case?"

"Of course. We'll need to sit down tomorrow and organise the sales figures for Keith. I don't know why he wants them now but his PA said something about it being very urgent."

Gavin raised his eyebrows in surprise. "Really? OK, let's do it when I get back."

"Oh, and Arthur Beljean needs you to call him. Just about the translation of those brochures. Have you had a chance to go into Athlone?"

"No. Might go for a walk later. Got stuff to do tonight and then a couple of phone calls. Didn't you say you had a link with here or something?"

"Mum and Dad. Well, Dad wasn't born here. He was born just outside the town. But the Dunne clan are all hereabouts."

"Are you going to visit them?"

"I don't think so. Only Dad comes over now. I haven't been for years."

"Were you saying you're from here?" interrupted Rhona.

"No, I said my family were from here, you nosey fat fucker."

"Oh, my mistake. It's a lovely place this. I love these Irish bars."

"You call this an Irish bar? It's about as Irish as the Berlin Wall. Just because they put sepia tinted photographs of Westmeath cottages with old black-smocked ladies sitting outside, doesn't make a bar Irish. But then it's probably about as authentic as your hair colour."

"That's what I heard. But I can't tell the difference. It's all Guinness to me."

"Have you eaten? Rhona and I were just talking about a quick bite. There's a bar menu which will be enough for me."

A bar menu. After all of her anticipation of eating somewhere intimate, staring across a table where the kindness of the candlelight smoothed out her seamed brow and eyes and would make her skin 21 again, she had to agree to a three-way bar meal with Gavin and the whale that was Rhona.

"That sounds ideal. I couldn't eat anything too heavy."

Gavin and Hope quickly chose a baked potato, but Rhona couldn't make up her mind.

"It's all very fattening."

"Then there won't be a problem because you're already the size of an industrial office block."

"You're right, I could replace the chips with salad. But salad's so boring."

Rhona then called the barman over and asked him if they did any other food besides what was on the menu.

"We can always put something together for you. Have you something in mind?"

"Not really. I mean it's all lovely but I was hoping for something…"

"I could ask the restaurant to bring it through. They won't mind. You can still eat it in here."

"Oh, would that be all right?"

"Of course. Shall I get the restaurant menu for you?"

"Oh, you're just divine. Are you sure it's not going to be a bother?"

The barman winked at Rhona and hared away from behind the bar.

"Give me a minute now," he called back.

"Isn't he lovely? Are all Irishmen that lovely?"

"Not all of them," replied Hope, now inwardly seething as the barman's departure meant that they would have to now wait longer before putting their order for food in.

"Excuse me, Ladies. Just need to recycle some of this beer."

Gavin walked off towards the toilet, leaving Rhona and Hope to wait for the returning barman with the other menu.

"How do you think Gavin is?" Rhona asked, peering over the top of her glass to look at Hope's reaction.

"Gavin? Fine. Why d'you ask? Is something wrong?"

"I should say so. Someone's told me he's been a naughty boy."

Hope shifted her position, physically trying to mask the desperate discomfort that had seized her.

"What do you mean a 'naughty boy'?"

"Oh come on, Hope. If anyone knows then you do. You're his eyes and ears. Don't tell me you haven't twigged."

"Sorry, Rhona, but I really can't be doing with gossip. What Gavin does is his affair." The irony of the last word was not lost on either Hope or Rhona.

"Maye it's all a bit to close to home, eh?"

"Have you been speaking to Barry Bufton?"

"Oh, so you do know something?"

"I know Barry's a… he just makes things up."

"Oh, he might, But I know what he told me is true."

Hope couldn't think what to say next. Was Rhona bluffing? Was her conversation cleverly designed to disabuse Hope of the belief that Rhona and Gavin had been secretly seeing each other? Or was Rhona merely telling the truth? Maybe she just had her suspicions and was manoeuvring to see if Hope might admit all? That it was Hope and Gavin who had been having an affair.

Mercifully for Hope, the barman returned and with a short bow and the address of 'Madam', gave the restaurant menu to Rhona.

"Oh, that's so wonderful of you. Thank you for doing that. You really shouldn't have."

The barman's face broke into a beautiful smile and then he glanced quickly at Hope, winked once more, before walking away, picking up a beer glass as he went and spinning it skilfully between both hands.

"Another Magners, sir?"

Hope followed him as he drew up smartly against the beer tap. She tried to think how old he might be, late 40s, early 50s? His dark brown hair was threaded with grey yet his skin seemed very youthful and smooth. His thin, tall frame moved quickly along the bar, preparing drinks for one group whilst asking the next in line for their order. How did he remember everything? Within a minute he would have poured a beer, taken an order, doled out change, passed the credit card machine to a customer, and still found time to greet people – some by their first name – and ask after the trivial events and happenings of their day.

Without warning, he looked across at Hope, who eventually had to look away, unable to meet his confident – almost insolent – stare.

"Do you know what?"

"What?"

Rhona looked up from the menu.

"Two things. First thing: I'm going to have the same as you. Second thing: I think that barman has the hots for you. He's staring at you right now."

"The barman?" Hope tried to look taken aback.

"Ah, oui, Mademoiselle. C'est le regard de l'amour."

80

"You're a rare one, Denis. I thought you were dead."

"Oh, hello Frankie. How are you? It's been an age."

Frankie looked at Denis with a peculiar smile on his face, his hands thrust deep into his pockets.

"It certainly has. So how come you're deigning to visit the town? Is it a romantic call?"

"Not at all. I've to see the Curristans about their herd. I wouldn't call that romantic."

"Right so. But I hear you've been seeing a lot of little Carol Maguire. Isn't that right?"

"I'm not rising to your insinuations, Frankie."

"Fancy a drink? I'll stand you a pint."

"Not really. I've these people to see. You know I normally would."

"Well 'normally would' now. Come on. I won't keep you ten minutes. Or have you forgotten all your friends now that you're nearly spliced?"

"Ah, why not. I'm a bit early."

Frankie put his arm around Denis's shoulders with an approving squeeze. "Good man now. Let's have one in the Oak. For old time's sake."

Denis always had mixed feelings about drinking during the day. The beer, he always claimed tasted better because his taste buds were still fresh. But he always added that he worked less in the afternoon because of it.

Frankie took off his cap and hung it on an adjacent peg.

"How's it with the farm."

"Could be better. Could be better now. How's it going at Gentex?"

"Grand. Mary's working there now as well. She loves it."

"She's a lovely girl."

"She is, right enough."

Frankie turned to lean on an elbow to look at Denis.

"And Carol? I'd say you were both seeing a good deal of one another."

"I see her when I can. No more, no less."

"Any plans?"

Denis drew hard on his bitter and, as he always did, inspected the foamy ring that marked off each long swallow.

"Not really."

"You know, Dunne, Athlone's not big enough for a man to keep a secret. Tell it to Mary in a whisper and Mary will tell it to the parish, as they say."

"We've nothing firm just yet. But I'm thinking of going to England. But I suppose you already know that."

"I had heard. And I also heard that you were to have company. Cigarette?"

Denis shook his head. "That's more of a dream than a plan."

"Well, if I were you, I'd make sure it stays a dream."

"Meaning what?"

Frankie shook the match and looked to the barman for an ashtray.

"Meaning that I think that Carol Maguire's a lovely girl but she's not right for you."

Frankie could see that Denis was offended and wondered if anyone else had already mentioned it to him.

"I think you've overstepped the mark, Frankie. Good friend or not."

"It's because you're a friend, and a good friend, that I wanted to speak to you. You know, there are some things which are sweet to drink but bitter to pay for. And there aren't many girls sweeter than Carol Maguire, but I know the family, believe me."

"What the feck are you talking about? Who gave you the right…"

"Hold it, hold it now… would you rather I said nothing?"

"I think I probably would."

"Look, calm down for Chrissakes. Listen to me. Just listen. Once I've said my piece I'll be done and you can see whom you like. Fair? Is that fair now?"

Frankie took Denis's indignant silence as an indication of a reluctant consent.

"My cousin Conor, you remember him? Lives out at Ballinasloe. Well he'd do this and that for old man Maguire. Put up a piece for him on the back of the house. Well, he would tell me some stories, I mean Deirdre's bad enough, but Carol."

"Like what?"

"It's... it's like she's in this dream world. That's what Conor said. Film star thing. She thinks she's going to be a feckin' film star."

"Maybe she might. Are you saying she's wrong to have dreams?"

"Course not. And God knows she's got the looks and everything. But Conor said it's like she's not there. Talking to you but not talking to you."

"And Conor's a psychologist is he? I mean, we can be sure he knows what he's talking about?"

"He's not joking. You know he's a good man. He never has a bad word for anyone. Oh, and he said she has these moods."

"Oh, so she has moods as well?" Denis couldn't hide the scepticism as Frankie persevered with his observations.

"Look, all I'm saying is people have noticed."

"No, Frankie. Conor has noticed. I've met her and been with her and she's a wonderful girl. Right, she's got her dreams. And right, they may come to nothing. But so have you and I. It's just our dreams are boring. Hers aren't – so we immediately think something's wrong with her. And what if she's a bit serious? I like a woman like that. I don't want a giddy woman. Sure there's enough of those in this town."

Frankie relented. "Well, maybe you're right. If it was any man other than Conor then I wouldn't have said a thing. Maybe the man was right, 'There is no cure for love other than marriage.' Hey, drink up now. You'll be late for your meeting."

They stepped out of the bar and both looked up at the shreds of grey-white clouds drifting serenely by. Young men, both conscious that life was drawing them in new directions.

"You know you're right, Frankie. It's been a while since I've seen you. Are you free on Monday? We can have a drink or two."

"I'll be there. Meet here first?"

"Meet here."

"No offence taken, Denis? About what I just said?"

"No. I'd have done the same thing me self, but Mary Tuohy's a decent enough woman. Look, I know she may not be perfect to you, but she's perfect to me. We're good for each other. If I'm taking a risk then, that's how it's got to be. To be honest, I have no choice. She's the girl for me really. There, enough said now."

"And arc you still set on England?"

"With her or without her. There's no future in Athlone."

"So have you proposed?"

"I have not. And I don't want to rush into things just yet. Here, what I told you in there, that's for you and I to know; I don't want it coming back to me from another direction."

"I'm a mouthy one all right, but I don't betray my friends."

Denis smiled and held Frankie's elbow affectionately.

"And see to it you don't."

81

Try as she might, Patsy couldn't get the cups to stand up on the red chequered plastic cover. The shingle of the beach was too uneven and, even though Martin had assured the group that this was the ideal spot, Denis suggested that it still might be worth looking elsewhere. A few yards from the small group, a gun metal North Sea was throwing a thin succession of waves listlessly against the shoreline, as if the vast, disinterested ocean was acting more out of habit than conviction.

"Here," said Martin irritably, "you pour the tea and I'll hold the cups. We'll be here all day otherwise."

"Do you want some pop, Hope?"

"Please, Dad." Denis poured out a glass of Fanta into a scuffed, highly coloured plastic beaker and gently pressed it into her hand.

When they had left the holiday home that morning it was in the hope that the clouds would give way to allow the heat of the August sun to stream through, but they had stubbornly remained and the long strip of oily cloud that crested the sea's distant horizon looked to all like a portent of heavy rain.

Eventually the three adults dug small wells in the stones to rest their cups, leaning across at intervals to take thin-lipped sandwiches and quarters of pork pie from the unruly plastic picnic sheet. As they looked out on the gently rolling ocean, they watched the shadows of the clouds spread like dark bloodstains on the surface of the water.

Hope sat beside Patsy, who had promised her that they would go in the sea together later. Almost fearing that the promise might be broken if she ventured out of Patsy's sight, Hope sat adjacent to her, resting her small sandaled feet on Patsy's shins.

"Did you see those darkies last night in the pub. You can't get away from them. I don't know what this country's coming too. You can't move in London with the immigrants. I hear there's shiploads coming in to Southampton. Bloody thousands of them."

"Martin! Watch the language with the child here. You're not in the bar now."

"Well, it really irritates me. There's darkies and Jamaicans and what nots pouring in and taking all the jobs. You can't get a bus in London without one of them telling you there's room upstairs."

Patsy looked at Denis and slyly rolled her eyes.

"There are places now you won't see a white face. You'd think you were in Bombay so you would. Not a white face to be seen anywhere. I know you don't believe me now, but if I were to take my wife to Southall, she'd be the only white woman for miles. There's a street there where they're selling all sorts of garlic and whatnot, not a cabbage or a potato to be seen."

"A woman can get fed up with cooking potatoes every day. Bit of variety would be a good thing."

"That's not variety, woman. And there's nothing wrong with a man having a potato on his plate when he comes home. Some of this darkie food, you couldn't tell what it was. Of course you know that that's *why* they have their curry? Did you know that? They have their curry 'cos the meat was so rancid that they had to make it edible. Now tell me, fine cook that you are, is that a suitable starting point for any meal?"

"I've nothing against them. My conductor is Indian and he beats any conductor I've ever had hands down. He's a decent man enough."

"Well he'll be decent to start with, but mark my words: they'll soon take over the country. They'll breed like rabbits, you watch.

Soon this country will just be a colony of Pakistan. That's what immigration will give you."

Patsy started to laugh, "Immigrants? Surely we're all immigrants. Hope's the only one born here amongst us. What does that make us?"

"We're not immigrants. Not like they are. We've the same skin colour. The same religion. Well, almost. The same God then. We look like each other. For Christ sakes, you could swim between the two countries they're so close. But these people, they're a different culture. They don't do things like we do. They belong in their own country and not here. You don't want to live with a lot of black men do you, Hope?"

"Hey," quickly interjected Denis, "Don't be dragging the child into it. Let it go and talk about something else."

But Martin wouldn't be deflected. "Something else? I'm not making this up. Are we to stop talking about something that she'll have to grow up dealing with? When was the last time you heard a good American singer that wasn't one of these black men – or women – singing about 'Baby, Baby' and that feckin' awful 'Da Doo Ron Ron' or whatever that pile of shit was. What's that supposed to be about? It's hardly Shakespeare is it?"

"Martin, I won't tell you again. Have you finished your pop, Hope? Shall we go for a swim? Come on."

Patsy led Hope away, helping her out of the small dress to reveal an already sagging swimming costume. The wind was now picking up, carrying fine spray against their faces. Far out to sea small white-tipped crests peaked and subsided.

"Keep with your Aunty Patsy, now." Hope, excitedly ran down kicking her feet at the water's edge.

With Patsy and Hope now paddling away from them, Denis began to remonstrate with Martin. "I still say we're all immigrants and I don't care where you're from. They came for the same reasons you and I did, to get work. If we'd stayed in Ireland, what would we be doing now? I'd still be shovelling cow manure and milking every day."

"Talk for yourself. I had a nice thing going back home. When I've made my fortune here I'm going back to Athlone. That's not being an immigrant, that's being an economic visitor. These darkies are here to stay, believe me."

"How do you know they're not, what did you call it... economic visitors? Maybe they have the same idea as you."

"I'll tell you why they don't have the same idea as me: they're bringing their mothers with them! Uprooting their poor mothers who, I might add, wouldn't have one word of English between a thousand of them, and living with them. How many Irish men have brought their mothers?"

"That's because most Irish men want to get away from their mothers. Seeing them once a year is bad enough."

"Oh, he is scant of news that speaks ill of his mother, Mr Dunne. Anyway, you're just muddying the water here and you know it. There'll be fucking hell to pay one day and no mistake. Thank God we've no worries about that back home. You wouldn't see Lemass letting the darkies in. Your man Wilson can't get enough of them."

"Well, I only go on what I see, and its live and let live' as far as I'm concerned."

"Let me tell you what I can see."

Martin stood up and pointed towards the Sizewell Nuclear Power Station; its large, brooding concrete shell dominating the beach to the north.

"Look at that now. Do you know who built that? I'll tell you who built that: the Irish. Not the Pakis. The Irish. That's what we bring to this country. Heat and light. There's our legacy big and proud. A fucking modern Cathedral."

But Denis had tuned out of the conversation and wished that it was Carol now splashing water on to Hope's legs, not Patsy. It was kind of Martin and Patsy to invite them to Thorpeness but he'd now regretted saying 'yes'. Perhaps he should have let them take Hope so that he could stay at home? He just felt that home was near Carol and he wanted to be – and feel - near to her. Visiting Carol, those precious moments of closeness, was probably more of a comfort for him than it was for her. Sometimes the medication she had taken was so severe that she almost didn't seem to recognise him.

Martin was sucking on a cigarette, pleased that he had had the opportunity to convince Denis of the perils of the immigrant invasion and to lay out his own thinking of what he would be doing when the 'dark invaders' were, in Martin's fevered mind, swarming over every inch of the country.

That night, as Denis was putting Hope to bed, she sat up and asked, "Daddy?"

"Yes, my angel?"

"You wouldn't let a black man take me away, would you?"

82

Hope's head lay on Neil's chest and both watched the orange glow from the artificial fire. She'd put her blouse on again after they'd made love; it felt like a token of modesty as this was still their first time. Neil's torso was already well defined and firm. It was, in contrast to Tony's bony frame, the body of a man. She smoothed her hand over his stomach, across his damp penis that still twitched as her hand ran across it and rested on his thigh.

"Why did you phone me, Neil?"

"Isn't it obvious? I've never stopped thinking about you."

"What did you think about?"

"Oh, why we'd never seemed to get together. Why you didn't like me."

"Didn't like you? I always liked you."

"Well you had a funny way of showing it. I was in pain for days after the last time we met."

Hope recalled jerking her knee into him and smiled to herself.

"Well, you were being a bit forward."

"I only wanted to kiss you. Is that being forward?"

It had all happened so quickly. Neil saying to Hope that his mum was away in Dawlish on a short holiday and would Hope want to go back and have a coffee before he took her home?

They had been kissing in the car after he had parked it up outside the house; the air inside Neil's Morris Ital heavy with arousal and desire. After he had opened the first door that led into a small glazed porch their kissing became heavy and urgent. Neil's hands had pushed inside Hope's clothes and long fingers were deliberately rubbing and pressing against her nipples.

Hope felt inflamed by animalistic desire to fuck him right there, turned on by the fact that anyone might walk by and witness their frantic love-making. The front door fell open and Neil pushed Hope hard against the hall wall, kicking the door closed with his foot. Clothes were soon discarded and Hope felt Neil's arms surround her to forcefully recline her on the stairs.

She breathed deeply as he entered her, kissing his hair and forehead feverishly and pulling at the skin on his back to try and enclose and embrace him completely. She felt herself lift and fall against the stairs as he took slow, deliberate thrusts into her. Her naked legs wrapped around him so that her feet came to rest on his small buttocks. She could feel herself sinking… sinking…

Neil and Hope were laying on the floor of the living room, both staring at a ceiling they could barely see in the dark.

"How long can you stay? Do you need to get home?"

"No, I'm fine. I told Dad not to expect me before I left. I told him that I might go on to Tony's after seeing you. His parents have a spare room."

"Christ, I forgot about Tony. How did he take it?"

"How did he take what?"

"When you phoned him earlier in Marlow."

"He wasn't happy. I'll call him again tomorrow and explain everything."

Hope had forgotten she'd told Neil in Marlow that she'd need to call him.

"And what about the wedding? Will you lose any money?"

Hope flinched at the rapidity by which her lies were being thrown back in front of her.

"We'd only got engaged. We actually hadn't fixed the date."

"I thought you'd told me June. That I could go to the reception in the evening."

"Oh, that's all loose plans. We'd still to confirm everything. Neil, I really don't want to talk about Tony. Not tonight. Not after what just happened."

"Sorry."

Hope pulled herself up and buttoned her blouse.

"So where do you live? You know, your flat."

"Oh, by Bloomsbury Tube Station."

"Is it nice?"

"Yeah, very nice. Nice area."

"Can I meet you there next time? Prefer it to here."

"Of course. I'm away for a couple of weeks in France, but I can call you as soon as I get back. Perhaps we could eat in town somewhere?"

"That would make a nice change. Tony and I don't seem to go out with all this saving up for the wedding."

"Let me call you at your Dad's. Fancy a drink? I think Mum's got some brandy in."

"Hmm, please."

"Tell you what, you go upstairs. Mum's room is straight ahead. I'll get a couple of glasses."

"Perfect."

"And don't worry about your blouse."

83

As Hope pushed the front door to, she called out to let her Mum know she was home. Her Mother appeared at the top of the stairs, dishevelled and still with her dressing gown on, seeming to point towards the front room or the front of the house. Hope wasn't sure which.

Hope took off her coat and gingerly opened the door to the front room. Inside she found Martin sitting with his head sunk into his shoulders. She instantly saw that he'd been drinking heavily.

"Is your Mother coming down to see me? She let me in and disappeared up the stairs like a frightened rabbit."

"Have you had some tea?"

"I don't want any tea. Have you a drink in the house? That's the only sort of tea I want."

Hope could see that another drink would only make his mood worse, so sat down to show that she wasn't going to add to however much he'd already had

"Is something wrong?"

"Oh yes, something's wrong all right. My wife of thirty-six years has gone. Just like that. Not a by-or-leave if you please. The bitch!"

"What do you mean gone? How do you know she's gone?"

"Because she fucking told me. As cool as you like. I got home last night and she wasn't there. I thought she'd gone shopping or something. The next thing, the phone rings and it's her. Telling me she'd moved out. Her leaving *me*! I should have left that barren cow years ago."

"Maybe it's temporary. Perhaps she just needed some space."

"Space? What fucking space does she need? I'm hardly ever there. I've been in the Middle East busting my gut and she says she's had enough of me. A woman couldn't have any more space!"

"I don't know what to say. Does Mum know?"

"As if I got a chance to tell her. She opened the door, saw it was me and skedaddled upstairs. Anyway, she's not all there. I can't get any sense from her."

"So you just thought you'd get plastered again."

"Wouldn't you get plastered? Your wife of, of… whatever it was runs off with someone else and you wouldn't take a drink?"

"How do you know she's run off with someone else? That doesn't sound like Patsy."

"Of course it's someone else. It has to be. And I'll wring both their bloody necks when I find them."

Maybe she'd finally had enough, thought Hope. Ever since she was a small girl, she'd watched leering Martin make passes at every woman he seemed to come into contact with. 'Just flirting' he called it. And Patsy had pretended not to notice. Poor, put-upon Patsy, who never had an unkind word to say to anyone. Saint Patsy. And now she'd finally come to her senses.

Hope rose from her chair.

"I'm going to make Mum a cup of tea. We've coffee if you'd prefer."

But Martin pretended not to hear.

"What have I done to deserve this? What have I done? I've supported that woman year in, year out. I've given her a home that any woman would be proud to live in. You've been there, Hope. You've seen it. I told her one day we'd live in Moor Park and I kept my promise to her. That house cost me a fortune. You don't get houses like that sitting around on your arse all day. You get it by working and, by God, I've worked for it. And what does that cow do? She throws it straight back in my face. Well, let her. I hope she's living in some dingy flat. She'll not see a penny off me.

I'd die first rather than give that bitch one farthing of what I've earned."

"Do you know where she's gone?

"Do you think I'd be sitting here talking to you if I knew where she was? I'd pull the bitch by her fucking hair back to our house if I knew where she was."

"I'd say you got what you deserved."

"Maybe I shouldn't, but wouldn't you drink? Thirty-six years of marriage."

"Well look at you now. Self-pitying and absolving yourself of all responsibility. Ask anyone to speak the truth to you and they'd say they'd have left a disgusting, lecherous old goat like you years ago."

"Ah, not coffee. I need something stronger. Are you sure you've nothing?"

"There's one tin left over in the cupboard. I'll see if it's still there."

"Oh, you have no idea how happy I am to hear you say that. God bless you."

Hope gave Martin the tin of beer and a glass and went back into the kitchen and started to make the tea. She opened the fridge door to get the milk when she saw a half-empty bottle of white wine from the weekend.

She poured herself a generous glass and raised it towards the back door window.

"To Patsy!" she whispered.

"Oh fuck!" she heard Martin exclaim, desperately, in the front room. "I've only gone and spilt the beer."

There was no mistaking the fact that Gavin looked very distracted when they sat down to eat. An unsmiling waitress placed cutlery and paper serviettes on their table.

"Thank you, love." said Rhona, cheerfully, unaware that the service seemed almost resentful. She caught Hope's eye and raised her eyebrows conspiratorially.

"How's Thuong?" asked Hope.

"Hmm? Oh good, thanks."

"And the children?

"Oh yeah, they're fine."

"So how long have you been speaking French?"

Hope was ashamed to reply that, barring a few learned words and short phrases, she didn't. But she also didn't want to talk to Rhona and ask her why her French was so good. Faced with the dilemma, she chose the honest response.

"I don't speak French. Well, just a 'petit peu'.

"But you'll often use French words."

"No, silly childhood thing. Don't know why I do it really."

Rhona turned to Gavin. "Any languages, Gavin?"

"Just bad language. No, not really. Schoolboy stuff. Restaurants and that."

"I worked in France for a couple of years. It's great because you're surrounded everyday by it. People speaking it. Road signs. So you soon pick it up."

Gavin interrupted: "Rhona, have we got the utilisation figures for tomorrow? I need to nail those down before we go in."

"I've covered all that. I doubt that Declan will want to go into that level of detail."

But Gavin didn't seem to be looking at Rhona, his mind seemed wholly taken up by something else.

Hope realised that, just maybe, Rhona and Gavin weren't seeing each other. But that call on the way to the conference, who was he speaking to so intimately? Maybe it *was* Thuong. But that didn't seem to hang together somehow. He'd seemed agitated that day, as if he'd been told something that had shaken him. The old, self-assured Gavin was missing. They were meant to drive back from Bristol together when the conference was over but he'd found an excuse to stay behind.

To Hope's dismay, she suddenly realised how closely Gavin's face resembled Neil's. Neil. Where was he now? How had life treated him?

"Well, what a couple of right dreamers you are! I feel I'm on my own here. Hello! Rhona to Ground Control! Speak to me! It's like a séance at this table."

"Grub's up," announced Gavin.

The surly waitress deposited the plates petulantly in front of them. She had just turned to go when Rhona called after her.

"Have you a wee bit of ketchup there?"

"No problem," the waitress replied, yet looking like the very request had burdened her short life immeasurably.

The meal limped on and it wasn't long before Gavin made his excuses to them both and left. By this point a succession of glasses of wine had lightened Hope's spirits and she found herself actually warming to Rhona's seemingly unquenchable thirst for life.

"So that thing you were saying about Gavin. What did you mean?"

"Well, Barry Bufton said that you'd told him that you and Gavin were… you know?"

"No, I don't know. Me and Gavin were what?"

"An item," Rhona whispered. "Doesn't bother me. You're a big girl and what's private is private."

The alcohol had deprived Hope of her normally cautious approach. She was feeling much more open with Rhona.

"I thought it was you."

"Me! Are you having me on? With Gavin? Me? Oh, no offence…"

"Why should I be offended? I'm not doing anything with him. He's not my type."

"Well, that's the last time I listen to Bufton. Goes to show…"

But Rhona couldn't think what it was exactly that it did 'go to show', so left the sentence hanging. But soon her energy welled up again and she placed her small hand on Hope's arm.

"But you've got to admit, he's not himself. He wasn't great company on the plane. I thought he'd something to tell me. At first I asked him if he were worried about the sales figures but he said his and Arthur's regions were fine. So, I thought, it can't be that."

"Maybe he's got marriage problems."

"Might be. Always look like the golden couple to me but you never can tell. She's a beauty, though. A bit brittle perhaps, but a real stunner."

It depressed Hope to hear Rhona talk so glowingly of Thuong. She offered a weak "Certainly is" in reply, but did relish the idea that the relationship might be fracturing.

The gradual thinning out of the bar's patrons seemed to prompt the same idea in Rhona who, draining her glass, declared that she best be going up to phone "her better half".

Hope said that she would finish her nearly full glass first, before also going back to her room. Rhona insisted on their hugging before she left, something which Hope found a little uncomfortable but, now past caring tonight about such things, responded in kind.

What a strange day it had been. First, Gavin failing to show up at the airport and the depths she had plunged to as she was driving back to Athlone. Then the appearance of Rhona in her room, before, finally, witnessing Gavin's strange behaviour. And then suddenly recalling Neil so strongly. True, she still thought of him most days, despite the passing of so many years. Was that why she wanted Gavin? Was he merely a substitute for someone – the only one – who had made her life so immediate, visceral and real?

"You're not from round here."

The barman's question took Hope completely by surprise.

He skilfully gathered up the empty glasses and placed them on a tray he'd placed on Rhona's chair.

"How did you know?"

"Well, I'll have definitely remembered someone like you now."

He flirted so winningly, so easily. Hope found herself enjoying it.

"Well, you're right, I'm not from round here. But my Mum and Dad are from the area. I'm here on business."

The barman sat down, looking first over his shoulder to check that he wasn't needed at the bar.

"I knew you were Irish! You can take the girl out of the bog, but you can't take the bog out of the girl."

"You just said I wasn't from round here."

"Wrong choice of phrase. I meant you don't live here now. But you're an Athlone girl right enough."

"I bet all the women you talk to get that old line. The one about the girl and the bog.

But he ignored her question.

"You've got freckles! My mother said…"

"I know. 'A face without freckles is like a sky without stars'. I've heard that a hundred times."

"Guilty, but there was never a woman who demonstrated that old saw as beautifully as you."

"A saw?"

"A saying. A proverb. Do you not know your own language?"

"Obviously not."

"Then I put myself at your service. Why don't I take the opportunity tomorrow night to treat you to a little dinner and we can visit the glories of the English language whilst we eat."

"Sorry…"

"The name's Cormac and, if you know your Irish history, he was the most famous of the ancient kings of Ireland. It's a severe mantle I must carry, but I do so with good grace."

"Well Cormac, it's very kind but I've…"

"That's sorted then. I'll call for you in Reception at 6pm. Sharp. Don't be late now!"

He whisked the tray of glasses from the chair and was soon chatting amiably to a waiting customer at the bar.

Hope felt a deep flush pass over her. She'd just been 'chatted up' by a strange good-looking Irish man and she'd enjoyed every second. He was so confident, so good with words. He was so…

So like Martin Whelan.

85

"Oh, Denis, I can't tell you how delighted I am!"

Patsy threw both arms around him and pulled him close.

"Carol, you don't look very happy about it all? It's an exciting day!"

"Oh, it's the shock of it. I still can't quite take it in."

Patsy looked at them both beaming with pleasure.

"Do you want a boy or a girl? I put money on it you want a boy, Denis?"

"No, I've no thoughts either way. Here, let me see if we have any of that brandy left from Christmas. This calls for a little…"

Denis was on his knees, his hand searching out the bottle in a low kitchen cupboard.

"You'll need a bigger place. You can't bring up a child in a little flat like this. Not with the damp and everything."

Denis held up the brandy bottle like a trophy.

"Ta-ra! Now, we've two glasses and I'll have mine from a cup. Hold on while I pour."

"Well, this is such news for you both. I'm so jealous. Martin and I have been trying for so long but, God willing, we'll be following you soon."

"Here we go. Carol, want to make a toast?"

"Oh no, you do it, Denis."

"Right so. Well, here's to the boy – or girl – and may he – or she – have a long and blessed life. Cheers!"

"Cripes, that's a bit much for the morning. But, well, it's a special occasion."

"Have you thought of names yet? What will you call it?"

"Oh Denis, I think I'd better go and lie down for a bit. Sorry, Patsy, perhaps it's all a bit too much for me."

"Of course. And I hope this man here is going to look after my lovely sister. Mr Dunne, don't be neglecting your fatherly duties!"

Carol hugged Patsy and gave her hardly touched drink back to Denis.

"You finish this, love. Just give me an hour or so. See you, Patsy."

"You take care of yourself now."

"Denis, don't let me sleep too long."

"I'll be in later with a cup of tea. Go and lie down."

Patsy sat at the kitchen table and hung her handbag off the back of the chair. The small kitchen was part of a flat in a house that had once been grand and spacious. Where once it had served handsomely for a middle class early Victorian family just moved to the spreading and leafy development of Kilburn, it now housed five different sets of occupants. Denis and Carol's flat was at the back of the first floor, their kitchen affording a view of a small, overgrown garden that housed greenery such as a sink, the front wing section of some long forgotten car and a recently discarded mattress.

"How's she been?"

"Oh, up and down. She went for an audition. Someone Martin had put her on to. Well, it didn't go well. There's not much more to say."

"Is she still sticking with this dancing thing? I'm afraid my sister was always the dreamer in the family."

"Well. I'd say that dream has ended. I don't know what happened but she just seems to have given all that up. When we first moved here it was like living with a linnet in the flat. Now I don't even hear her humming to herself. Not a peep."

"She'll come to her senses. You know I tried to have a talk with her? About all the dancing thing. I told her she's great, but she's not great enough. Sure, Athlone's a small enough town, and it's so easy to make yourself stand out there. But London..."

"I think she's wonderful. And if she has ambition then I'm all for it. But, between ourselves, it's kind of hollowing her out. Do you know what I mean? She just seems empty. Perhaps this baby will change her. Give her something new to think about. God knows she could do with something."

Patsy put her hand behind her and felt in her bag for her cigarettes.

"Would you mind if I had a smoke?"

"Course not." Denis walked over to the small, mould ringed sash window and jerked it up.

"Look at us now. Drinking and smoking and it's only just gone ten! Here's something for your ashtray."

A small saucer was placed by Patsy's tumbler of brandy.

"So, have you thought about names?"

"If it's a boy, we thought Stephen. If it's a girl, we might go for Hope."

"Hope? That's not a very Irish name."

"Who said it had to be Irish? Besides, we don't live in Ireland. We live in England, so let's do something a bit different."

"Don't tell Martin. He'll think you're betraying the cause."

Denis laughed. "I'm sure he would. But that only makes me more determined."

"Maybe I'll get used to it. But you've a long time – God willing – so you might change your minds yet."

"We might. But it seems, I don't know, apt."

"Well good luck in getting it past the Father Cooney. He'll want a list of saints' names following it."

"Anyway, it's probably going to be a boy. I'm from a family of fellas so let's not get too carried away."

"What's Stephen the patron saint of?"

"I haven't a clue. Carol said that the only thing she ever remembered from school is that they stoned him to death."

"Perhaps Hope isn't such a bad name after all."

86

Hope looked once more at the calendar; it confirmed what she already knew, it was now over three weeks since she had seen Neil. She recalled that he had said that he would only be a couple of weeks in France. Perhaps he left later than he'd originally planned? His new job was probably always like that, things chopping and changing at the last minute. There was the other, worrying and dark consideration which was always eating away: perhaps he'd just wanted a fling. Had she committed herself too early? Perhaps she should have played more 'hard to get'?

She'd promised to walk to Mass with her father and took a light jacket off the back off the settee, where she'd discarded it the day before. It was rare that she went to Mass these days, preferring to use the excuse that she would stay and look after her Mum, who rarely left the house.

Denis came heavily down the stairs, deciding that the weather didn't warrant a tie: as much a sign to Hope that it was summer as fresh strawberries or the ever-circling flies in their front room.

"Have you locked the back door, Hope?"

And Hope, still looking at the calendar, nodded that she had.

"Have you a couple of pound for the envelope?"

"I've done it already. There by the phone."

"You're a good girl. Let's go."

The warmth of the day was already rising in the air as they closed the garden gate behind them. Denis, as always, made sure that Hope walked on the inside of the pavement, taking up his position without even thinking.

"So it's still all off then, this wedding?"

"All off. Like I said, I just… I couldn't go through with it."

"Well, it took me and your Mother aback, I must tell you. He was a nice enough boy. The Lennons are decent people. But, you know your own mind I dare say."

"Will they be at mass?"

"The Lennons? I shouldn't think so. They're early risers. Usually at the eight-thirty. But you're going to run into them sometime."

"I know. Just not yet."

It was an easy pace as they walked together, both taking in the houses as they strolled past, saying 'hello' to the occasional person they knew. Denis surveyed the gardens whilst Hope peered through the windows that didn't have curtains or nets drawn across. Denis was genuinely disappointed that he'd no longer be seeing Tony, whose company he always enjoyed. They traded football and other sports gossip and even enjoyed *Match of the Day* together if he had brought Hope home late on a Saturday night. The relationship had grown so easy that, as soon as he heard them come in the back door, Denis would be reaching for the ring pull of a new beer can to pass to Tony.

"How did he take it?"

Hope recalled his astonishment as she broke the news. How he had kept repeating what she was saying, unable to accept what he was hearing.

"We both knew it was for the best. It was just a case of 'when' really."

"Well, what with all the wedding arrangements, you both seemed enthusiastic enough."

Hope could tell where this conversation was leading: Denis was unconvinced about Hope's explanations. These questions were his attempt to get to the truth and Hope recognised his quietly interrogative manner.

"Don't go thinking there's more to it than there is, Dad. Couples are always breaking up. Some break up on the morning of the wedding. There's nothing unusual in Tony and I calling it a day. Look at all you've had to put up with. I bet there isn't a soul at work who knows what you've been through. You're the best actor of all."

"You're telling me to shut up. Right, no more questions. But he was a grand young man."

"He still is. And someone's going to make him a lovely wife, but it won't be me. That's all."

"Well don't go rushing into something else. Give yourself time."

"Oh, Dad. As if I would. I need a break. I'm not going to go careering back into another relationship. Not after what just happened."

"Anyway, who am I to give advice? I've only ever loved your mother so I'm hardly the expert."

Hope leaned across and kissed his cheek. "You're my expert."

"I forgot to mention, there was a call last night. Whilst you were at the pictures. I've a mind like a riddle."

Hope responded with a cool, "Oh yes?" even though she instantly felt a fluttering sensation in her stomach

"It was that same fella. The one that called a few weeks ago. I forgot all about it 'til I saw the envelope by the telephone pad back at home. Should have mentioned it then."

It had to be Neil. Please let it be Neil.

"Who was it?"

"He didn't say. Said he'd call back today. I wrote out his number for you. But it was the same one."

Hope realised that her bluff about the demise of her and Tony's relationship had just played straight into the hands of her canny Father. He knew she was seeing someone else and had been artfully playing her along.

"Oh that's probably just Neil. The one I used to go to school with. He said he might call back."

"Now look at those. They're a beautiful colour. Hybrids possibly. I wonder how he gets them to flower so early."

"Did he leave a message?"

"I don't think so. Just to call back today. Neil you say? Not Mrs Dowling's Neil? The University lad?"

"Yes, that's him. Nice. You'd like him."

As they neared the grounds of the church, which sat incongruously amongst the surrounding houses like a slumbering spaceship, they found themselves gradually subsumed into the growing number of people making their way to Mass. Denis and Hope started to thread their way through the parked cars so that they could enter the church through the side door, allowing Denis to get to his favoured pew to one side of the altar.

It was just as Hope was about to pass through the door that she was struck by something she'd just seen. Stepping back a few steps she looked again to make sure. It was a Morris Ital. Neil's Morris Ital.

"She's frightening! Hang on to your hats!"

Jamilla, eyes wide in mock terror, had walked dramatically back into the office. She threw her notebook on her desk and sat upright, still with the same stare on her face.

Hope looked up, irritated by what she saw as Jamilla's constant need for attention.

"Who is?"

"That Liz Clancy. She is ice!"

"Oh, her." Hope pretended not to be moved and returned to the email she was writing.

"I mean it. You know what they've brought her in for, don't you?"

Jamilla drew her forefinger across her throat.

"I dare say she has. She can fire the lot of us for all I care. She probably will."

"You mean that? You think she will?"

"Sorry, Jamilla, I've got to get this email out to the team."

Martina entered holding a bottle of coke. Hope still couldn't see any change in her figure. Maybe she's done the unthinkable, she concluded; that's the way to get the tide of leering men beating the path to her desk again.

"Martina, do you know who I just met?"

Martina was concentrating on unscrewing the cap of her drink.

"Don't know. Who?"

"Liz Clancy. The new Director. Keith's replacement. She is *scary*."

"How scary?"

"Icy scary. White witch scary. Eat your children scary."

Martina became interested. "When did you meet her?"

"In the project meeting. Everyone was frightened of her. You could have heard a pin drop! I mean it, it was so tense."

"What did she do, put a spell on them?"

"No. She just sits there and asks questions. 'Where did you get those figures?' 'Why has this taken so long?' Gary Vaughan was taken apart in his presentation. Taken apart I tell you. 'Where is the justification for that deadline?' 'What made you think the customer would ever pay for that?' Oh, it was embarrassing."

"Gary Vaughan? From Project Management? I've never seen him look flustered."

"Oh, believe me, he was flustered. He'll have sleepless nights before he sees her again. Sleepless nights."

"She's only human," said Hope. "She's just trying to make her mark. Show the men she's not afraid of them by trying to be like them. She'll calm down."

Martina became visibly irritated by Hope's observation. "I don't agree. Just because a woman is strong doesn't mean she's 'being a man'. You Brits always say the same thing. A tough man manager is just a tough man manager. But a woman manager who's tough is a bitch. It's bad enough when the men go round saying such things. But women who go round saying it are the pits."

"I don't remember calling her a bitch. Did I call her a bitch? Jamilla, did you hear me say that she was a bitch?"

"Oh Hope, of course you didn't."

"I said that she's acting like a man. Throwing her weight around so that they know they won't be able to take advantage of her. And good luck to her, 'cos she's going to need a lot of it."

Martina placed down the coke bottle – its cap still in place.

"We do not have to behave like men to be on level terms with them. That statement is what holds women back in this country. And the fact it comes from a woman makes it worse.

"So if things are so bad in this country, why are you here?"

"I beg your pardon?"

But Hope had committed herself too far now. Day after day, month after month, she had sat seething with a bitter resentment. All those years ago, when she had first joined Jupiter Rent a Car in that summer of 1984, it had been almost entirely populated with British staff: white white-collar working people. 'Foreigners' were people who worked for the company overseas. For Hope, they existed as variations of their national stereotype: the Scots were mean, Germans were humourless and abrupt, the French smelled of garlic. Her world conveniently consisted of eyeties, spicks, wogs and little-Johnny-foreigners. But gradually – as each successive year dragged by - all had changed. At first, it was young second and third generation Indians and Pakistanis that started to occasionally appear in the offices. Then came the Greeks, Polish, Lithuanians, Italians, Spanish, Romanians, Bulgarians…

"You heard. No one made you come here. But you're only here because we gave you a job. More than you'd get in your own country…"

"Hope, what are you saying..?" It was Jamilla, trying to ease the tension.

"I'm saying that… I'm saying that…"

Hope slumped back in her chair.

"What am I saying?

Martina's face had turned red in anger. "I'm going to HR. I am going to let them know what I have just heard. Jamilla, you're my witness. You heard what she just said!"

To Hope's horror, she knew that it could have been Martin Whelan speaking. His poisonous thoughts had seeped into Hope's soul and thinking; she was now his mouthpiece from beyond the grave. Years of listening to the bile of his thinking had left a stain on her. This was now Hope Dunne: bitter, resentful of life, entirely devoid of whatever promise she once had. Her eyes brimmed with tears as she stared across the small office.

Jamila had left with Martina to try and comfort her and persuade her to change her mind. The office was empty and Hope suddenly felt very alone. Friendless. Hopeless.

88

Patsy put the tumbler of whiskey on the small table by Denis' chair.

"Here now, love. Drink some of that."

"Do, Denis. We all need something medicinal this evening." Martin drained his own glass and raised it towards Patsy for some more.

"Where's Hope?"

"Now don't worry about Hope. She's next door with the Williams. They're great with her. They've little girls themselves.

"But what do I tell her?"

"We'll work that one out later. Carol told her she'd have to go away."

"No, she didn't. Carol told her she was going to heaven."

"Well, leave that one to me. It's probably not a good thing for her to go home straight away anyhow. You know you're welcome to stay here too, Denis."

"Why did they put her in jail? Could they not see it's a hospital she needs? I can't bear to think of her in a jail."

Martin, unsure what to say, stared down into his drink. Eventually he felt he had to try and say something. "Well, Denis, when a mother… kills her son, that's all they'll see. We know that Carol's been ill. But that just doesn't seem to be enough for them."

Patsy could see that it would be down to her to try and find some light, some glint of hope, in the misery of the situation.

"She'll only be in prison for a short time. You see now, they'll realise she's ill and put her in a hospital. Pray God they do."

Denis sat forward and, with elbows on his knees, joined his hands over the back of his head and rubbed slowly.

"I have to see her. I've got to see her."

"We can go into all that tomorrow. You'll see her and… and who knows? They might cut the sentence or something. They're always doing that. She'll be out in a few years and you can start again. Move somewhere else. Don't stay in Ruislip. There's lovely places they're building now. You'd get a lot for your money elsewhere."

"She's right, Denis. And you know I'll help. I have a bit put by. A fresh start would do it. Patsy's right."

"I need to be near Stephen's grave. It's Hope's home. It's our home. It's the home I want her to come back to."

Patsy and Martin exchanged glances, tacitly accepting that the best they could do was to just be with Denis.

"Why did I not see it? Why did I not get help? She only needed help."

"None of us could see it. Christ, I told Patsy Carol was always depressed. I thought it was just something she'd get through. None of us thought she'd do what she did. God love her."

"Oh I saw it, all right. But I didn't want to look. I just couldn't bear to look. She kept saying she was seeing things. I told her, Carol, love, there's nothing there. Look, I said. Nothing. But there was something there, wasn't there? Oh, I couldn't see it. But she could. It was there all right."

Patsy sat on the arm of Denis' chair and put a hand on his shoulder.

"Do you need to lie down, Denis? It's been an awful day."

Denis lurched up and stood unsteadily upright.

"Actually, I need some air. Excuse me."

He walked slowly to the living room door and looked back at Martin and Patsy. Too stunned to weep, eyes shadowed with a quiet despair.

"Thank you both."

They heard their front door softly close and said nothing, unable even to look at each other. After almost a minute had passed, Martin threw back his whiskey in one noisy gulp.

"Look what that fucking twisted sister of yours has done to that man."

89

Hope had regretted bringing such a limited choice of clothes to Ireland with her. The trip was only meant to be for three days and most of what she had brought had already been used. She took the suit jacket off deciding that it was too formal for a date.

She sat on the end of the bed and studied herself in the long hotel room mirror. What was she doing, preparing to go out on a business trip date? What for? Was she ever going to see him again, this Cormac, King of the Irish? Wasn't he just the sort of man who preyed on women like herself? He'd probably developed the radar that allowed him to spot the vulnerable, the lonely and the emotionally needy. They probably appeared on his scanner from the moment they entered the bar. Perhaps they looked around too much? Smiled too much? Tried to please whomever they talked to too much?

Hope couldn't look at herself any longer and looked through the windows instead. It was the same fields of course, but the sunlight was brighter and had lifted and intensified the colours of the countryside.

She took a small bottle of wine from the minibar and poured it into a slim tumbler. It was five thirty. Still had half an hour or so. Didn't want to turn up early or on time. That would send the wrong signal.

The taste of the wine mixed a little with her lipstick. She knew she drank too much now. In fact, she tried to think of the last time she hadn't had a drink. Looking down at the small glass of wine she was aware of a long-distant memory, but she couldn't grasp its tail. What was it? A night recently or from her youth? It was pleasurable, that much she could remember.

She really wanted a bar of chocolate, but knew it would probably kill her appetite, especially if the plan was to eat early. What if he was a killer? He had the smoothness and patter of a 1920's bounder. An easy charm that was so unforced that Hope had succumbed all too easily to it. She'd need to tell someone. Then she could let him casually know that people knew she was with him. Rhona? Despite their closeness last night, she wasn't sure it was the right thing to do. Besides, she'd woken up this morning unconvinced about Rhona and Gavin, despite Rhona's insistence the previous evening.

She could phone Gavin. That would show him! Now he'd see that she wasn't some adoring thing that was waiting for him to click his fingers for her to then run to him. Yes, she'd tell Gavin. She reached for her mobile and speed-dialled him.

"Hullo."

"Hi Gavin. Did you have a good day?"

"Yes, not long back from the meeting. I think we're there with the contract. They certainly seemed happy with what we'd proposed. Rhona was excellent. They really like her."

Hope was surprised when she realised that her usual vitriolic response to any praise given to Rhona didn't kick in. Maybe she wasn't his 'amour' after all.

"That's good. All set for getting away tomorrow."

"Yeah, nearly all done. I have to see Keith at nine but that won't take long. Rhona's staying on so it will just be you and me going to the airport. Still got the car?"

"Yes. Rhona can return the other one."

"Hope, there's something I need to ask you. Are you free this evening. Just needed to have a quick chat."

Why hadn't he called her 'Hopey'? The old Gavin would always have used that affectionate address when asking for something. It was always his usual way of inveigling his way past her defences. What did he need to talk about? Was this the chance she had hoped for? Would she, in two hours' time, be resting her head on her hand looking lovingly into his soulful brown eyes?

"What about?"

"I'd rather talk about it to you in person. Would you mind?"

"Well, I was due to go out for dinner this evening."

"Oh, really? Who with?"

Hope didn't like the manner with which he'd said that. It had a tone of surprise she found slightly insulting.

"A friend. To be honest, I'm supposed to be meeting him at six."

"No, you go. Maybe we can talk about it tomorrow. That would be better anyway. I'm not feeling too bright."

"I could cancel…"

"Course not. That would be wrong. You go and enjoy yourself. Why don't we meet up for breakfast again?"

When Hope had thrown the mobile on to her bed she remembered her glass of wine and picked it up. Had she just blown the one chance she would ever have? But, strangely, there was something suddenly unappealing about Gavin. The thought of him holding her for real, undressing her for real and she undressing him, now all seemed quite appalling.

What had she been doing for the last three months? What had she been doing with so much of her lonely life? When was the last time that she had lain naked next to a man? Was it all over? Was that it? Marginalised by life to remain in a constant, secret state of fantasy until the last vestiges of her beauty slipped behind creases, varicose veins and limbs heavy with the mottled, chicken skin of old age?

She reached for her jacket and held open the hotel room door. And paused.

90

It was warmer than Patsy had expected and she now regretted having brought her overcoat. She looked again at her watch and saw that she was a little too early. The bridge across the Serpentine in Hyde Park , the rendezvous for her meeting with Hope at 11 o'clock, was busy with a small group of well-mannered, elderly Japanese tourists who seemed to be part of some walking tour.

"Patsy?"

Patsy turned to see Hope walking towards her. She should have known that Hope would be early also. They hugged warmly without speaking for almost a full minute, small tears running down Patsy's face and on to the shoulder of Hope's jacket.

"Look at me? I must look a right mess?"

"Here, have one of these." Hope pulled out a small bag of tissues.

"I'm sorry. I'd told myself I definitely wasn't going to cry, and now look at me!" Patsy laughed and sniffed before holding the tissue to her nose.

"How have you been? Why haven't you been round?"

"Oh, because Martin might be there. I couldn't cope with that."

Hope noticed that, even though Patsy's eyes were a little red from the few tears she had just shed, she was looking remarkably fresh and smart. Underneath her coat, Hope could see a simple, well cut blouse that co-ordinated perfectly with a patterned skirt and new shoes.

"You're looking so much better. Are you on the way to somewhere?"

"You're not the first person to say that. Marriage to Martin is a funny thing. The more he tells you that you've lost your youth, the more you believe him. I must have looked a sight."

Hope recalled the endless line of large cardigans that Patsy had worn that she had always just thought were Patsy's 'thing'. Barring social events, Patsy had always dressed in muted or neutral coloured clothes that flattened the lines of her figure.

"Mum was asking after you. She's been worried."

"How's she coping? She wasn't too good when I saw her last."

"The doctor has given her some new medication. That's helped."

"Shall we walk? I could do with talking to someone. I wouldn't mind finding somewhere for a cup of tea later."

Hope had been surprised to receive a call from Patsy at work the day before. Her mind, being Friday, had been thinking about weekend TV and a promise she'd made to herself to begin decorating her bedroom.

Patsy had been calm when she answered, telling Hope that she couldn't talk for long as she was in a call box, but would Hope be free to meet? Patsy had insisted that it wouldn't be anywhere near Ruislip, so they eventually agreed the bridge over the Serpentine and shared a brief joke that it had sounded like they were in MI5.

Hope had enjoyed the journey to Lancaster Gate, and then found the unexpected walk through the park strangely comforting and peaceful.

After walking for a little, they sat on a bench that gave them a fine view of the calm Serpentine water, its surface skimmed and smoothed by a thin breeze.

"Your Mother was here once. Said she came after an audition. I think she told me in the secure unit one time. I think she'd been trying get into some show or something?"

"Mum? In a show?"

Patsy sighed. "Did you not know? Oh yes, she was quite the 'hoofer' when she was young. And a powerful voice too. Not that anyone would know it."

"She never told me."

"What does she tell anybody? You've only ever known her as she is now; the family's 'dark secret'. But she was once very different."

"I've seen her wedding photos. But there's not much else."

"Well, people didn't take photos like they do these days. But she was a fine looking woman."

"Martin was over last week. He's still very angry."

"He'll get over it. Does he know you're meeting me?"

"I haven't told him. Do you want me to?"

"No. I'll keep out of his way for a good while yet. I've no wish to see him."

"I couldn't believe it when he told me. I came home from work a few weeks ago and he was there in our front room. Really drunk. He couldn't take it in. "

"I bet he told you I'd run off with someone?"

"Something like that."

"The arse. He wouldn't be able to bear the fact that he was the reason I'd left. He thought I'd always put up with him and his philandering. He's an ego the size of a planet."

"Where are you living? Have you got somewhere?"

"With a friend from work. She's a flat in Edgware. Bit of a come-down, eh? From Moor Park to a little room in someone's house. But it's done me a power of good."

"What will you do next?"

Patsy pursed her lips before she answered.

"I'm going home. I want you to tell Denis and your Mam but no one else. I've no family but you and your Mum here. Over the years I've put a little by when I could. Now I have the money, I mean to start over. There it is. That's what I wanted to tell you."

"Where will you live? In Athlone?"

"No. I've somewhere on the coast. There's nothing for me in Athlone any more. I'll send you the address. There's a telephone there so you must promise to phone. Will you do that for me?"

Hope nodded and now found that she, too, was tearful. In the years that her mother was away, Patsy had been more than just an Aunt to her. Whenever she visited the Whelan's home she had always checked that the small photo of her and Patsy sitting on the Thorpeness beach was in its right place on the kitchen cabinet. Her father had always been there for her, but he wasn't the woman she needed in those confusing and difficult teenage years.

"You know the funny thing is," Patsy continued, "Your uncle and I came over here, like your Mum and Dad, full of expectation. Young people with all this exciting new world to experience. I can't tell you what that was like, how thrilling that was. I kept pinching myself and saying, 'Patsy, it's like you're having a holiday that's never going to end'. Even the awful flats and the bigotry with the 'No Irish or dogs' hanging in the window didn't matter. I had just married the most handsome man in Ireland and I was young and wanted everything. But the trouble was…."

Hope held her breath, wondering if she should say something. Patsy sat up and smiled unconvincingly.

"Well, will you listen to me rabbiting on now? Let's get that cup of tea, eh?"

Patsy stood up and pulled her coat together. They walked slowly down the path.

"Can I ask you something, Hope?"

"Me? Of course."

"Why did you never settle down? You're such a lovely looking woman. God knows you must have had your share of admirers."

"Just didn't work out that way. I always wanted to. There's still time."

"You know your Grandad used to sing a song when we were small. I don't know what the song is or where he got it from, but there was always a line he sang which ran: 'When he fancies he is past love, it is then he meets his last love and he loves her as he's never loved before.'"

"I think I did love someone once and… well, it wasn't what I thought it was going to be. I don't think I ever got over it. So there you have it. Now you know my secret!"

Hope laughed to try and lighten the delivery, but Patsy just smiled at her.

"Are you afraid of being hurt? But who am I to talk, after what I've just told you!"

Oh, but I have been hurt, thought Hope. A different hurt. Not like yours, Patsy. Not a single hurt but slowly overwhelmed by a thousand small hurts. Where I live now no one can hurt me. Not Martin, or Mum, or Dad, or you, or…

91

The Church was three-quarters full as Hope and Denis entered. Hope tried to look casual, not wanting Neil to know that she knew he was there. Denis whispered an 'excuse me' to a couple at the end of the pew, who both moved their knees to one side to let him and Hope through. Hope sat down and picked up a mass sheet that happened to have been left on the pew in front. She desperately wanted to look up but felt that it wouldn't be somehow 'becoming' to look too interested.

St. Osburg's church was deemed architecturally 'very modern'. Its steel and glass roof was a pyramid that let copious amounts of light in whilst managing to liberate what little heat there was in the church at the same time. Consequently, despite all of the garish hangings that draped the walls, it was a cold, ironically soulless space which was – whatever time of the year – a wintry aircraft hangar of worship.

After reading and then re-reading the first lines of the page, Hope affected to disinterestedly look up and take in the congregation. Moving her head slowly she scanned each set of pews arranged in a semi-circle that was wrapped around the stepped altar. Once she thought she saw Neil, but soon realised that it couldn't be him. Perhaps he had temporarily gone back outside again. The doors at the back of the church were still regularly swinging open as people entered, but those who trailed through were not him.

She then thought that, if Neil's car was parked to the side of the church, the side that she now happened to be sitting in, then surely he must be near her? Discreetly, she tried to find reasons for looking behind her. She then dismissed the idea that he was sitting on her side of the church. After all, she would have seen him as she entered and he certainly wasn't there then.

All the while, Denis was kneeling, his right hand covering his eyes as he lost himself in a rehearsed litany of favourite prayers. Hope relaxed and looked again at the groups kneeling, whispering, staring, all lost in their own prayers, thoughts or quiet conversations around the church.

The thought struck her that there were so many *different* people present at mass to what she remembered. In the six years or so since she had attended St. Osburg's, the composition of the congregation had changed. There were two, what seemed to her, Indian families. Large families, with children whose faces were scrubbed up into angelic, washed features. At different points again she noticed individuals who were definitely West Indian. Didn't they have their own happy-clappy church? What were they doing in a Catholic church?

She became angry as she considered that yet another area of her life was losing its 'Britishness'. In her mind she could hear

Martin, drunkenly ranting about 'nig-nogs', 'darkies' and 'golliwogs', and yet saw that there was a real prescience to his words, however mangled the message may have been by too much alcohol.

As the mass moved drearily on, Hope eventually gave herself up to the tedious cycle of kneeling, sitting and standing that she knew so well from her schoolgirl years. Even those prayers that she hadn't spoken since her aborted time in the convent fell all so easily from her lips.

It was only when the queues started to form once more for Holy Communion, did her keen observance of the congregation recommence. Every dark-haired young man was scrutinised, as if she feared that Neil might in some way be cleverly disguised. But again he wasn't there. Perhaps it wasn't Neil's car? She entertained this notion for a while but knew in her heart it had been his.

As always, with Mass now over, Denis waited until the train of priests and altar boys had closed the doors behind them before beginning to move out of the pew.

"I'm going to light a candle. Won't be a moment."

"All right, Dad. I'll wait outside."

With as much speed that still yet had some degree of decorum to it, Hope quickly went through the door and out into the car park. Neil's car was still there. She again adjusted her hair and tried to look composed for when Neil should come round the corner of the church. It was only when a middle-aged woman appeared and walked towards the car did Hope realise the error she had made.

It wasn't Neil's car. It never had been Neil's car.

It was his mother's.

92

When Hope had finally reached home and opened the door, she failed to notice the post card at first. With her coat and bag thrown onto the sofa she went to the fridge and took out the bottle of wine she'd almost finished the night before. It tasted crisp and satisfying and she went back through the hall, now seeing that there was some post. She dropped the two letters onto the telephone table but took the postcard into the front room.

The postcard showed a photograph of a Suffolk beach, boats resting on the shingle and houses almost hyper-real in their garish seaside shades. The deliberate, neat characters of the writing revealed her father's hand and she swung her stocking feet onto the length of the settee.

'Dear Hope, we are having a very lovely time. Your Mother enjoying herself. We walked to Aldeburgh today. Weather quite nice. Home on Saturday. Much love – Mum and Dadxxxx'

Pardew pulled the length of her flank against the front room door and looked up at Hope to remind her she needed to be fed.

"Go away."

Undeterred, the cat settled down next to the coffee table and pulled her front paws in under her.

Hope thought how the world had quickly become hostile to her. The scene earlier in the afternoon with Martina would have consequences. Gavin had phoned in sick, but had done so from his mobile. He was probably going for another interview. She'd watched him nonchalantly place the manila folder containing copies of his updated CV into his bag. Doesn't he realise that there are no secrets he can keep from his EA?

So Gavin was feeling the heat of Liz Slater as well? She knew that Keith's departure had shaken him, after all it was Keith who had brought Gavin in, and Gavin was probably seen as 'Keith's man'. Hope had often fielded calls for Gavin which she knew to be from head-hunters; it wouldn't be long before some other organisation snapped him up.

And what about her own tenuous relationship with Liz? Since they had first met Hope had noticed that Liz – on the few occasions that their paths had crossed – had behaved as if Hope was invisible. Even when Hope had tried to counter this by making a show of saying 'Hello' to her, Liz had responded with a distant, curt 'hello' that was almost inaudible. Liz's intention seemed to be to make Hope feel she didn't exist and, as Hope now suspected, encourage her perhaps to think about employment elsewhere.

Ironically, after the first meeting with Liz, she had already reached the conclusion that her future probably lay elsewhere: either through being forced to leave or finding something herself before that happened. To even consider leaving Jupiter was something that had never entered her mind. Over the years, with all that she had endured at home, work had become a dependable crutch: one that was always there. Of course there had been ups and downs over the 30 years that she had worked there, but somehow clear-outs of staff were things that only happened to other people, never to her. There had even been occasions when she had been privy to the imminent demise of members of staff, when she had found herself enjoying this secret knowledge of their fates whilst pretending that the situation was 'normal'.

She was now certain that others were now carrying that secret information about her own fate, and were probably enjoying the same thrill she got during those occasions.

That was why the depressing realisation, that she had arrived at only this morning, had been so difficult. She'd received an email concerning a recent position she'd applied for in Pinner; the position was one which, she felt, suited her so much she would have struggled to have written a more perfect job description. The agency had confirmed that the employer had called several people in for interview, but not Hope.

With everyone out of the office, she'd contacted Gez (which she suspected was an anglicized version of some unpronounceable foreign name) at the recruitment agency who told her, no, it wasn't a mistake and that they had done their best to get her into the next stage.

"Do I need to change my CV? Have I missed something out?"

"No, the experience is great. Look, Hope, let me be honest: you've been a long time at Jupiter Rent a Car and that doesn't always stand you in good stead, if you see where I'm going, like."

"No, I don't see where you're 'going like'. Don't people value loyalty? They could get some blonde airhead who only stays with them for six months and then they'd be right back where they started.'

"Yeah, and I do take your point completely. It's just that you and I say 'loyal' and they say 'stuck in her ways'. It's a young company; average age is only about 26. They don't value long service like you and I do."

Hope sensed that the recruitment agent was ingratiating himself by carefully making sure that he 'appeared' to be looking at the problem from her side.

"And something else that might help, Hope."

"What?"

"I'd take your date of birth off. And maybe get rid of those jobs from the early 80s."

"Am I supposed to lie about my age? Don't they want to know about my experience?"

"I wouldn't say that. Look, I want to get you in front of our clients. Once they see in an interview how fab you really are, then they'll..."

"Forget that I'm so old? Oh, piss off." She'd slammed the receiver down so hard it had bounced up again and slithered down the side of her desk.

Hope took her glass back into the kitchen, dealt with Pardew's food, and then poured the remainder of the bottle into her glass. She slipped another full bottle into the freezer to chill it, telling herself that this will probably be her last glass but, well, you never know.

It was only when she had passed again into the hall that she noticed that there hadn't been two letters in that morning's post, but three. Intrigued, she picked them up. The third letter was between the two uninteresting buff-brown envelopes which, being slightly larger had cleverly hidden it. She slipped it out and looked at the handwriting which showed that the letter was addressed to her. She didn't recognise the handwriting; the envelope seemed very thin, almost as if it was empty.

She took it back into the room, set down her wine glass on the table and ripped the letter open. There was one small piece of paper inside, which simply read: *'Come live with me'.*

She snatched up the envelope again and, this time, saw that it had a London postmark.

93

As soon as Denis and Hope had returned from the church, Hope checked to see that the telephone was properly on its cradle. She picked it up and put it back again, just to make sure. Her father had been quite sure that the caller had been the same man as before, so it *had* to be Neil.

Yet, somehow, the situation had changed. Seeing Neil's mother had first made her shrink back inside the entrance porch of the church, not wanting to be recognised, although she knew she hardly knew her. The easy way that Neil's mother had opened the door, set down her bag and prayer book on the passenger seat, convinced Hope that the car undoubtedly belonged to her. Hope desperately tried to rationalise what might have happened.

At first she tried to convince herself that she had borrowed it off Neil, but the absence of awkwardness that an occasional driver might betray was completely lacking. She handled the car as if it were own.

Then Hope's mind returned to the previous thoughts she'd had in the church: maybe it wasn't the car Neil had taken her to Marlow in. Eventually she had to accept that the coincidence was too great and that explanation was, reluctantly, dismissed.

Earlier, as she and Denis had quietly walked back to the house, both lost in their own thoughts, Hope realised that there could only be one answer: Neil had lied to her. Once she had bitterly come to accept this, she occupied her mind thinking about the reason for his deception.

Surely he had only done it to impress her? What does that say about Neil? That he was desperate to make a good impression? This seemed to sit well in her mind. Yes he may have lied, but only because he was trying to make sure that she would like him. Doesn't everyone lie at first? Doesn't everyone present themselves and their situations in the best possible light because they want to win the other over? Once Hope had settled on this line of reasoning, she started to feel much better.

As Hope went up the stairs to change, a second dark thought entered. If he had lied about the car, what else had he told her that may also be untrue? This question was, she now accepted, more unsettling than the first one about the car.

Hope heard Denis moving plates around downstairs, fixing a light lunch before he went off to the Unit to see Carol. Hope began to feel unsettled in her mind and quickly began to undress, just to occupy herself in an activity.

At two o'clock, Denis checked his hair in the hall mirror and shouted back to Hope that he would see her later.

Hope finished washing the few plates and glanced at the clock, pleased that she would be able to talk to Neil in private.

But Neil's call never came.

94

"Do you only drink white? Can I not offer you something a little duskier?"

Hope, still standing after having taken off her coat, shook her head. "I prefer white. Is that OK?"

"Of course. It's just that I've a little beef thing going but you do as you please."

Hope took the glass from Cormac.

"Sit down, Hope. You don't mind cats, do you?"

"No, we've got a cat at home. Pardew."

"Pardew?"

"Yes, some footballer Dad liked. I don't know who."

"Oh, Alan Pardew. The Newcastle manager."

Hope shrugged her shoulders. "Is he? I wouldn't know."

"And why should you? You've a mind that I'd say lifts itself above trivial things like football."

Hope couldn't decide if Cormac was serious or not. Was he cleverly taking the rise out of her and viewing it as some kind of easy enjoyment for himself? She decided not to continue with the subject of Pardew's name.

"Are these your children?" Hope looked at a small arrangement of photographs on a nearby table.

"They are!" he called from the kitchen which was divided from the living room by a low wall. That's Niamh on the left and Kevin on his graduation day. Have you children of your own?"

"No; no children."

Cormac walked casually in from the kitchen and sat by Hope on the long, fawn settee.

Everything was exactly how Hope had imagined it not to be. For some reason she thought that, as a middle-aged man, he'd somehow have a small, untidy flat which he'd bought after a divorce. But the house, which was less than a mile from the hotel, was bright, spacious and well cared for. The next surprise was his openness about the past. He was a widower, had been for 11 years. With the help of his sister, who lived in a neighbouring road, he'd brought up the children on his own.

"What's the music?"

"Piazzola. Argentinian I think. Niamh put me on to him. Were you expecting something Irish?"

"I don't know what I was expecting."

Yes, he was an easy talker, but there seemed nothing unsettling or creepy in his effortless patter. At first she feared the unctuous charm of a salesman, but somehow that never materialised. Also, there was something penetrating about his eyes. When he sat next to her they seemed to uncover her, as if closely following the thoughts and emotions that raced beneath her skin. Hope began to feel uncomfortable and drew herself in as she sat on the edge of the settee.

"So what do you do for work? I bet you're very senior?"

Was this being provocative? Was he playing with her?

"I'm an EA, to a Vice President of Sales." The easy exaggeration; the wall of lies she so easily constructed around her.

"Oh, and what does an EA do?" Cormac sprang up and went back to the kitchen for the wine bottle.

"I am really his right-hand man. I try and take away the things that hold him back, deal with people who want to speak with him. Field calls. That sort of thing. You have to be very discrete."

Hope watched him pour the wine with the same professional flourish he exhibited in the bar. The actions of dealing with alcohol were so part of him that, even when relaxing, he behaved exactly the same way.

"And was that him last night with you? He seemed a nice enough fella."

"Yes, that's Gavin. The other lady was Rhona; she's a sales manager for him. She looks after Scotland and Ireland. That's why we're here. There's an important negotiation going on in Athlone."

"Athlone? I didn't think we were that important? Who are they? I probably know of them."

"Oh, I can't say. I'm afraid it's confidential."

"Ah, discretion, eh? Then I won't ask any more questions. Here you go."

"Are you not drinking?"

"I'll have a glass with dinner. Occupational thing."

Cormac looked so relaxed in an open-necked pale blue shirt. Although slim, he lounged with the grace of a resting lion. His sinewy frame composed, limbs carefully arranged, but all conveying a feeling of strength merely at rest.

"I've not done this for a very long time."

"Eat? I do it every night."

"No, you know what I mean. This... just being with someone. I've forgotten what I'm supposed to do."

"Are you serious? A woman like you? I can't believe that."

Hope shook her head and found that, for some unknown reason, her eyes were prickling with tears.

"Oh no, it's true."

Cormac leaned towards her. "Are you divorced?"

"No. Never been married. Hard to believe, really. I think that probably makes me a frumpy old spinster."

Hope sniffled and tried to make light of it, "So just think what a night you're going to have!"

"Well, I'm speechless. I really am. Here, would you like a tissue?"

Hope declined his offer and took one of her own from her handbag, glad of the opportunity to avert her eyes.

"It's wrong of me to pry, Hope. I shouldn't have asked."

"No, I'm just… I don't know. It's probably this trip. There's so much resting on it."

"The stresses of high commerce, huh? I see it every night."

"How long have you worked there?"

"At the hotel? About six or seven years. It's a nice enough place to work."

"What did you do before?"

"I've always been in bar work. I love it. It's what I do best."

"Well, it is a night for revelations. I must admit I thought that…"

"That it's all a man at my age can get? It doesn't earn much, but tips are good and the house is paid for. There's only me except when the children come home to visit their decrepit old man."

"I didn't say that. It's just you seem very clever."

"Oh, but I am! I'm a genius really, but there's not been a job advert for a genius for years, so I must comfort myself with something menial. Seriously, I know which side of the bar I'd rather be on. The whole human race assembles itself along that long bit of wood. You hear a lot of stories."

"Like middle-aged women whose life has passed them by? I'm sure you have them back here all the time."

"Oh no, hold on there! Do you think I'm some sort of predator now? Are you thinking this is a little side-line I have for myself? Let me put you straight on that for a starter."

Hope wanted to unbutton his shirt. Were they going to have sex tonight? Would she be ready for that? She'd probably freeze.

"Well don't you? You looked very sure of yourself when you asked me here."

"And why have I asked you here? You tell me."

"For dinner?"

"For dinner and for some company with a woman who was the loveliest thing I've ever seen walk into that bar. I'm afraid if you think it's going to be anything more than that, then you'll be a disappointed woman."

Hope couldn't think what to say. She was pleased and disappointed at the same time. She didn't want him to make any advances at her but would feel somehow wronged if he didn't.

"It smells lovely. What is it?

"Beef."

"Beef what?"

"I don't know. She didn't say."

"Who didn't?"

"My sister. She made it. I'm just warming it up. Oh, you thought I cooked it myself?"

"Yes, I did! Why did your sister cook it? I thought *you* were making it."

"What? And poison my first female visitor for years? I don't think that would be a good start."

They shared the joke together and Hope felt herself beginning to relax.

"Do you know what? I'm about to break Cormac's rule and have a drink now after all. I've got a feeling this is going to be worth it."

95

"Hey, put that bedside light on. The switch is on the base."

Hope leaned across, her fingers fumbling in the dark for the lamp switch. Neil put down a melamine tray on the bed and transferred the bottle and two tumblers to the opposite bedside table.

"Mum's got no brandy. Rum I'm afraid. Is that OK?"

"Has it got alcohol in it?"

"I'll do my best."

Neil passed the glass over to Hope, and apologised about the rum he'd spilt on his fingers. In the dim light, Hope looked down at the pinpricks of light that sat on the fluted patterns of her glass. This was such a perfect night. The scent rose up from her glass and she breathed it in, wanting every sense to savour this deep and delicious happiness.

Hope felt Neil's naked, warm torso as he climbed into bed next to her. She leaned against him and closed her eyes.

"My Mum is very much alive. I'm sorry for lying to you. I'm afraid that lying is a bit of a defence. Creating a life you don't have can be a very good form of defending yourself."

"Defending yourself from what?"

"Oh, being hurt by other people."

"But I don't see why you had to say it in the first place. I mean, we were good friends. Or I thought we were."

"Look, I've told you. I've said sorry. Something happened that… well, that changed everything."

"It was your Mum, wasn't it?"

"What was?"

"That killed your brother. It wasn't you, it was your Mum."

Hope nodded. "How did you know?"

"I asked Mum about your family. She said your brother had something wrong with him. She couldn't remember what, just that she'd hit him with some rock in the Lido."

"I was there. I don't really remember it much. Just him floating on the water. And Mum crying."

"Was the bit about moving true? You said something once about you and your Dad having to move, when we were at that party."

"No. that wasn't true. Dad couldn't leave the house. He wanted to. My uncle offered him money apparently. But he just couldn't do it. I don't know why. I don't know what he went through with the neighbours and things. He just changed my school and hoped things would pass. And they did. Strange, really."

"What is?"

"Your mother's a killer. You grow up at first not being told the truth. You slowly begin to work it out for yourself. And the more you find out about the truth, the less you want to know. Is this making sense?"

"Where is your Mum?"

"In a secure unit. But Dad's hopeful they'll release her. I'm not sure how I'm going to cope with that."

"Do you see her?"

"Sometimes. Not often. More to please Dad, really."

"I don't know what to say."

"Oh, I can tell you what to say. You can say 'Goodbye. Hope. And goodbye to your fucking awful family.' Believe me, I wouldn't blame you."

"But I'm not going to say that. I suspected something bad had happened, but your Mum was probably very ill."

"She was. Dad thinks that if he'd done more at the time then Stephen would still be alive today. It eats away at him."

"I love you, Hope."

"Don't be silly."

Hope shivered with pleasure just to hear Neil say it. She turned to him, eyes pleading for him to repeat what he'd just said.

"I mean it. When we were at school. Even when you nearly put a stop to my fathering children."

Hope laughed into the duvet cover.

"Oh, I'm so sorry about that. Do you mean it? About loving me?"

"Why do you think I called you? I have tried to forget you. Told myself it was a crush. You know, one I hadn't grown out of. A teenage thing. But I couldn't get you out of my head. I'd go out with girls and really get on with them. But you've always been there somehow. Was never fair on them really."

"I can't believe that you've just told me that. That could have been me talking. It is exactly what you have been to me."

"Would you like some more to drink?"

"Will you hold me?"

96

When Hope arrived in the Hotel Reception, she could see Gavin outside, walking around with his mobile phone held fast against his ear. She settled her room bill and, pulling her case behind her, walked outside.

Gavin was talking to Rhona, imploring her to do something that Hope couldn't quite make out. He turned, saw Hope was there and held an acknowledging hand up as he continued to speak.

"No, we stick to our guns on that one. We've already compromised on the payment terms; he's just pushing for whatever else he can get now."

Hope found the car, opened the boot and started to load her case into it. Her mind still swimming with the events of the evening before.

"Shall I drive?" asked Gavin as he loaded his own case into the car.

"Suits me. Was that Rhona?"

"It was. Nearly there with this deal. She just needs to close it off."

The early miles passed quietly, as both turned over their separate thoughts. It was Gavin who eventually broke the silence.

"Good night, last night?"

"Very good, thank you."

"Dinner wasn't it?"

"Yes, really nice. You said you wanted to talk about something."

Gavin seemed to press his lips together in uncertainty. "Oh no, it was nothing. All sorted now."

Hope wasn't sure how truthful Gavin was being. She thought about how differently everything seemed to have turned out on the business trip.

She furtively looked at Gavin and berated herself for what she had been doing. How could she have spent so much time fixating and fantasising about this man? How many hours had she filled with creating scenarios that had filled her mind like the fevered yearnings of a teenager? She glanced at him, and watched the self-satisfied air that he always casually exuded, now finding him quite repellent.

"I'm sure that Thuong and the children will be glad to see you."

"I guess so."

Hope was struck by the neutrality of his manner when he answered her. Something had changed quite profoundly in him and she couldn't quite determine what it was. Last year, when they had journeyed together to the Bristol conference, his whole existence centred on Thuong, playing her music and talking about what she had brought to his life. Now she and their children merited just three indifferent words.

Hope thought of her own scheming attempts to create mistrust between Gavin and Thuong. Perhaps she had been doing him a favour all along?

What a complete prick he was.

97

Hope turned into Glenavon Road and took in the long line of bungalows and two-storied houses that lined the cul-de-sac. They were depressing in their determinedly suburban appearance of uninspired frontages, stone driveways and cheerless gardens.

When they had driven up from Marlow that wonderful evening (was it *really* only a few weeks ago?) she remembered that the house stood out, even by lamplight, with its mock-Tudor beams intersecting the front walls.

It was Denis who had set the ball rolling in her mind. Only that morning, as they enjoyed the rare treat of a lazy breakfast that only a bank holiday Monday could allow, did Denis toss out an innocent enough question.

"And how's your new romance?"

"It's not a romance. He's just a friend."

"Oh, a 'friend' now. So how's your new friendship?"

"You don't normally ask about my friends. Well, not a particular friend."

Hope wasn't sure that this was a conversation that she really wanted to pursue. Especially as she was still smarting by Neil's broken promise of calling her back.

"Where does he live? Is he local still?"

Hope buttered herself another slice of toast.

"Bloomsbury. By Bloomsbury tube."

"Bloomsbury tube? There's no Bloomsbury tube."

It wasn't what Hope wanted to hear. She paused for a moment and then carried on looking for the marmalade jar.

"Are you sure, Dad? He definitely said Bloomsbury tube."

"I'm sure I'm sure. God know I've driven enough buses to know London like the back of my hand."

"Maybe I misheard him."

But Hope was equally sure that she hadn't. Denis rubbed his hands together to rid them of the toasted breadcrumbs and took up his Daily Mirror again. Hope affected a quiet patience, but she soon found an excuse to leave the kitchen and seek out a dog-eared A-Z that was kept in the front room.

She picked it up and closely followed the lines of tube stations that were arranged on the back cover. Dad was right. Desperately she opened up the book and found Bloomsbury Square. Russell Square, Holborn, Goodge Street but no Bloomsbury. Was she going mad? Why was all of this happening? She could stand it no longer, she called to her Dad that she had to go out and rushed through the front door before he could ask her why.

It took her almost 30 minutes to walk to the road where Neil's Mum's house was. As she walked towards where she remembered the house being, she could hear only the chirrup of bird song and the drone of a distant vacuum cleaner. Halfway down the cul-de-sac, she instantly recognised ahead the blue roof of Neil's – no, his Mum's – car.

Her steps slowed as she approached; the moaning of the vacuum cleaner told her that it was Neil's Mum's car being cleaned. His mother bobbed unexpectedly up from the car, where she'd previously been hidden by the roofline; she looked up at Hope. Hope hadn't expected to meet his mother. She hadn't even thought about meeting Neil. The stupidity of going to his house was becoming increasingly apparent to her.

"Oh, Hello, Mrs Dowling."

"Hello love. I'm, sorry, do I know you?"

"Yes… I'm a friend of Neil's. From school."

"From school?" Mrs Dowling looked even more confused. Why would someone from school suddenly turn up six years after he'd left?

"Sorry, this must look a bit silly. We're having a school reunion and no one had Neil's telephone number. Someone remembered that this was his address and so I got sent to ask."

"Oh right. Come on in and let me write it for you. What's your name?"

"Hope. Hope...Whelan."

"OK, Hope. You just wait in there and I'll be in in a second. Won't be long now."

Hope was ushered into the room that she and Neil had first made love in. It all seemed exactly the same and yet so utterly different; she noticed now how the sun, though a little muted by the net curtains, filled it with light. No, there was something else that was different. It was the bookcase. There were pictures on the bookcase. She certainly couldn't recall those being on there before. She walked over and picked up the largest one. Neil was looking back at her, smart in a hired suit, smiling so happily, his newly married wife threading her arm through his.

Hope stopped breathing and held her hand to her mouth to stifle the sob that had automatically leaped within her. And there, just by where the first picture had been was a smaller one, not yet framed, unsteady with the cardboard arm at the back weakened by use. Hope never knew whether the picture was of a baby boy or a girl. She threw the wedding picture onto a nearby chair and ran from the house. It was only when she felt that she might be sick did she stop running and made for an entry that ran between two houses.

Crying uncontrollably she pressed her forehead hard against the pebble-dashed wall, oblivious - in her mental torment - of the incisions the sharp stones made on her forehead. She repeated 'Oh my God' over and over, until it became a rhythmic mantra that tried to quell the searing pain she felt inside.

When she could weep no more, she looked up and down the entry to see if she was alone. She wiped her eyes with the back of her hands and looked for a handkerchief she luckily remembered having placed earlier in her bag. She saw the spots of blood when she'd removed it from her eyes and realised what she had done.

As Hope walked slowly back towards home, the world looked a very different place. Never again, she decided, would she or could she trust anyone. It was her against the world. Of course she would lose – but who would know or care about that?

It had always been just her and Denis. And that would be how it would stay now. That was how it was meant to be.

98

"I wouldn't give you fucking that for your cheap psychologists!"

Martin snapped his fingers loudly to demonstrate his point.

"I'm not who I am because of all this 'someone's-done-something-awful-to-me-in-the-past' shite. You are who you are. You're born with it. Only Freud and his mob would tell you it's all the teeny-tiny, little things that happened to you on the way."

"So what's your excuse, Martin? Were you just born unpleasant?"

The small group laughed and even Martin, beery and lary as he was getting, turned and smiled at Patsy.

Denis and Carol had just moved into their flat and, of course, had invited the Whelans over. The neighbours, Howard and Colin, who were sharing a flat above, were also asked to stay after helping them move in. The confined spaces of the rooms were littered with boxes both full and empty, but all that had been forgotten as the wooden beer crates – courtesy of Martin – were emptied and bottles hissed open.

"If I didn't love you like I do, I'd put you over my knee and beat you for saying that, wife or not!"

Martin leaned over to Patsy and kissed her tenderly on the forehead. Patsy pulled him close to her, before mocking him with "Now get off me you great lump."

"Now, Denis, don't let your wife talk to you like that. Beating them is the only way to make them come to their senses."

"You just try, Mr Dunne. I'll divorce you soon enough."

"It's too late, Martin," Denis soberly interjected, "She's already too wild."

Carol set down her glass and sat on Denis' lap

"We're going to love you and leave you," said Colin. "We're out tonight to the theatre. Lovely meeting you all and thanks, Martin, for the beer."

"Not at all. Good men yourselves for helping." Martin raised his glass to them as they left and, when the door was closed turned conspiratorially to the others: "Do you think they're queers?"

Martin pulled Patsy out of her chair, sat himself upon it and then heavily drew her down on to his lap.

"God, this all seems very unreal," sighed Carol.

"Only at first, Carol. Martin and I had to keep pinching ourselves but you soon get used to the freedom. A quick letter every so often to mammy and daddy and you've done your daughter's duties."

"I'm just glad we found somewhere. I thought we'd be in that dirty hotel forever. I can't quite take it in." Denis looked around and started to mentally list the jobs he would need to do before he started the bus driver training the following week.

"Take it in, Denis. Your happiness and freedom start here. We've shaken Athlone off our feet and come to the Promised Land. I'm here for good. Burn my passport and stake my claim in this wonderful, dirty city!"

"Me too," added Patsy. "I could never go back to Ireland."

Denis, thin and handsome, looked up at Carol with an unashamedly adoring look.

"I'll just go wherever you go."

99

Hope took the piece of paper with the number her father had written down and held it in front of her. How deceptive a string of simple digits can be? She remembered how she'd first thought it might be for Mr Reynolds following her interview for the role she now had, and the surprise she'd experienced – and pleasure – when Neil had answered. But where had it led? To a farrago of lies and an experience where the intensity of pleasure had been answered by the torturing depths of mental despair and disappointment.

She had one more lie to nail. Trembling a little, she keyed in the numbers once again, this time knowing that it would take her directly to Neil's extension. The phone rang for a while, before another voice, an unexpected voice, responded.

"Accounts Receivable."

"Oh, hello, could I please speak to Mister Neil Dowling."

"He's out of the office at the moment. Can I get him to call you back?"

"No, it's.. I'm returning Mr Dowling's call and I'm not quite sure who he is, can I ask his position."

"Neil? He's one of the clerks. Can I ask what it was in connection with?"

"Yes, but can I just ask first, was he away very recently on business? I just wanted to make sure I've got the right person."

"Erm, not to my knowledge. He sits opposite me and he's been here all the time I've been here."

The young woman laughed uneasily, perhaps not sure of the reason for the question.

"Look, can I take a number for Neil to call you back on?"

"No, there's no need. Could I just leave a message? Just let Neil know that Hope rang and there's no need to call me again. That's all...."

"Oh, actually, he's just..."

Hope quickly put down the receiver and leant against the wall. She was past weeping now. Only yesterday, after going to Neil's mother's house, had she somehow managed to find her way home. She'd cried so bitterly and so fully that there was nothing inside but a hollowed-out and aching mind.

She picked up the receiver again and phoned Mr Reynolds to let him know that she was not feeling well and would need to go to bed.

His only retort was that she should let him know if she'd like tucking in. She couldn't even pretend to laugh and dismissed him with a curt "See you tomorrow."

As she dragged her feet wearily upstairs the phone rang. She knew who it was and she didn't want to answer. From her bedroom that day it rang several times more. Eventually, when passing the phone on the way to making herself a hot drink, she took it from its cradle and left it off the hook.

100

Hope sat on the side of the bed and stroked her mother's hair.

"Do you want this tea, mum?"

Carol slowly sat up and asked for her dressing gown. Hope placed it tenderly around Carol's shoulders and eased her pillows upright so that she could lean back against the headboard.

"Are you getting out of bed today?"

"I will, but not just yet."

Hope handed her the tea.

"Shall I get you some toast? It won't take a minute"

"No, perhaps later."

The best efforts of Denis and Hope couldn't persuade Carol to eat more and it alarmed Hope to see her as she was. Her dishevelled hair was now almost chalk-white, her skin grey as ash. Hope worried that she was declining, she always would make her way downstairs at some point of the day to a favourite armchair and watch television, but that was becoming an exception lately, so seldom had she left her bedroom.

"She'll rally, you watch", Denis had repeatedly told Hope, yet even he seemed less convinced every time he said it.

"Mum, I'm thinking about getting another job. I've been at Jupiter for so long now and I thought it would be good to change. I'm also a bit worried that they might be moving so now would be a good time."

Hope spoke brightly, determined to convey that she was master of her own destiny.

"Moving? Are you sure? They've been good to you."

"Can't stay there forever, Mum. Got to move on sometime."

"I guess so. Be pushed to find somewhere as good as that, love."

"I think they'll be pushed to find someone as good as me!" Hope maintained the positivity; she'd not been looking forward to having this conversation and needed to carry her Mother along with her.

"Well, I suppose you know what you're doing. Where's your Dad?"

Her Mum spoke slowly, always looking at a fixed point at the bottom of the bed and never once looking to make eye contact with Hope.

"Gone for the paper. Anyway, I'd better get to work. Don't want to lose the job I've got, do I? See you later."

Hope kissed her and went slowly downstairs. She'd already phoned in sick on Monday and taken yesterday off as well. She picked up her resignation letter and eased it into her bag. As she did so, she pulled out the small note she'd received that previous Friday. It was simply written in blue ink: 'Come live with me.'

At the weekend, she'd told herself it was someone having a joke with her. She couldn't think who would do such a thing, but a joke definitely seemed the most likely scenario. Why the mystery? Why didn't they sign it? Asking herself those very questions made her realise that she was cheerfully wishing it to be something quite different. If it was a joke, it was cruelly teasing her.

It wasn't Neil's handwriting. She could easily recall the letter she had once received (was it really 20 years ago?), a desperate request that they keep their meeting quiet which masqueraded as a pitiful – and somewhat self-pitying – apology. No, it wasn't Neil.

Somebody at work? But that didn't appear likely. Who would know her address and be so presumptive to write such a…

Cormac. Was it Cormac? Of course she had thought about it previously but had discounted it when she'd looked at the London postmark. But what if he was in London? She hadn't considered that. Of course, at one time she would have told herself it was Gavin. He'd thrown off the yoke of marriage and seen, once and for all, that it was Hope he wanted to share this life with. Hope blushed at the thought of her own embarrassing childishness over the past three years.

Denis bustled in through the kitchen door. "You off, love?"

"I'm off. Mum's got her tea. I'll see you later."

She made a decision that she thought she might come to regret, but opened the pedal bin and tossed the note inside. Before she could even think about retrieving it, she had walked from the house and opened her car door.

She wished the mournful Mr Snipe good morning, and he nodded without even turning his head. For some reason, his misery was an affirmation of singledom. She rifled through her CDs and found what she was looking for. As she pulled away, Mr

Snipe winced at the music that spilled out of her open car windows.

Well there's a rose in a fisted glove
And the eagle flies with the dove
And if you can't be with the one you love, honey
Love the one you're with.

101

With dinner over and a vague promise that he'd wash the brown streaked dishes later, Cormac had suggested a walk. He drove them out to a lough, suggesting that it might be 'worth a stroll'.

"So what happened?"

"Nothing. I had his letter and I threw it away. It wasn't written for me anyway. It was written for himself, I just happened to be the one that it was sent to."

"Have you seen him since?"

"No. Dad says that he would be at Mass occasionally, but that was all. I didn't want to see him ever again after that."

"Hope deferred, eh?"

"Sorry?"

"Hope deferred. It's line from a poem. Who was it now? Rossetti, Christina Rossetti. I can't remember the title of the poem, I was always reading that slushy romantic Victorian stuff as a teenager, but I still remember one verse:

I looked for that which is not, nor can be,
And hope deferred made my heart sick in truth:
But years must pass before a hope of youth
Is resigned utterly.

That's it now."

Hope went very quiet, before finally answering, "I haven't heard that before."

"It's just a poem. Nothing but words."

They walked along the pebbled rim of the lough in silence, enjoying the softness of the evening and the water reflecting the many layers of high, sun-tipped cloud.

"Is it all an act? Your job? Is it what people expect of a barman?"

"It's not an act, but it is what people expect. But that's no different to anyone's job, really. Doesn't everyone put on a bit of a show at work?"

"What if you lived your whole life like that? Not just work, but all the time."

Cormac looked inquisitively at Hope, trying to decipher the veiled intent of her question.

"Well, that would be a strange thing. Surely you wouldn't do that to the people you were close to? Your parents or your children."

"Didn't you act after you lost your wife? I bet you were brave for your children. That was an act."

"True, true. But that was to protect them. They were young and they were heartbroken. They needed protecting."

Hope smiled. "I needed protecting once."

"You mean after Neil?"

"No, it wasn't Neil. It was someone else."

"Can I ask who?"

"It doesn't matter. He's dead now. Sometimes talking is no help at all really."

Cormac gestured to reply, but then decided against it. Instead, he took off the sweater he'd brought with him and carefully draped it around Hope's shoulders.

"Jamilla?"

Jamilla, turned abruptly in her chair. "Oh, hello, Hope."

"Why's Martina's desk cleared?"

Jamilla didn't reply, but moved her eyes in the direction of Gavin's office. Hope walked and opened the door. His desk was empty. The chair neatly pushed in; his photographs and personal effects cleared. Even the scarf, a present from Thuong that he never wore - and which had always hung forlornly from a brushed steel coat hanger - was gone.

Hope's eye was suddenly drawn to the winking orange light on the telephone, telling her that there were messages on Gavin's voicemail. One of them was probably hers, saying that she was ill and wouldn't be coming in.

"Bit of a shock, isn't it?"

Hope didn't answer, but pursed her lips and looked back at Jamilla.

"Like a coffee, Hope?"

"Please, Jamilla."

Hope switched on her computer, uncertain as to what she might find on it. She first tried her email inbox. There was nothing of note, just a few emails that she had been copied into. She looked through her drawers one by one, as if expecting the mystery to be unravelled by something stored in one of them.

Jamila returned with two mugs, putting one by Hope's keyboard.

"They've both gone. I walked into an empty office on Monday. It's just like a ghost town in here."

"I'll be next after my little outburst on Friday."

"Oh, I think you're all right. It was just the last straw really, what you said."

"Did Martina go to HR?"

"No, she got as far as the toilet. I went in to see if she was all right and she just burst into tears. Said she couldn't take any more and that Gavin was making her life impossible."

"I'm not sure that's true. I don't think Gavin…"

"He's the father. Martina's baby. It's his."

"Gavin? Gavin's baby? Are you..?"

"I was astounded. I couldn't think what to say. What can you say? I just told her not to worry, but she couldn't stop crying. Said she was leaving and that was that. Poof! She was gone!"

Hope's face was still caught in a rictus of astonishment. Her mind pitched back and forwards between conversations and events: Gavin's call at the service station, Martina's depression, Rhona's insinuations in the bar… why hadn't she seen it?

"Hey, I can't believe it either, Hope. I thought it was her boyfriend's child! You could have knocked me over with a feather."

"Gavin…" Hope mouthed. "So why has he…?"

Jamilla's eyes narrowed: "Hatchet woman. I told you. And the next ones to go will be you and I, you wait."

"Gone? Sacked? Oh, Jamilla, this is all too much. But he was doing well. He told me this region was…"

"Well, if that was the case, Liz Slater's got a strange way of showing her appreciation."

Hope sat back in her chair looking at Jamila. Her first thought was to quietly get rid of her resignation letter. She had been certain that Martina would go straight to HR and tell them that she had been racist to her. That would have given Liz Slater the perfect grounds to get rid of her. Even if she'd not been thrown out, the thought of working alongside Martina every day knowing that Martina had bleated about her to HR would have been insufferable, never mind how she might have been perceived elsewhere in the business. But now Martina was out the way, why should she walk the plank as well?

“Oh, and a man has called for you. Cormac. He asked if you’d got his note. That’s all he’d say.”

Hope heard herself thank Jamilla, but it was almost as if she was hearing someone else speaking the words. It *was* Cormac. Was this morning real? Would she wake up soon and find herself in bed, her alarm clock telling her there was only 9 minutes before it would knell the arriving day?

Live with Cormac? How could she live with him after only a few brief hours together? Was he mad?

Hope collected her things together and took out the resignation letter.

“Give this to Liz for me, will you?” She kissed Jamilla’s cheek, smiled warmly at her and walked out.

103

Hope looked down at the small smudge of red wine at the bottom of her glass.

“I have to go. That wine was lovely.”

“You know what I’d like, Hope? I’d like to introduce you to a whole world of red wine. A life’s journey of pleasure.”

Hope wanted Cormac to kiss her and looked across the room with the confidence she had lacked the night before in the bar.

“I’ll get your jacket.”

He turned off the music, put on his own jacket and opened the door for Hope to step out into the still-warm night air.

“Did you walk here?”

“Taxi. Only a few Euros.”

It’ll only take half an hour or so, and it’s a lovely evening.”

“Why did you ask me over? I’m intrigued to know.”

“Like I said, how could I not? You’re a very lovely woman.”

“If I was such a lovely woman, why didn’t you try and do what every other man would try and do?”

"It's not my style. It'd be an awful presumption to make wouldn't it?"

"I wanted you to seduce me. Did you know that?"

Cormac stopped. "Did I disappoint you?"

Hope took his arm and put her head against his shoulder.

"Tell me, Hope, will you ever come this way again? With the job and everything."

"Might do. Hard to say really. You know, Cormac, I lied to you tonight. Gavin's not a VP. He's a regional sales manager. I was trying to… Oh, make more of myself in your eyes."

"Ah, well that's good that you've told me. I'll not mark you down for it this time."

"I'm not sure I can see you again."

"Oh, that's disappointing. Tell me why. Is it my cooking?"

"No, it's just that you are very good and I am not. There is someone, some very lucky woman that is out there for you – and I envy her – but it could never be me."

"Don't talk nonsense."

"No, your little poem was right. Some lives aren't meant to be happy. I wasn't meant to be happy. My Mum is very ill and my Dad can't cope and I am doing penance."

"Penance? For the love of Christ what would you be doing penance for?"

But Hope didn't answer. She felt the warmth of his jacket against her face, and looked on at the pinpricks of stars above the blue-black hedges, rising and falling in time with their walking.

104

Bubbles and blood. It was the absence of both that struck her. The blow had been heavy; his surprise genuine. He must have registered her murderous intent in a micro-second, much too short for that recognition to give way to fear, his eyes opening wide by a degree almost impossible to notice.

After the blow his young body reeled comically and slid – to her pleasure and surprise – silently into the enveloping water. She lifted her arm again, the stone still gripped to deliver a second blow; but a second blow wasn't needed.

She released the stone beneath the surface of the water and allowed it to sink to the lido bed. As the pale, thin, white body arched upwards she gripped his hair with her right hand and pushed into the small of his back with her left. Easing him down into the water again, feeling his chilled torso slide smoothly against her thigh.

She then calmly looked up but all were occupied with their own dramas: lovers splashing each other in a watery courtship; children noisily flopping around from the inside of supporting inflatable rings. She turned back to see if there was any movement. But there was none.

Carol, who had been swimming nearby, had stood up when she heard the screams. Blood began to billow from the small boy's battered skull.

"Oh my God, Hope… Oh my God! Oh Jesus! Oh Jesus! Oh God, Hope. What have you done?"

Carol desperately thrashed her way through the water.

Hope calmly held up the stone.

Also by Michael Heath

Swimming Out to Sea

16 Short Poems

This small selection of poetry explores the themes of loss, memory and the longing for those fleeting flashes of happiness that are all too brief in our lives.

From the tragedy of a young child's death in 'Shooting Star' to a small moment in time perfectly captured in 'The Rise from Castle Combe', his verse recalls the melancholy of Thomas Hardy and the easy narrative of John Betjeman.

Available now in Kindle format only

52175475R00182

Made in the USA
Charleston, SC
06 February 2016